Shadow of DEATH

The Protective DETECTIVE SERIES 3

ALSO BY YOLONDA TONETTE SANDERS

In Times of Trouble

Day of Atonement

Wages of Sin

Shadow *of* DEATH

The Protective DETECTIVE SERIES 3

A Novel

YOLONDA TONETTE SANDERS

SBI
STREBOR BOOKS
NEW YORK LONDON TORONTO SYDNEY

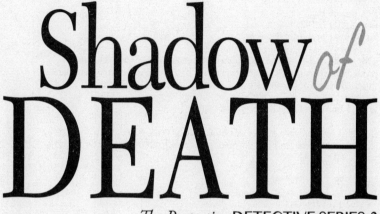

SBI
Strebor Books
P.O. Box 6505
Largo, MD 20792
http://www.streborbooks.com

ISBN 978-1-59309-528-4
ISBN 978-1-4767-4459-9 (ebook)
LCCN 2014943296

First Strebor Books trade paperback edition May 2015

Cover design: www.mariondesigns.com
Cover photograph: © Keith Saunders/Keith Saunders Photos

10 9 8 7 6 5 4 3 2 1

Manufactured in the United States of America

This book is dedicated to Sanders, Tre, and Tia
who are daily reminders of God's love.
I am so blessed to have each of you in my life.

ACKNOWLEDGMENTS

This is it. The third book in the Protective Detective series. Whether or not there will be a fourth adventure for Troy Evans is a question that has yet to be answered. I'm taking it one day at a time as God leads and opens doors. As one who enjoys movies and books in the mystery/suspense genre, it has been an amazing journey to write such. I am grateful to have the opportunity to glorify God even through my works of fiction. It's an honor that I don't take for granted. He's also blessed me to have the love and support of many, some who've had an impact on my completion of this story.

David Sanders, it's because of your unconditional love and support that I have been able to spread my wings. "Thank you" doesn't seem like enough. I love you, dude!

Tre, I miss you so much that sometimes my heart aches. I'm so proud of the young man you have grown up to be. I look forward to the amazing things that God has in store for you. The Navy can take you all around the world, but it can never take you anywhere that my love can't reach.

Tia, you are so beautiful. (No, I'm not saying that because you're in denial about looking like me! Lol.) I admire your dedication to excel academically and outside of the classroom. I am proud of you, baby girl! I enjoy our special moments together.

Dad, I don't think a girl ever outgrows the need for her father.

I am no exception. Even at my age, you play a vital role in my life and in my children's lives. I appreciate all that you do to support my writing and for us, in general.

Mom, you are the best telephone salesman ever! Forget email and social media, you work what you know to keep others informed about my projects. Thank you for doing what you can to help spread the word.

Janice, also known as "Mama J" in my heart, thank you for not only being a great mother-in-law, but also a good friend. It's a blessing not to have any monster-in-law stories to share. I thank you for the many ways in which you support me.

Teresa, I've said it before and I'll continue to say it, you are irreplaceable. Besides David, there has not been anyone who has consistently been in the trenches with me through all the ups and downs of Yo Productions as you have been. Thank you for believing in me and all that I do, and for working to help Yo Pro reach its full potential.

Jenn, there are very few people I would declare as lifelong friends simply because I know that seasons and circumstances change. I think it goes without saying that you, my dear, are a lifer. I love you and I appreciate your support. With all that you have going on, you still make time to read my books. You were there in the beginning when the idea to write my first novel came to fruition. I have no doubt that you'll continue to stand by my side. Your support means much more than I can express in words.

I'm happy to have found a new friend in Dana Hall, also known as my rap partner, "Devastating D." ;-) Dana, I love how genuine you are. You have such a pure kindness that is not easily found in many. It was an honor to share my public rap debut with you. (Ben and Sanders can hate all they want, but they know we blew up the spot! Lol) Thank you for the "widow before ex-wife" line used in *Shadow of Death.* It's way less morbid than what I'd always said! I also want to thank you for your excitement about my books, in general. It has been a blessing to me.

Jeff Lucas, thank you for going above and beyond duty to help me work out a few kinks in this story. I would say more, but I don't want to give anything away. ;-)

Aaron Dagres, what's up, buddy? I bet you thought I'd forget to acknowledge you when I used the story you told me about Anthony's potty mishap at school. ☺ That was hilarious! Thank you for sharing and for allowing me to tweak for creative purposes and share publicly.

Angela, thank you for being a faithful prayer partner. I enjoy our weekly sessions. They and you are an encouragement. Thank you for sharing in the ups and downs of this season in my life and allowing me to be transparent.

Sara, whenever we speak, it's always a pleasure. I appreciate the way you labor on my behalf. It is a great honor to have you as an agent. Thank you for the times when you've allowed me to vent (and freak out). You are a wonderful listener and you have such a calming effect. I'm grateful to have you in my corner.

Stephen, though we haven't actually spoken in years, I'm kept up-to-date about you through Sara. Congratulations on the newest addition to your family. Whenever I think of you, I smile because I know that you are rooting for all things to work in my favor. Thank you!

Working with Simon and Schuster/Strebor Books has honestly been one of the *best* publishing experiences that I've ever had. I was nervous when I signed on with *In Times of Trouble.* My writing style is so different from many of the other books published under this line that I didn't know what to expect. From the bottom of my heart, I thank you for allowing me to be *me* and for respecting my voice during this entire journey. It has been wonderful to work with you all. Thank you for giving me a platform to share my stories.

Mitzi, I will never forget the day I met my "super fan." Little did you know, I was having a spiritually and emotionally rough day. God used you in a mighty way to remind me that my work is not in vain. Thank you so much for your support.

Pastor Howard, your trust in me is beyond belief. I really don't know what else to say. Your support and encouragement means a great deal. Thank you for walking with me on this journey of faith as I explore new ventures.

It would be remiss of me not to thank my biological family members, in-laws, and my church family at Family Fellowship Church of Christ in Gahanna for your consistent support. I love y'all so very much.

A special shout-out goes to Afonda Johnson, leader of the Butterfly Book Club, and Daniela of Ruby Readers Book Club for throwing book launch parties for me. I'm astonished that you would do something like that for me. What a blessing it is to have the support of you ladies and the other members of your clubs.

Robbie Banks, Lynnette Grace, Alisa Graves, Angela Gude, Valerie Hayes, Janice Hilliard, Shelby Kretz, and Charmel Mack, y'all were there for the very first weekend writing event held by Yo Productions and witnessed my efforts to wrap up this story. All of y'all served as my accountability partners and I thank you. Part of my drive to finish was knowing that I would have to report my progress to you. I didn't want to disappoint or discourage anyone.

To the Columbus Literacy Council, the Ohioana Book Festival committee and other festival planning members around the country, bookstores, libraries, clubs, readers, churches, Facebook friends, Twitter followers, *Yo Notes* members, friends, and acquaintances,

THANK YOU, THANK YOU, THANK YOU for all that you do to support and tell others about my work!

If I have neglected to mention anyone specifically, please forgive me. I would never intentionally overlook you. Please charge it to my head and not my heart.

Much love and many blessings,
Yolonda

Website and Social Media Info:
www.yoproductions.net
www.facebook.com/yoproductions
www.twitter.com/ytsanders

Prologue

"That was her, huh?" Robert asked Troy one evening when they were sitting in Robert's basement watching the basketball playoffs while their other halves were upstairs. The women were having their Wise Wives meeting, a group that Robert's wife, Lisa, had started some time ago. Natalie, Troy's wife, had been a somewhat regular attendee for the past couple of years. The meetings were held monthly on the third or fourth Friday evenings. Whenever possible, Troy made sure he was able to watch the kids. Most times he stayed home, but occasionally they all accompanied Natalie to the meeting and hung out with Robert and his little one, Chandler. Having a feeling that he knew where this conversation was headed, Troy wished he would have chosen to stay home tonight.

Troy deleted the text message that had immediately followed the call he'd ignored moments ago. He hadn't said a word to Robert about this situation, in general, for quite a while, and he certainly didn't tell Robert about the phone call and text. But, somehow he knew. *How?*

"Your whole demeanor changed," Robert responded to the question that Troy swore he hadn't spoken out loud. "I've been around you long enough to know that, due to your line of work, you generally don't ignore phone calls. I also know that you would never ignore a call from a friend or family member without good reason, and chillin' down here with me doesn't qualify. You need to tell Natalie before this thing gets any worse. Keeping secrets from your spouse isn't good."

Troy found himself getting irritated by Robert, or RJ as he'd suggested Troy call him many times. That's what all his friends called him. Subconsciously, Troy wondered if he insisted on calling him Robert to maintain a little distance between them. Robert was cool, but their wives were friends. They were acquaintances and acquaintances minded their own business. Troy had shared something with Robert during a moment of frustration and weakness, but it didn't give the man the right to interject his opinions into Troy's personal life.

"Chill, man, I got this under control." Troy tried to sound convincing. There were times when he did feel like he was handling things. Sometimes he wouldn't hear from her for months. Other times, she was relentless in her pursuit to get in touch with him. Somehow she knew things about his family, personal things that made him uncomfortable. Their only mutual contact was Troy's best friend, Elvin, who, after learning about the havoc she'd been wreaking in Troy's life, had removed her from his social network world. If Troy consistently ignored her long enough, she'd have to eventually leave him alone for good...*hopefully.*

"For the sake of your family, I pray that you do have things under control."

The word "family" pricked Troy's heart like a needle. He glanced at his children. His family meant everything to him. The twins, who'd turned one last month in March, had been a little fussy the last hour or so. Not surprising since it was way past their bedtime. Nate, Troy and Natalie's oldest, would be five in June, and was busy entertaining himself and the others by singing and dancing. Troy shook his head in amusement. That boy always found a way to be the center of attention. Nate had amped his silliness up a few notches from normal, which indicated that he, too, was tired.

Troy took pride in his family, including his stepdaughter, Corrine, whom Natalie had as a young teen. There was nothing he wouldn't do for any of his children or his wife. After several years, he and Natalie were finally getting a grip on this thing called marriage. The twin addition to their family had required some tough adjustments this past year, but they'd made it! Things had been peaceful between him and Natalie for the last six months or so. Telling her about his craziness with his ex would only upset her and possibly disturb the tranquility of their relationship. Troy believed that it was better to let sleeping dogs lie.

It would b in your best interest 2answer my calls, her first text had read.

Now a new one came through. *Soon u will wish that u had never ignored me. Consider yourself warned.*

She was trying to scare him, he thought, as he deleted the message, refusing to even look Robert's way while also pretending that he didn't feel Robert's eyes boring into him. *It's better to let sleeping dogs lie*, Troy reminded himself. His only concern was that he may not ever be able to get this particular dog to sleep.

Chapter 1: Leap of Faith

"Hey, babe, I'm going to the gym before coming home," Troy called to say.

"Okay," Natalie replied, though Troy could hear the disappointment in her voice.

"Don't worry. I'll be home well before you need to leave for your meeting."

"Who said I was worried?" The lightness in her voice brought a smile to his face. He'd remembered the meeting without a reminder from her. Surely that would somehow work in his favor later tonight. "Are you and the kids coming?"

Robert had texted him earlier and asked the same question. "Naw, I don't feel like it," Troy stated matter-of-factly. "It's been a long week. I want to kick back and relax when I get home." He'd skipped going in May and would probably do the same next month when July's meeting came. Robert was too much in his business and avoiding being around him was the only way Troy could think to keep him out. After the April meeting, Robert had followed up with Troy to see if he had handled the situation with her. She hadn't contacted Troy since that night she last texted him at Robert's. As far as Troy knew, everything was fine and he told Robert as much, hoping what he wanted to believe was actually true. Troy still suspected her of being the one who sent anonymous presents to the twins and Nate for their birthdays.

When Ebony and Ean received a package back in March, neither Troy nor Natalie knew who had sent the engraved souvenir baby blankets. Troy assumed that Natalie had traced down the sender, but forgot to ask her about it. It wasn't until Nate received a fifty-dollar gift card to Toys R' Us and a mini remote-controlled car earlier this month that Troy remembered to ask Natalie if she'd found out who'd sent the presents. Both boxes, the one to the twins and to Nate, came with fake addresses, and none of their friends or family admitted to sending the items. Natalie wasn't alarmed. She believed one of their loved ones simply wanted to give without receiving credit for doing so. Troy, however, was a little more suspicious. Perhaps he was being paranoid. How would *she* have even known the kids' birthdays? Then again, he remembered the congratulatory message he'd received from her only moments after the twins had been born last year. Somehow, she was keeping up with the ins and outs of his family's lives. Still, sending presents to his children did not fit with the tone of her last text message to him. He got chills when he thought about it.

"*...Consider yourself warned.*"

What was that supposed to mean? Was she threatening to harm him? Troy was certain that if he went to one of her superiors about her antics, she would be severely reprimanded; maybe even fired. He didn't want to open a can of worms that may lead to admitting to Natalie all the things he'd neglected to tell her previously. Besides, Cheryl was a forty-six-year-old federal agent. Surely, she would come to her senses and not destroy her entire career by doing something crazy to him because of a relationship they'd had over two decades ago. It didn't make sense. Then again, shows like *Snapped* existed because there were women who killed for reasons logical people would not understand. He wasn't so much concerned about himself as he was his family. What if Cheryl had some crazy fatal attraction to him and tried to take it out on Natalie? The thought alone was enough to send his blood pressure skyrocketing. If Cheryl ever laid a finger on Natalie, he'd…

"*Hello!*" His wife's screaming voice sobered him.

"I'm here, babe. I'm sorry. I started thinking about something else."

"Let me guess…a case, right?"

"Do I detect sarcasm," he teased. "I'm sorry, for real. What were you saying? Something about putting the kids to bed early and skipping tonight's meeting so you can put me to bed when I get home?"

She laughed. "Not quite. Nate, get that toy from him before he puts it in his mouth, please!" Her instructions had obviously been followed. Troy heard Ean start to wail. His twin sister, Ebony, quickly chimed in. "Honey, I have to go. I'll try to get them bathed and into pajamas before I leave so that'll be one less thing you'll have to do."

"Thanks, babe. I'll see you in a couple of hours. I love you. Tell Nate we'll play a game together when I get there if he behaves."

"Okay. I love you, too."

Perfect timing. They hung up as he pulled into the gym parking lot.

"*Heeyyy, Troy.*" Shay, the ghetto-fabulous evening receptionist, was the first to greet him upon his entering. As usual, Troy nodded, got a locker key, and kept it moving. Shay had a nickname for him and she made it no secret that if he wasn't a married man, she'd snatch him up in a heartbeat, but she, as she put it, "respected his vows." Still, Troy always kept his interactions with her brief as not to give any indication that he was the least bit interested. He already had one psycho stalker chick he couldn't shake.

Shay could claim she'd snatch him up all she wanted, but she was overlooking one fact—she was not his type! Her hair was dyed an unnatural shade of blonde with red and black tips at the end. She was loud with multicolored fingernails so long that it should be a health and safety violation, and Troy had yet to see Shay wear a pair of earrings that didn't hang to her shoulders. The culmination of Shay's look always included low-cut shirts showing all of her cleavage, proudly displaying the word "*Delicious*" that was tattooed across her breasts.

The woman might actually be cute if it weren't for her exaggerated appearance. Shay was short with brown skin and a tiny indentation on her left cheek when she smiled. She managed to be thick enough to exempt her from the thin category and yet small enough to keep her from being considered fat. Somewhere under the super-shiny lip gloss was an intelligent person. According to Will, Shay had several years of college under her belt until she was forced to drop out for financial reasons.

Shay would tell anyone who'd listen that working at the gym was only temporary until she got her big break. She was an aspiring actress waiting for her chance to come. She'd been pursuing acting for more than a decade and had yet to make it. Troy could certainly see her playing the part of a sistah-girl. She was, by all means, a natural. He had yet to witness the brainy side of her, but he'd take Will's word for it. Will, of all people, would know because he and Shay were friends with benefits and no strings attached. He apparently enjoyed those benefits; Troy could think of no other reason why Shay was working the front desk. It definitely wasn't because of her people skills or professionalism.

After securing his cell phone, keys, and wallet in the locker, Troy headed to the aerobic machines, stopping briefly at the bulletin board as he sometimes did to see if there was anything that piqued his interest. One half of it contained announcements pertaining to the gym; the other half advertised the businesses and services of its members. Every blue moon, Troy would find something that caught his eye. Today, there was nothing. He didn't need a deejay or a landscaper, nor did the adorable picture of newborn puppies compel him to want to bring one home as the flier suggested, so Troy went about his business. When he got to the workout area, he said "what's up" to the familiar faces as he became situated. Occasionally, Troy would run into his neighbor there whenever she was able to find someone to sit with her daughter. Charlie, Fudago, Miriam, and Ted were the only ones present today that he knew by name.

Charlie, who was probably in his late fifties, was known as the old-timer because he seemed to come to the gym more to socialize than anything else. As usual, Charlie was on the treadmill with his baseball cap walking at a pace that was laughable. No matter how long he was on the machine, he never seemed to break a sweat and might as well be standing still.

Fudago was a young dude from the Bahamas with dreads and a Caribbean accent that seemed to become thicker whenever there were attractive ladies around. Fudago and Charlie had a love-hate friendship. They were always comparing themselves to one another—their tattoos and who went through the most pain, their cars and whose cost the most and went the fastest. Troy believed in good-old-fashioned male competiveness, but Charlie and Fudago were nauseating. They would also get into it via playful banter, making jokes about each other's appearances, mamas, and anything else that came to mind. Sometimes they got on each other so badly that Troy expected a fistfight to break out between the two, but things never went that far.

Miriam and Ted were married and quite an odd pair. It wasn't the fact that she was a red-haired white woman and Ted was Asian, it was *everything!* Miriam was a fitness freak without an ounce of fat on her body. Ted, whose name surprised Troy considering his heritage, had his fair share of fat and then some. The two had been married for over a decade and had several children together, but it didn't appear to be a match made in heaven. Ted had only started coming around the gym in the last six months, and it appeared he did so only to keep an eye on Miriam who'd had an affair with Charlie at one point. Troy had seen Miriam and Charlie together before and didn't know she was married until Ted started coming. Troy hadn't a clue what Miriam had seen in Charlie. Despite his slow-paced walking, he had an athletic build for an "old-timer," but he was admittedly a ladies' man. He joked that his full-time job was as a hustler and his side gig was working as a mechanic. Troy would never understand why some women, including his neighbor, traded common sense to be arm candy for a man with money and a nice ride.

After giving everyone the hello nod and opening the radio app on his iPod Touch, Troy hopped on the elliptical, setting it for forty minutes. The song that was currently playing was fast paced about a guy declaring his feelings for the girl of his dreams. It made Troy think of Natalie. Man, he loved her—every inch of her! From her used-to-be-black-but-now-dyed-golden-brown, shoulder-length hair, to her professionally painted toenails, there was nothing he would change about her. At least nothing physically. At times he wished the good Lord would make some adjustments to that high-maintenance personality she occasionally allowed to get the best of her. He attributed that to her former years as an aspiring model, and perhaps having no siblings along with being the only female grandchild when she was younger. He smiled, thinking about how melodramatic she could be at times. Underneath the prima donna that would sometimes rear her head was the most tender-hearted and loving woman that he'd ever known.

Things were rough between them for a little while after Natalie first had the twins. She'd tried going back to work full time, but the stress of a toddler, two babies, and an eight-hour workday, was too much for her to handle. She'd gotten herself into a situation at her job where she was given the choice to resign or be terminated. She chose the former while resenting Troy for not "being there" like she felt he should have been. He was a homicide detective and his schedule often involved late nights, early mornings, and everything in between. Natalie used to frequently vocalize feeling like a single mother, and it would spark a verbal storm between them.

From the beginning of last summer through the fall, they argued like the Hatfields and McCoys. Troy hadn't been sure that their marriage would survive the hurtful words that had been exchanged by both of them. The root of their issue had been trust. Natalie had trouble fully placing her trust in him to be a financial provider for their family because of her issues about depending on men in the past. He had difficulty trusting her to handle the family's finances; he'd been used to paying his own bills ever since he could do so. He and Natalie had a joint account that they each transferred money into from their paychecks that was used to buy groceries or other things for the house or their family. They'd also maintained separate checking accounts until last fall when they took a leap of faith. They combined everything so that each had access to all the money that came into their household. Natalie was no longer employed and he was the family's sole provider. Their action was symbolic of them surrendering their independence and becoming more interdependent on each other.

It was a scary leap for them both, but things had been going very well these last six or seven months. They were no longer at each other's throats, but had become as carefree as Adam and Eve running around in the Garden of Eden before the fall. Natalie loved being a stay-at-home mom; he enjoyed bringing home the bacon and letting her distribute it. It took the birth of their twins and the situation at her job to get them to this place. Perhaps the Lord does work in mysterious ways, Troy thought to himself, wondering if that saying was actually scripture or something someone had made up.

Troy finished the elliptical around the same time Charlie called it quits for the day. Fudago had left about twenty minutes earlier for a private session with a trainer and the old man apparently didn't appreciate the evil stares he was getting from Ted. *Drama…*, Troy thought as he went to the weight room, noticing how Charlie stopped to flirt with Shay before leaving. Troy shook his head. Though Will and Shay were "free" to date other people, Shay didn't give Charlie the time of day. Troy wondered what his neighbor would think about Charlie's actions seeing how the two of them had been dating for several months. Charlie was a frequent visitor at his neighbor's and though disgusted by Charlie's flirtatious behavior, Troy ultimately decided not to get involved.

The music, plus pleasant thoughts of Natalie, caused time to fly. Concentrating on Natalie's tall, semi-slender frame could work miracles in his mind. His wife had always had curves in all the right places. Those places had been further enhanced after the birth of the twins. Though she'd lost most of the weight she'd gained during the pregnancy, she was a little thicker than she'd been previously. Nothing diet-worthy in his opinion. He knew many women who would kill to have her post-pregnancy body and yet, she complained about her butt being "too big." *I don't have any complaints*, he thought smiling as the severely overplayed "Happy" song soared through his iPod.

When Troy rested after a set of reps, he saw a guy on a machine across from him staring at him before quickly looking away. The dude was young, likely in his early twenties, with a height and build that seemed somewhat similar to Troy's own six-one, one hundred seventy-three-pound frame. The hard lines in the dude's face, combined with his many tattoos, indicated a life experience, and maybe even a criminal background, well beyond his years. Dude had an Uzi tatted on one arm and the words "Naughty by Nature" etched on the other. It seemed like everyone in the place had tattoos. Troy, the oddball in that respect, continued to stare at Naughty to see if he would look his way again. He did and, when Troy caught him, Naughty did something on his cell phone and then went back to doing reps.

The guy was a newbie to the gym. Troy had only seen him a few times over the last several months though the two had never spoken. It felt as if Naughty by Nature had been staring at him those times as well. If all was indeed true, Troy wondered if it was because the guy had finally been told that he was a cop. Will had told Troy once that he was bad for business after a few guys stopped coming when they learned that Troy worked for the Columbus PD.

Troy didn't take Will's comments to heart. He knew his long-time acquaintance had a tendency to embellish. The two of them had attended the police academy together, but Will got kicked out for falsifying information on his application and for testing positive for marijuana. Troy was certain that Will still had a little bit of wannabe cop in him. He was constantly coming up with theories about unsolved crimes and sharing them with Troy, who indulged him merely for the entertainment of it all. The only reason that most people around the gym knew of Troy's occupational status was because Will always referred to him as "Detective." It was much better than the "Southie" nickname that Shay sometimes tried to put on him because she liked his accent, or "Country Bumpkin" that some of his colleagues were known to say behind his back. "Detective" was a term of endearment and, if Troy didn't know any better, he'd think it gave Will a sense of security to have an officer on the premises, but Troy knew that Will wasn't always walking a straight path. Will still got high and Troy also suspected that he might engage in the distribution of weed, though he had no concrete evidence to prove his hunch. It was a feeling he got sometimes by Will's mannerisms, especially when people would ask if they could see the gym manager in private. Troy partly believed that the "Detective" nickname Will gave him was likely a warning to others that law enforcement was in their presence and they should straighten up and fly right.

Nothing ever went down in Troy's presence and he didn't break his neck to look for activity. Overall, Troy thought Will was a decent guy. The extent of their interaction was at the gym, except for a few occasions when they would run into each other at special preschool events where both Nate and Will's nephew attended. If Will was at the gym today, Troy would ask him about Naughty to get a better understanding since the dude rubbed him the wrong way. *Why wait for Will?* Troy would be able to figure out for himself by striking up a conversation with the guy and he'd intended to do just that. Unfortunately, by the time Troy finished his next set of reps, Naughty was gone.

Maybe next time. Troy could ask Shay, but learning more about Naughty wasn't so serious that he'd initiate a conversation with her. He still couldn't fathom how Will and Shay had ever hooked up. The one thing he and Will had in common when they were at the academy is that they'd both vowed to never get married or have children. Will kept his promise. Troy thought he would as well, but...*along came Natalie*. He smiled and glanced at his watch. *5:53!* He needed to get out of there so he'd have time to shower before Natalie left. He did one more set of reps before calling it a wrap and went to retrieve his things.

Outside, Troy caught the tail glimpse of Will's car leaving the parking lot. *Strange.* He hadn't seen Will inside the gym. Will's car was easy to identify because it was a black BMW 2 series coupe with a specialized license plate that read, *WILL DO.* Figuring that the gym manager had probably come in and out unnoticed, Troy attempted to deactivate his alarm only to find it acting up again. For several weeks now, the alarm to his truck had been giving him problems. He'd turn it on; it would automatically turn off. He'd leave it off and somehow it would turn on. It was driving him crazy, and when he got a chance, he would take his truck to the shop. He'd had his Navigator well before he and Natalie ever met and it was high time for an upgrade. "You'll have to do for now," he said aloud as he hastily threw his duffel bag across the front to the passenger's side of his truck and peeled out of the parking lot.

He hadn't been on the freeway for thirty seconds before a figure sat up in the back, pointing a gun at his head. "Get off at the next exit."

Chapter 2: Simple Life

After getting off the phone with her husband, Natalie tended to the crying storm of her one-year-old twins who were eerily connected beyond simply sharing the same birth date. The only thing they didn't share was gender and skin color. Ebony had taken a darker tone like Troy and Nate; Ean had taken after his mother. Other than different parts and complexions, they embodied every meaning of the word "twins." If Ebony got sick, so did Ean. If Ean pooped in his diaper, his sister did as well. If Ebony wouldn't eat her food, neither would Ean. It came as no surprise then that, when Ean started crying after Nate snatched the tiny kids' meal toy away from him, Ebony felt the need to imitate though nothing had been taken from her. For several minutes, Natalie was in need of a "Calgon, take me away" moment while she was trying to calm the twins. She even said as much under her breath, forgetting that the five-year-old human tape recorder picked up everything.

"Mommy, who's Calgon?" Nate asked after the cry fest had ended.

"No one, honey. It's a brand of bath soap."

"What's a brand of bath soap?"

Knowing that this could inevitably lead to a never-ending Q&A session, she was able to redirect his attention with another statement. "Honey, Mommy needs your help while she finishes dinner. I'm going to put your brother and sister in their playpen and I need you to babysit them, okay?"

"'Kay!" His face lit up as she knew it would. Nate liked being "in charge."

Natalie wasn't crazy enough to solely leave her youngest children in the care of her oldest son. She put the playpen in the middle of the walkway between the kitchen and the living room where she could clearly keep an eye on everyone. The twins cried for a split-second when they were moved into the confined space, but their attention was quickly diverted by the lights and sound of one of their noise-making gadgets.

Things went smoothly while Natalie whipped up dinner. The twins laughed heartily at Nate who would put his face against the net of the playpen and make silly faces and call them "monkey babies." It was something he'd picked up when Natalie had been pregnant, thanks to Troy's mother's crazy superstitions. Natalie usually tried to discourage Nate from referring to his siblings as such, but she let it slide this time; she was concentrating on finishing the task at hand. Besides, the kids were all having fun and she didn't want to impede on that moment with unnecessary verbal correction.

It brought sheer joy to Natalie's heart to witness moments like this when her children interacted with one another. It also stung a little when she thought about all the times she'd missed similar occasions with her oldest daughter, Corrine, whom Natalie had at the tender age of thirteen and gave up for adoption. It wasn't until Corrine was in college that Natalie learned she'd been adopted by a family member and the two of them reconnected. Now, several years later, she and Corrine had an unbreakable bond.

With dinner finally done, Natalie made Nate's plate and then chopped up food tiny enough so that Ean and Ebony could eat with ease. As expected, their messes mirrored one another's. As she'd promised Troy, Natalie got everyone bathed and into pajamas. It was only about a quarter after six when she'd finished. The babies were usually put to bed by eight whenever they were home. Since Nate was a "big boy," he got to stay up until eight-thirty or nine, if he was well-behaved. When Natalie relayed Troy's message to him about playing a game, Nate was thrilled.

By six-thirty Natalie and her brood were back in the living room. Nate had gotten tired of entertaining the little ones by having them chase the remote-controlled car he'd gotten for his birthday, so he put it out of their reach and sat on the couch playing with Natalie's iPad until Troy arrived to make good on his promise. Ebony and Ean were crawling around babbling and gurgling in a language that only the two of them understood. With her purse and keys in hand, Natalie kept glancing out of the front window, expecting Troy at any second, and anticipating the wild reaction of her children when he walked in.

Nate and the twins often reacted to Troy like he was a superstar, and he didn't have to do much to earn his stardom. Simply walking in the door after being gone for a while would spark Nate to do his "*Daa-dee*" squeal while Ean and Ebony would babble "dada" and bounce with excitement. It was cute to see and Natalie sometimes teased Troy about being the favorite parent since she didn't routinely get such warm receptions when she came home after being gone for a while. "It's because they see you all the time," Troy had explained.

"Um hmm" was Natalie's playful response. She found it delightful to watch and it brought back memories of how she would react to her own father when she was younger. She'd only known him for five years because he was killed in a car accident, but his memory continued to live in her heart. "*Daddies are always favored*," she remembered her mom saying once. It certainly seemed true in her household. Sometimes Natalie would have to repeat herself or even threaten to spank Nate before his behavior changed. Troy could say something once and Nate straightened up. The one thing Natalie didn't do was make a habit of being one of those "I'm-going-to-tell-your-father" type of moms. The thought of having a child who disobeyed all day only to turn things around when the father came home made her cringe. She was strict and made sure Nate ultimately listened to her, even if it meant following through on one of her threats.

Natalie glanced at the time. It was 6:40 p.m. Her meeting started at 7:00 and Troy still wasn't there. She began to get concerned and tried calling his cell phone. Voicemail. She waited a second and then tried again. Still no answer. She texted Lisa explaining why she would be late. Not surprisingly, Lisa suggested that she bring the kids. If it was only Nate, she would, but Natalie wasn't about to put the responsibility of her twins on RJ's shoulder. Natalie called Troy once more. This time she left a message. "Hey, where are you? Quit working on those biceps and come home so I can go. You promised you'd be here on time." She also decided to look up the number to the gym. "May I speak with Will, please?"

"I'm sorry, huh-nee," a woman responded. "Will ain't here today. Can I help you wit' sumthin'?"

"Yes, can you page Detective Troy Evans for me, please?" She felt asking for him in that manner made her call seem more legitimate. She'd intended on having Will deliver a message to Troy since the gym's policy on paging people was technically for emergency situations only.

"Oooh, I know him! You talkin' 'bout Southie, 'dat cute, dark-skinned police offisa wit' a li'l country twang to his speech."

This had to be Shay, the one Troy had told her about with the tattooed breasts that had a crush on him. Natalie had to push aside the thought of this woman salivating over her husband every time he went to the gym and, that perhaps, he went for that very reason. *Unfounded jealousy.* That had been the topic at the last Wise Wives meeting. They had discussed how men and women could create issues in their marriages by being unreasonably jealous, failing to realize that jealousy was actually based on some personal insecurity. Such insecurities then caused husbands and wives to react on scenarios that had only taken place in one's head. Besides, someone who couldn't put an intelligent-sounding sentence together was not her husband's type. And Natalie couldn't fault Shay for telling the truth. Troy was cute…and muscular. At forty-three, he had a six-pack that would put even Hollywood A-listers to shame. She quickly reminded herself of the wisdom imparted from last month's Wise Wives meeting as she listened to Troy's admirer explain, *in detail*, what he'd done at the gym and that he'd left at least a half hour ago. "Are you sure?" *Dumb question.* Any woman who could describe Troy the way Shay did would know when he was no longer in her presence. "Okay, thank you."

After the call, Natalie didn't know if she should be concerned or mad. Did he get into a car accident or had he been called to a crime scene and didn't have the decency to let her know what was happening? She was so deep in thought that the call from her best friend, Aneetra, scared her.

"Are you on your way to Lisa's?"

"No. Troy still hasn't gotten home yet."

"Where is he? Is he on his way?"

"Girl, I don't know." She explained the whole scenario to her friend, from her phone conversation with Troy earlier, to what she'd made for dinner, to getting the kids in their bed clothes and waiting on Troy to arrive.

"Well, you know I don't like going by myself. I'm coming over and waiting with you until he gets home."

Between the two of them, Aneetra was the most extroverted, which is why Natalie found it so ironic that her friend had refused to attend meetings alone. Natalie had done so without Aneetra on several occasions and she tried to encourage her to do the same. "No. You should go," she urged. "I don't want you to miss because of me." Aneetra and her husband had recently reconciled after being separated for well over a year. Aneetra's feelings still fluctuated sometimes and Natalie knew she could use the encouragement and support of the other Wise Wives women.

"I'll see you in a few," Aneetra said, ignoring Natalie's suggestion and hanging up.

Natalie snickered lightly before her mind quickly reverted back to Troy. In the past, Natalie would have been livid with him about not being home on time, but concern began to overshadow any possibility of anger. She turned to the local news channel, sighing in relief when there weren't any breaking reports about a fatal car crash.

What could be keeping him? Assuming that perhaps it was a lead about an open case that had distracted her overly committed detective husband, Natalie decided she would cut him some slack. Things had been good between them lately and Troy had been doing everything possible to be there with the kids for her meetings. Sure, there were times he'd missed because of work, but unlike depicted in TV, there was no machine that could predict or prevent murder. Still, a courtesy call would have been nice and Natalie would be sure to tell Troy about himself later. Right now, she needed a Plan B if she had any chance of getting to the Wise Wives meeting before it was over. "Hey, Corrine, I need a huge favor." She explained the situation to her daughter.

"Aw, Nat, I would, but I'm still at the office working on a new campaign." Corrine was a marketing analyst for Victoria's Secret. Her job could be challenging at times, requiring out-of-town trips and long hours, but Corrine seemed to love it. She was young and, as far as Natalie knew, still single so she could keep up with the demands of her position. Corrine was also very helpful with the kids. Natalie didn't need her quite as much now that she wasn't working, but she knew how much Corrine loved her younger siblings, especially Nate. She wore a locket with his newborn picture in it. Whenever Corrine was able to lend a helping hand, she was always a godsend. "I feel bad that I can't watch them for you."

"Honey, there's nothing for you to feel bad about. It's not the end of the world if I miss tonight's meeting."

"Okay. Well, call me this weekend if you need me for anything else."

"I might take you up on that offer the next time Ean and Ebony have one of their crying fits. They are cool now, but they showed out earlier. I'm no longer wishing that Calgon would come take me away." Natalie laughed, expecting her daughter to do the same.

"Who's Calgon?"

She gave Corrine the same explanation she'd given Nate, this time adding information about the old commercial which featured the lady in the bath and the bubbles.

"Uh, yeah, okay. I'm gonna need you to stop with that joke. It's not working. You make yourself sound old."

Sometimes Natalie felt every bit of thirty-nine and then some, trying to keep up with her three little ones. And the grays didn't help, which is why she'd decided to dye her hair. She'd also gotten the cartilage on her right ear re-pierced. It was something she'd done in her early twenties, but let it close because the healing process was too painful. She suffered through it this time, wondering if she had been going through some midlife crisis. These last couple of years had been like a roller-coaster ride. She didn't purposefully get pregnant, despite Troy's desire for more children. And when she did, she certainly hadn't expected twins. Considering that her father had been a twin, it shouldn't have come as any surprise, but it was more than she'd bargained for. And then there was the thing at work...

Becoming a full-time homemaker was far from her goal. Natalie had enjoyed her job as a financial analyst with Dennison Financial Solutions. She had been in charge of small business accounts that grossed less than $100,000 each year. Though there was the typical office drama, Natalie stayed away from it. She was cordial with everyone, but the only one she spent any time with was Aneetra, whom Natalie met at Dennison. Aneetra, who had been there for several years before Natalie began, was also well liked by the other employees and favored by their boss. Natalie was sure it was their boss's affinity for Aneetra that worked in her favor coupled with the lack of solid evidence that Natalie had done anything malicious that kept the company from doing a formal investigation. It was perhaps why Natalie was offered any type of severance. Overstressed from her work caseload, Natalie had brought some files home and logged into the Dennison portal. Somehow she accidentally deleted years' worth of electronic financial records that one of Dennison's clients needed for a court proceeding.

Natalie still didn't know how in the world she'd managed to not only delete the files, but also erase the backup copies as well. From the outside looking in, it appeared that Natalie was purposely trying to sabotage things. The only thing she could think of was that she'd somehow been careless in trying to balance home and work duties at the same time. Troy had been working late that night, and of course, Natalie felt his absence and inability to help care for their children consistently, contributed to her stress load and indirectly affected her job performance. In retrospect, she'd unfairly placed blame on him. In the end, losing her job worked out for her benefit as one well-known scripture in Romans stated, "*And we know that in all things God works for the good of those who love him, who have been called according to his purpose.*"

The job thing didn't only work out for Natalie's good, but for the good of her entire family. Through that ordeal, her marriage was strengthened because she and Troy were forced to communicate openly and honestly with one another. They now had a level of intimacy that they'd never had before. All of her guards are down, no hesitation, no reservations... just pure, unadulterated trust.

Being forced to leave her job also benefited her children who now had more access to her time. The twins were with her all day every day, but she and Troy had decided to keep Nate in preschool on a part-time basis—Mondays, Wednesdays, and Fridays until noon. They thought it would be good for him to have that structure since he'd be starting kindergarten in the fall. Nate was now home with her in the early afternoons on those days versus the times he would have been in aftercare until the evenings if she worked late. In addition, Natalie gained a whole new level of love and respect for motherhood, in general. To think that she, former miss fashion model wannabe, would find joy in the complex and yet very simple life of snotty noses, dirty diapers, and *Blues Clues* was nothing short of a miracle. She still wasn't crazy about the stretch marks that sprinkled over her abdomen and thighs, and she faithfully used cocoa butter, shea butter, and all kinds of other butters and creams in hopes that they would one day fade. Her bikini-wearing days were in the past, but Natalie couldn't imagine life without any of her children, including Corrine, who, thankfully, had been kind enough not to leave permanent pregnancy reminders on her body. *Ah, if only my skin had the elasticity in my thirties as it did when I was thirteen.* She smiled. That was the model in her talking. Most days, the mommy in her saw those same scars as badges of honor.

Speaking of badges...her husband had better be utilizing his right then. That's the only excuse he'd have of not being home in time for her meeting!

Chapter 3: Second Shift

Aneetra arrived a few minutes after 7:00 p.m. with a couple of Redbox movies in hand. "I figured if Troy doesn't come home, we'll need something to do." She handed the movies to Natalie and walked into the living room to give hugs and kisses to her godchildren.

Nate loved "Aunt Nee Nee" to no end and proudly ran into her open arms. Ean's and Ebony's love had been conditional ever since Aneetra had done the big chop about six weeks ago. Her relaxed, shoulder-length hair was resting in a landfill somewhere and a new teeny-weenie Florida from *Good Times* 'fro had taken its place. The twins perked up when they heard her voice, but the new look was still foreign to them so they briefly cried when she approached them.

"You got my babies so confused." Natalie laughed and picked up Ebony who reached out to her. Ean followed suit.

"Whatever. They should be used to my hair by now. They didn't act crazy when you dyed yours."

"The keyword is 'dyed.' I didn't go from Goldilocks to nolocks overnight."

Aneetra playfully stuck out her tongue and sat on the couch with Nate who told her about his day at school before reoccupying himself with Natalie's iPad and having "Aunt Nee Nee" play, too.

Natalie observed the two of them with delight. She felt like she had her old friend back. Aneetra's happy-go-lucky personality was refreshing and something Natalie greatly missed during the time that Aneetra and Marcus had been separated. Natalie hadn't been sure if their marriage could be repaired after the damage that had been done to it, but she was glad that they'd worked through their issues. Aneetra had said that being a part of the Wise Wives ministry group helped her, which is why Natalie really wished Aneetra had gone without her. The meetings helped Natalie as well. Neither she nor Aneetra had gotten comfortable with the whole group-sharing thing and generally were non-talkative participants during the meetings. But, they were both good listeners and would discuss amongst themselves the things that they learned from the other women in the group.

Aneetra was eighteen years-plus into her marriage while Natalie and Troy were two weeks shy of their sixth anniversary happening early next month. Yet, there were things that both women learned from and taught each other. Natalie was proud to see that her friend had started to accept her fashion advice. When Aneetra cut all of her hair, Natalie wasn't feeling the new do. Aneetra, who had a darker skin tone close, but not quite the shade of Troy's, was only two years Natalie's senior, but always dressed much older. She was on the thicker side of the spectrum and Aneetra seemed self-conscious about her appearance. The original short hairstyle, combined with somebody's grandma's clothing, and the lack of consistent cosmetics and jewelry did not work in Aneetra's favor. It took Nate telling "Aunt Nee Nee" that she looked like a boy for her to spice up things a bit. Aneetra had a makeover party at her home a couple of weeks ago with her daughters, Natalie, Corrine, and a few women from church and Wise Wives. Since then, Aneetra's life—well, her appearance—had never been the same. Tonight, she was working that afro, along with a maxi dress, gold hoops, and shimmer lip gloss. Natalie would have chosen heeled sandals, or even wedges instead of flats, but at least Aneetra had chosen fashionable ones. Natalie didn't have to ask Aneetra if Marcus enjoyed her new look. They'd been together on several occasions when Aneetra cut out early because Marcus was home waiting on her; that had said it all.

Natalie again started thinking about her own husband whom she still had not heard from. By a quarter to eight, she was certain that he wasn't coming home. She simply wanted the assurance that he was okay. She'd tried calling him one more time. No luck. "It's unusual for him not to call or at least send a text when he knows I'm expecting him," she expressed to Aneetra. "Something isn't right. I feel it."

"You're feeling gas from those beans you made. Relax, Nat, I'm sure he's okay." Aneetra didn't sound as confident as she was trying to make Natalie believe. Still, Natalie appreciated her friend being there, especially when all three of her youngins decided to go crazy at the same time.

It was Nate who had led the way to the Evans children's group meltdown. Whenever he was sleepy, he got excessively silly or whiny. Tonight he'd chosen the latter and it seemed like every big-brother bone in his body had vanished. It started when the twins finally warmed up to Aneetra. She'd stopped playing with him on the iPad and turned her attention to them. They both sat in her lap on the couch next to Nate. Ean, as any one-year-old would be, was fascinated by the jellied objects on Candy Crush and grabbed at the game. Nate fussed at him about being too young to play, and when Nate moved it out of Ean's reach, he somehow accidentally ended the game. As luck would have it, that was Nate's last life and it would be twenty-something minutes before he got another one. That whole scene went down in less than thirty seconds, but caused at least fifteen minutes' worth of chaos.

Nate had a fit; jumping and screaming as if someone had died. Not one to take kindly to temper-tantrums, Natalie wanted to pop his butt except she'd only be doing so because of her own emotional distress. She was a firm believer in spankings, however, it wasn't her first reaction to initial episodes of misbehavior though she couldn't swear that she'd always had that mindset. Her tolerance had increased now that she didn't have the stress of working eight hours a day and then coming home for her "second shift," a term sociologists used to refer to the after-work responsibilities of wives and mothers.

"Let's pay for him to get extra lives," suggested Aneetra after Nate's tantrum about the game became infectious and rubbed off on the twins.

"Let's not." It didn't matter that she could acquire a new set of five lives for only ninety-nine cents. It was still a waste of money. Though Aneetra offered to give her "a freakin' dollar," Natalie would not give in. "No. He needs to know that acting crazy won't get him what he wants. It's time for them to go to bed anyhow."

Natalie took the screaming twosome and left Nate in the care of Aneetra. Of course, there was nothing really wrong with Ean or Ebony. They were out almost as soon as they were laid in their cribs. Nate was a little more uncooperative and Natalie figured out why. In addition to being sleepy, he was acting out because he missed his father. When Aneetra offered to read him a story from one of his Spider-Man books, Nate cried that he wanted his daddy to do it. The poor child lay in his bed and literally cried himself to sleep.

"I didn't know Candy Crush was that serious," said Aneetra.

"It wasn't Candy Crush. It's Troy. Earlier Troy promised to play a game with him when he got home." Remembering this, Natalie started to wonder again if something bad had happened to her husband. He wasn't one to make promises to Nate and not keep them. Troy's role as a father and his word were too important to him. When she and Aneetra went back downstairs, Natalie was about to call CPD headquarters and grabbed her phone only to see that she had a text from Troy.

Chapter 4: Dead Man Walking

The blaring noise brought Troy to full consciousness as he awoke in a pitch-black room trying to make sense of his surroundings. The red light flashed on the ringing phone that sat on the nightstand next to the bed. Without giving it much thought, he answered it, if for no other reason than to stop the noise.

"Hi, Mr. Evans, this is the front desk with the wakeup call that you had requested."

"Huh?"

"I have a note here that you asked for a six a.m. wakeup call this morning. When you're ready to check out, leave your key on the dresser. We'll charge the room to the credit card on file unless you have changes."

Troy begrudgingly thanked the lady, trying to comprehend everything. If it wasn't for the sticker posted on the telephone, he wouldn't have even known what motel he was in. What day was it? *Friday*. No, that was yesterday. He tried to piece together how he'd gotten there. It was all coming back to him now. The phone call with Natalie...the gym...Naughty's Uzi tats...Will's BMW. The last thing Troy remembered was getting in his truck and her surprising him by sitting up in the backseat, holding a gun to his head.

"Get off at the next exit," she'd ordered.

If he hadn't known her voice, he would not have immediately recognized her. The last time he'd seen her was about a year and a half ago when Natalie was about six months pregnant with the twins. Her hair was short then. It was long now; much longer than it had been when they dated. "Cheryl, what are you doing?"

"Do as I said or I'll pull the trigger. Get off!"

He obliged, more annoyed than scared. Once he pulled over and she stopped pointing that thing at him, his plan was to overpower her. It would be easy. She was almost an entire foot shorter than him and Troy was certain he could bench press her weight and then some. Taking that gun from her would be like snatching a pacifier from a baby. He simply had to get her and the gun from behind his driver's seat.

Troy never got the chance to enact his plan. He pulled over on the side of the street and all of a sudden, she pricked a needle in his shoulder. The next thing he knew, he was waking up in the motel room with a major headache.

Troy jumped out of bed, thinking she could be lying beside him. She wasn't. He could see clearly into the bathroom. It was empty. Troy was angry and alone. When she called his cell phone only seconds later, he, in a not-so-Christian manner, asked what she'd done to him.

"That's no way to start off the morning, my dear. Did you get a good night's sleep?"

He opened the window to let natural light into the room and peeked out, wondering if he'd see her car nearby. His keys were on the dresser, underneath a black thong, which he carefully laid to the side with disgust. "*What did you do to me!*"

"Not nearly as much as I wanted to." She laughed and hung up.

Troy left the room, ignoring the "do not disturb" sign hanging outside on the door and deeply praying that he had not been violated. As he mashed the alarm on his key chain, trying to find his truck, he wondered about Natalie and how he would explain this to her. He could kill Cheryl right now. He was so mad that he would find joy in strangling her and watching the last breath of air leave her body. He'd resuscitate her only to repeat the process of choking her until she could no longer be brought back to life. When he was sure that her heart had been permanently stopped, he'd empty his gun into her chest simply for fun. The thought of murder became so appealing to the sworn officer of the law that he literally had to fight to clear his mind. Thoughts preceded actions, and such an action, for him, came with severe consequences. He was able to get a little help controlling his thoughts by recalling the New King James Version of Romans 12:2: *[D]o not be conformed to this world, but be transformed by the renewing of your mind, that you may prove what is that good and acceptable and perfect will of God.* He wasn't convinced that God's perfect will was for him to take Cheryl's life. But, if there was the slightest possibility…

Finally! Troy found his truck parked in front of the motel lobby. Before entering, he made sure to check the back seats. Empty. He really had to get his alarm fixed to keep Cheryl or anyone else from unauthorized access to his vehicle. Right now getting home to his wife and children took precedence and Troy raced through the city as fast as he could. When he arrived, he stayed parked in the garage for a while, trying to figure out the words to explain to Natalie about what had transpired. He was supposed to watch the kids while she went to the meeting. He'd told her that he was on his way home. Sure enough, she'd tried to call him. Troy saw the missed calls, but he didn't bother listening to the voice messages that he was certain were words of discontentment.

Troy walked in the house, glad that Natalie had secured the alarm. Sometimes she forgot and that worried him. He didn't want them in the house unprotected. Their home was eerily quiet. He wondered if Natalie had turned on the monitoring system so she could hear him come in. He expected her to charge down the stairs at any moment to rip him up one way and down another. He stood still, waiting for the confrontation. She didn't come.

Troy didn't know whether he should be relieved or worried. He held on to the granite island for strength for a few minutes before going upstairs. His head was pounding. What happened to him last night? How did Cheryl get him from the truck into that room? Did the drug she'd given him knock him out or merely inebriate him so that he'd be more cooperative? Had something sexual taken place between them? He had so many questions and frustratingly, no answers.

The thought of cheating on his wife, even unwillingly, made Troy sick. The walk up the stairs seemed to take forever. He felt like a dead man walking. In a way, he did feel like he was headed to his execution. Before entering his bedroom, he checked on all the kids as was his custom. Nate's room was decked out in Spider-Man and li'l man was still in a deep sleep. Ebony and Ean shared a room for now. When they got older, the plan was to move one of them into the fourth bedroom, which was currently more of a storage facility than anything else. Their nursery had a Disney theme, half Mickey Mouse, half Minnie. They looked so peaceful. Actually, all of his children did. Troy hated that he'd missed the chance to play with Nate last night. He'd been looking forward to spending that time with him. Cheryl had robbed him of that opportunity!

Troy took a deep breath and braced himself for the storm that was brewing inside his bedroom. To his surprise, Natalie lay asleep like a log. There was a note on his side pillow.

Now I lay me down to sleep
I pray the Lord my husband to keep
I pray the Lord my husband to protect
May he come home unharmed without any defects
When he finally lays down to rest
May he arise again and be at his best
—Love Always, Nat

Troy didn't understand. He knew Natalie well enough to know that she was livid last night when he didn't come home. Was this poem a trick? Was her goal to be so sickeningly nice to him that he would forever be burdened with guilt? He was at least comforted that it wasn't an angry letter waiting for him though he was sure there was still damage control to do. Her being fast asleep bought him some time to think about how to make amends for last night.

Troy needed to take a shower before getting into bed. He wasn't sleepy, but he wanted to lie next to and hold Natalie. Before stripping off his clothes, Troy plugged in his phone charger as the low battery alert had sounded. That's when he noticed the text message icon. There were two messages waiting on him. One was from Cheryl who wrote, "You're welcome."

For what? Troy thought, but didn't dare reply.

The other was from Natalie to say that she understood and that she loved him. It didn't make sense until he scrolled up and saw a message that he'd supposedly written to her. *Hey, babe. I'm soooooo sorry. I got called to a triple homicide on the way home.*

So that explained why Natalie wasn't upset with him and left a nice poem. Was Cheryl's message her way of saying that he should be grateful that she made up a story to appease his wife? Unbelievable! Troy put down his phone and headed to the bathroom to shower. Before doing so, he inspected himself of any signs of sexual activity. There was no residue that he could see. Anxious to wash the stench of whatever had gone on last night off of his body, Troy jumped in the hot water, determined that the first chance he got, he was going to Cheryl's superior. When Troy finally got in the bed, his movement stirred Natalie.

"I'm glad you're home. I love you," she said in a still-half-asleep voice.

"I love you, too, babe," he responded and held her close.

Chapter 5: About Last Night

Later that Saturday afternoon, Troy and Natalie took their children downtown to Columbus Commons, the community nine-acre park located on the site that once housed the City Center mall before it was demolished. It was a nice open area with various family activities, featuring a twenty-seat carousel, café, free fitness classes, special concert events, and a reading room, which was a section of tables covered with umbrellas. It was Natalie's idea to go there. Troy's head still hurt so he wasn't feeling up to par. He'd speculated about the type of drug Cheryl had injected him with to cause such a side effect. In light of the recent incident with her, Troy didn't want to take his family anywhere until he made a visit to the local FBI office, but Natalie was in such a good mood. He didn't want to ruin her day by disclosing all the secrets he'd kept from her about Cheryl the last two years. Besides, either way, Troy's visit to the FBI would have to wait until Monday morning.

It was a little known secret that Columbus even had an FBI office. It was termed a residency agency rather than a field office. This meant that it wasn't listed on the national website and unfortunately, for Troy, it wasn't open twenty-four-seven. He would have gladly found an excuse to delay this family outing if it meant being able to get Cheryl off his back for good.

Troy had mixed feelings about how populated the park was. On one hand, he felt safe with the crowd. Cheryl would be beyond stupid to target him or his family in such an open space. On the other hand, a lot of people meant too many uncontrollable elements. What if Cheryl was hiding somewhere in the midst of all these people? It would be like her to pop up unexpectedly and engage Natalie in a conversation simply to put him on edge.

At first, Troy thought that a young, middle-aged Caucasian gentleman was being polite when he spoke to them, until Troy continued to see the man gazing at him and his family. He sat at a table with a black baseball hat pulled down to the middle of his forehead. He held a newspaper as though he was reading, but Troy caught the man several times intensely staring at them. The guy looked away every time. Troy bore his eyes into him so intensely that the man finally got up and left.

After that incident, Troy was having a hard time holding it together. He swore that everyone was staring at his family. In addition, he thought he'd seen a glimpse of Cheryl in every direction he turned, but when he'd blink and look again, she would be gone. It wasn't humanly possible for Cheryl to go from the north side of the Commons to the south side in the short time it took him to turn his head from one end to the other. His paranoia was starting to get the best of him and Troy wanted nothing more than to get his family home to safety. What made things even creepier was that some kid walked by with old school rap music blaring through his headphones. It was the song "My Mind's Playing Tricks on Me" by the Geto Boys.

"Here comes your friend."

At the prompting of his wife's voice, Troy looked and saw Will walking toward them.

"Hey, man! What's going on?" The two bumped fists and Will

said hello to Natalie and the kids. Troy was not surprised to see Will in tight workout gear showing off his tats. On one arm, Will had a tattoo of a black panther and on the other, he had a tiger. Troy never cared enough to ask him the meanings. Will seemed to love wearing things that accentuated his muscles and brought attention from the ladies, something he and Fudago had in common. Troy refused to look at Natalie for fear that she might be staring harder than he would feel comfortable with. He kept his focus on Will, whose glossy eyes indicated that he'd spent some quality time with herb recently.

When Natalie announced that she would take the kids to the reading area, his knee-jerk response was for her to "*wait!*"

She gave him an awkward smile. "We'll just be over here. Nice seeing you again, Will. I'm sure I'll see you around sometime at a pre-school event."

"For sure. Good to see you, too." Will, who had no children of his own, often stepped in as the father-figure for his young nephew who was being raised by Will's mom because Will's sister and the child's father were both serving life sentences. He turned his attention back to Troy. "So what's up, man? You get a good work-out in yesterday? I heard Charlie and Fudago got into it again."

"Are you surprised?"

"Naw, not really. Charlie's at the gym so much that he might as well apply for a job."

"Do you really want him working there? He'd run all of the female clients away."

Will laughed. "Yeah, you're right. Charlie don't know how to keep his mouth shut. How long were you there yesterday?"

"About an hour and a half. I don't how we missed each other. I saw you, though, when you were leaving."

"Leaving? I wasn't at the gym yesterday."

"Then how'd you know I was there?"

"Shay told me last night when she came over." Will spoke slowly as if Troy was hard of hearing, or maybe that was his high getting to him. "You know she has a crush on you, so I hear about *everything* you do."

"It's a good thing I don't do much then, huh? Are you sure you weren't at the gym at all yesterday?"

"*Yeh-uh.* You all right, man? Seems like you had a rough night. Hey, by any chance, have you ordered any personal training services?"

"No. Why?"

"No particular reason. Just wondering."

Diversion. That's the tactic Will seemed to be using to draw Troy's attention away from the fact that he was lying about being at the gym. But why lie about such a simple thing?

When Will's phone rang, he said, "I need to take this call. I'll see you at the gym next week." As Will was walking away, Troy thought he'd heard him say, "Hey, Cheryl."

Maybe it was Sherry…or, more realistically, Shay. Maybe he simply said "Hey" and Troy was imagining the rest. Confused, he set out to meet up with Natalie and the kids and almost lost his mind when he saw the guy with a black baseball hat standing in front of them. "What's your interest in my family?" Troy asked aggressively, shoving the man in the shoulder.

Natalie looked at him like he was a three-headed monkey and when the man turned around, Troy felt like one. There was no logical way that anyone could have confused this dark-skinned brother in his sixties with the Caucasian man Troy had seen staring at them earlier. The person talking to Natalie was Richard Griggs, a colleague and family friend; and the man responsible for introducing him and Natalie to each other. Richard was a district attorney and once the longtime boyfriend of Natalie's deceased mother. He was currently married to Natalie's godmother and, together, they served as surrogate grandparents to the Evans' children.

"Is everything okay?" Richard looked from Troy to Natalie with confusion.

"Yeah, my bad, man. I'm trippin'. I don't know what got into me. I guess I'm being overly protective."

Richard didn't take the assault to heart. Though Troy wasn't feeling conversational, he still engaged in small talk. Troy learned that Richard's wife, Sylvia, was also at the Commons and, thus, he and his family spent the remainder of their time there hanging out with them. Troy thought he saw the mysterious man with the hat again, but like the times when he thought he saw Cheryl, he'd blink and the guy would be gone. The Geto Boys' song was playing again. This time the music was all in his head.

When they got home around 4:30, Natalie made all the kids lie down for a nap. Troy was in the process of changing into more comfortable clothing when he heard Natalie yell, "*Danggit!*" before entering their bedroom.

"What's wrong, babe?"

"I tripped over this stupid car again." She came in holding Nate's toy vehicle. "I'm tired of finding it all around the house. I feel like getting rid of it and then pretending it's lost somewhere. I know…," she said before Troy could interject, "that would be cruel."

"Maybe put it up for a little while until he asks for it and then explain that he can only have it back if he agrees not to leave it everywhere."

"That's a good idea." Natalie sat the car on top the ottoman at the foot of their bed. "So, what's up with you? You've been pretty quiet today. Is your case bugging you?"

Troy opted to tell the truth, not wanting to drag out the triple homicide thing. "No. I have a headache and I've also been thinking about Will. Yesterday, I saw his car at the gym, but he told me today that he wasn't there. Then, out of the blue, he asked me if I had ordered any personal training sessions. It was weird."

"What was so weird about it?"

"Why would he lie to me about being at the gym yesterday?"

"Maybe he didn't lie intentionally. I could tell he was high. He could have easily forgotten or maybe someone else had his car."

"Naw, high or sober, Will's too crazy about that BMW to let it out of his sight."

Natalie came up behind him and wrapped her hands around his waist. "Is talking to Will what had you walking up on Richard like he stole something?"

Humored, Troy turned to face her and put his arms around her as well. "What-*ever.* I didn't know who he was at first. I had to make sure everything was okay."

"Um hmm. Everything *was* okay, but obviously you weren't. I think you're making way more of this Will thing than needs to be."

"If you're telling me that I'm making too much of things, I must be because we both know that I'm the level-headed one in this relationship."

"Oh be quiet!" She playfully shoved him in the chest.

Troy picked her up over his shoulders pretending he would drop her while she screamed for mercy. "Promise you'll never hit me again."

"Okay, *okay*! I promise," she said between giggles. When he put her down, she looked up at him adoringly. "I love you, crazy man."

"I love you, too, crazy woman," he responded as she leaned in for a kiss.

The overly exaggerated "*yuck!*" from their five-year-old both startled and amused them.

"If you were taking a nap like I told you, you wouldn't have seen that."

"I'm not sleepy," he said, yawning. "I wanna play a game with Daddy."

"You need to—"

"It's okay," Troy interrupted. "I need to make good on my promise from last night."

"Okay, but if he starts trippin' from the lack of sleep, you're on your own, buddy." After those words of warning, Natalie grabbed her iPad and headed to the restroom.

"You ready, li'l man?"

"Yep, 'cuz I'm not sleepy," Nate managed to say in the midst of another yawn. Troy could only chuckle at his son's denial and insistence to take his toy car with them to the basement. He'd spotted it on their ottoman. Troy issued the warning that he and Natalie had agreed upon. Nate said he understood, Troy gave him the car, and the two of them headed downstairs. Not twenty minutes later, Nate had fallen asleep on the couch with the Xbox remote control in hand.

As much as Troy tried to let go, both the strange man at the Commons and the thing with Will kept nagging at him. Perhaps the incidents were nothing, but as a detective, Troy couldn't ignore his hunches. He could do nothing about the stranger, but he could investigate things further with Will. Troy gave him a call.

"Hey, man, I need clarity about something from earlier. Why'd you ask if I'd ordered any personal training services? The question came out of nowhere and threw me off guard," Troy said into Will's voicemail. "I'm sure it's no big deal, but please give me a call when you get a chance." He decided not to mention anything about seeing his car again. He'd wait until they spoke in person. However, the more Troy thought about it, the more he wondered if he should let the car thing go. Will's lying could have possibly been because of something related to his extracurricular activities. If that was the case, Troy preferred not to know.

Later that evening, Troy's head had finally started to feel better. Natalie ordered pizza for dinner and then she and Troy watched a Spider-Man movie with Nate that they'd seen more times than they could remember. Each parent took turns running after Ean and Ebony who tried to get into everything their little hands could reach. Corrine called to see if they were home and then stopped by for a short while to hang out. Ultimately, she ended up taking Nate with her upon his request. She normally got him overnight at least once a month. Sometimes she also took Ebony and Ean, but three little ones were a lot for a young girl. Plus, everyone could tell that, though Nate loved his younger siblings, he didn't like sharing his sissy's time with them. Corrine was his and the two of them had a special bond that Ebony and Ean would have to learn to live with when they got older.

"Hey, honey, when you finish, please come here. I want to show you something," Natalie yelled down to Troy after Corrine and Nate had left and she'd put the twins to bed.

"Okay, give me a sec." He was in the basement on his Xbox playing The Outfit, a World War II combat game set in Europe. Normally football or basketball were his go-to choices when he wanted to relax, but every now and then, he'd knock the dust off of something else in his collection.

Despite having spent the entire day with his family, Troy had been too worried to truly enjoy the time with them. Ironically, not hearing from Cheryl hadn't given him any peace. He couldn't help but wonder what was going through that crazy mind of hers. He prayed God would hinder any plans she had until Monday morning when he would finally be able to put a stop to all of this. He also hoped that somehow it could all be resolved without getting Natalie involved.

Not knowing what took place in that motel room bothered him most of all. He wanted to tell Natalie everything, but he didn't know what to say. He, himself, wasn't sure what had happened last night. Had he been sexually assaulted? Who, in their right mind, would believe that someone as petite as Cheryl could overpower and have her way with him? He wouldn't believe it had he not been the victim. Though there's no concrete evidence that they'd had sex, there was also nothing proving that they hadn't. His thoughts spiraled into a thousand scenarios. All of them were still fresh on his mind when he went up the stairs to see what Natalie had wanted and nearly tripped over Nate's toy car, which had been left in front of the basement door. "Here's your chance to take this thing if—" Troy froze. Having been so preoccupied with what might have happened with Cheryl was the reason why he felt uncomfortable, instead of excited, when he saw Natalie dressed in one of his favorite lingerie outfits adorned with stilettos.

"Instead of playing the game, I thought you might be interested in playing with me," she flirted, seductively beckoning him with her index finger.

Under any other circumstances, Troy would have swept her into his arms and wasted no time exploring all of Victoria's Secrets. He'd actually been relieved when Nate came into their room earlier and asked him to play because, had all of the children been asleep, Natalie could have easily made her move then. Fearing such, Troy had remained in the basement after Nate dozed off until he heard the pitter-patter of the little ones. Now, Troy stood motionless, paralyzed by the unknown details about last night. If there was intercourse, was a condom used or had there been an exchange of bodily fluids? What if Cheryl had given him a sexually transmitted disease? He loved Natalie too much to put her at that kind of risk.

"What's wrong? I thought you'd like this."

"I do, babe. It's just that I, um..." *Think, Troy, think...* He began fumbling with Nate's toy. "Um, I got a call from the station. I need to go interview some suspects."

"Is it the case from last night?"

"Uh, yeah. Yep, the triple homicide."

"Phooey." Her bottom lip protruded, reminding him of their son sometimes when he didn't get his way.

"You have no idea how bad I want you." Troy spoke truthfully as he walked closer and drew her into his arms. They engaged in a brief, but passionate kiss. "I'm so sorry, babe."

"I'm horny, not mad." She gave a half smile. "I understand; duty calls. You go take care of things and I'll be here when you return."

They both went upstairs. Natalie put Nate's car on their chest so that it would be out of his reach. "I feel bad that we can't properly thank the person who sent this."

"Oh, I'm sure they're not worried about it at this point," he said, trying not to give too much thought that it could have very well been Cheryl. He watched in dismay as Natalie took off the heels and put on house shoes and a robe while Troy pretended to get ready for the fake call by changing his shirt and grabbing his service weapon from the safe. "Make sure you lock up after I leave," he said to her.

"Ah, my protective detective." She pretended to be annoyed by his instructions. "I love you for being so concerned about our safety. Now, hurry up and get out of here so you can get back home." She tried to seem normal, but he saw it in her face. She was about to go into prayer mode, which was her custom whenever he left for night calls.

He felt like an idiot, knowing he was causing her prayers to be in vain! After one last peck, Troy left, uncertain where he was headed. He remembered a time when leaving so abruptly would have eventually worked its way into a future argument where Natalie would have accused him of inactive parenting, and he would have said that she was irrational and unappreciative. The fact that his wife was so understanding made him more infuriated with Cheryl. Without thinking twice, Troy called her. When she didn't answer, he left a nasty message on her voicemail, using words he'd surely have to repent for later.

A few minutes passed and Cheryl responded with a text. In it, she sent her address and suggested that he come over so they could talk.

Troy looked at the message with disbelief. How stupid did she think he was?

Chapter 6: Zero to Sixty

Troy wound up at a different motel from the one he'd woke up in this morning. He had nowhere to go and no one to confide in. He thought about going to his ex-partner's home, but didn't want to drag him in the middle of it. He also thought about calling his best friend, Elvin, who lived in Chicago and was fully aware of the situation with Cheryl. Elvin had been through so much in the last couple of years that Troy didn't want to burden him by sharing bad news. As a last resort, Troy had even considered reaching out to Robert. However, the close relationship between their wives made that a horrific idea. All it would take was for Robert to tell Lisa that he called, Lisa to tell Natalie, and Natalie to wonder why he'd contacted Robert when he was working a triple homicide. It would lead to a whole bunch of questions that he could not answer. Monday morning, this would be all over. First, he'd head over to the FBI office, then he'd go get tested for sexually transmitted infections. By Monday evening, he hoped to be making love to his wife.

While lying in bed staring at the ceiling, Troy was worried that he'd left his family vulnerable by being gone. Unable to put his mind at ease, he left the motel and drove back and forth between his home and Corrine's apartment, looking for suspicious activity. He called them both to "check in" and make sure everyone was okay. He also apologized to Natalie about having to run out on her. "Just admit it…you didn't like my outfit," she teased.

"Babe, that couldn't be further from the truth. Red is starting to become my favorite color, too."

Convinced that Cheryl wasn't on the prowl tonight, Troy went back to his room where he lay awake until morning.

Sunday was relatively quiet. Not long after Natalie and the twins had gotten home from church, Corrine dropped Nate off. Troy wanted nothing more than to spend another day actively engaged with his family, but he had to continue the ruse of having a big case and his actions needed to reflect such. Thus, he barricaded himself in the basement to "work." Natalie knew how he was when he was concentrating on a case, so she didn't disturb him. Troy remained downstairs until he was certain that she was asleep.

Thankfully, Troy didn't hear from Cheryl that day either. The only text he received was from Will stating that he'd gotten Troy's message and asking if Troy would meet him sometime during the week to talk about *"some shady stuff that's been going down."* Though his interest was piqued, Troy never replied. Whatever Will had gotten involved in, Troy wanted to stay out of it. Will had lied about being at the gym Friday. Obviously, he'd been doing something that he didn't want to share with Troy. It was probably for the best as Troy had his own issues. He'd let narcotics handle Will.

Natalie awoke Monday morning to a note on the pillow next to her from Troy stating that he headed out early to run some "detective errands," as he called them. *Great!* This meant that she'd have to take Ebony and Ean with her when she dropped Nate off at pre-school. It would have been so much easier to leave them there with Troy as she was accustomed to doing most times. Occasionally, he did have to leave early and she understood that though a little advance notice would have been nice.

Natalie was concerned about the effect that this recent case was having on him. Troy hadn't been himself all weekend. He'd seemed edgy, more so than he normally was when he was working a case. She didn't know how he dealt with murder on a day-to-day basis. His job seemed too depressing for her. But, Troy was a problem-solver and took great pleasure in helping to bring closure from a justice standpoint to those who'd suffered traumatic losses. Troy felt like his work contributed to their family's safety and for that, she couldn't be mad at him. She appreciated his protectiveness of them. Though sometimes it could be a little overbearing, she knew it was coming from a good place.

Troy's motivation to work hard and not give up is one of the things she both loved and resented about her husband. Natalie had put on a good front Saturday night when he had to run out, but the truth was, the timing sucked! Oh, how she'd wanted, no *needed*, to be with her husband. They were pretty active, in general, but things were always a little trickier when Nate was present. She wasn't sure how long they could keep explaining the noise in their bedroom as "wrestling" now that their son was getting older. With him gone Saturday night, the atmosphere had been perfect and then Troy was called to work. After he left, Natalie changed into regular night clothes and watched a ridiculous number of hours of *Law & Order* reruns. No matter the time of day, the show always seemed to be playing on at least one cable network.

Natalie sighed to herself, reminiscing about what could have been Saturday night, as she hurried to wake Nate and get the twins ready. Getting herself and her babies dressed in the morning simply to take Nate and come back seemed like it was more effort than it was worth. She wished she could be like a few of the younger parents and arrive at the pre-school in pajamas and head scarves, but her model-mentality would not allow it, not even on her worst days. Ebony and Ean always looked nice as well. This mama made sure that her babies weren't out in public with dirty diapers, onesies, or filthy bibs smelling of dried food and milk. Consequently, it took her over an hour to make sure everyone was dressed and ready for what was only a ten-minute ride to and from Nate's pre-school.

No time for a proper breakfast, Natalie gave Nate a cereal bar to eat on the way. He only ate half of it. If Natalie didn't remember to get the other half when she got home, it would eventually end up crushed in the upholstery, on the floor, or finding a permanent resting place in the back window sill until Troy fussed at her about cleaning out the car. If only she could keep the back seat of her vehicle as neat as she tried to keep their personal appearances!

As they walked into the pre-school building, Nate held Ebony's hand while Natalie grabbed hold of Ean's. As usual, the staff *oohed* and *ahhed* over the twins who, like their brother, enjoyed attention. Natalie wondered how long it would be before they stopped sharing the spotlight and each demanded center stage for themselves. Before leaving, Natalie gave Nate a big hug and kiss as was her custom whenever he was receptive to it. He was increasingly becoming a "big boy" and sometimes his actions indicated that he could do without the affection because he would wave "bye" and keep it moving. Natalie knew her mommy moments would get fewer and further between as he got older, so she took advantage of every moment while she could. She'd just gotten Ean and Ebony into their car seats and was about to slide into the driver's seat when she heard someone call her name. "Yes," she said turning to see a petite, brown-skinned woman standing a several feet behind her.

"I'm not sure if you remember me. I'm Cheryl Hunter, a friend of your husband's."

"Oh, hey, Cheryl! I didn't recognize you at first." Cheryl, who was at least five inches or more shorter than Natalie, looked much different from the last time Natalie had seen her when they were in Houston about a year and a half ago for a funeral. Cheryl's hair, which was cut in a short style then, now hung to the middle of her back. It had to be a weave because no amount of biotin or conditioner could produce such miraculous results in that amount of time. "What are you doing here? Do you have a child enrolled here as well?"

"No, I wish. I was hoping to catch you and ask if we can go grab a cup of coffee or tea. I need to speak with you."

"Now is not a good time. They haven't eaten breakfast." She nodded toward the back seat, hoping Cheryl didn't glance long enough to get a good look at the mess. "I need to get them home before reality sets in for them. Trust me; you won't want to be around me if I have two hungry one-year-olds on my hands."

"Well, how about we go to breakfast. *Please*...it'll be my treat. What I have to say is important."

Natalie would forever be grateful for how helpful Cheryl had been when Troy was working on the Bible Butcher case, and even when Troy was trying to help solve the disappearance and murder of Elvin's sister. Natalie glanced in the back at Ebony and Ean who were communicating to each other in their special language. They seemed content for the moment and Natalie could easily get them something to eat at the restaurant. Besides, Cheryl looked like she was in desperate need of a shoulder, so Natalie said, "Sure."

Natalie followed Cheryl in an almond-colored sedan for several miles until they ended up at SuperChef's in Gahanna, a small Black-owned restaurant chain that first opened in Louisville, KY. Later, the best friends and co-owners decided to expand to their hometown of Columbus. Natalie first heard about SuperChef's from Aneetra whom she'd met there one morning before work. Soon after, their Wings and Waffles dish became one of her favorite breakfast meals and she was ecstatic when Cheryl picked the location.

Though she wasn't really hungry, Natalie ordered her usual. When it came, she got extra plates and gave Ebony and Ean each a quarter of her waffle and put her chicken in a "to go" box. Cheryl didn't order anything. After making sure her babies were content, Natalie said to Cheryl, "So, what do you need to speak with me about?"

"How are things between you and Troy?"

Taken aback by the question, Natalie looked at her without giving a response.

"I'm sorry. I don't mean to overstep my boundaries, but Troy and I have been friends for a very long time and I'm worried about him. When we were together Friday night, he was stressing about some things."

"I didn't know the FBI had been called in on the triple homicide case. Yes, I agree that the case does have him stressed. But then again, it's Troy. He stresses about every case."

Cheryl's smile was too wide for a discussion about murder. Natalie focused in on the small dimple in the middle of her chin that sunk in even further when she grinned. "So, he told you about the case, huh?"

"Yep. It kept him busy all weekend. It must be pretty serious if the feds are involved. I'm not sure what you think I can do to help. Troy sometimes talks about his cases with me, but it's not like he shares all the details." And even if he did, Natalie wouldn't be foolish enough to tell this chick. For Cheryl to come to her meant that there was some territorial conflict happening between the FBI and the police department. Whatever information Cheryl had about the case was apparently all that Troy had wanted her to know.

This time it was Cheryl who neglected to respond. She still had that stupid grin on her face, which was starting to become irritating. "Not trying to be rude, but I don't understand why you needed to speak with me. If you're concerned about Troy, he's okay. Like I said, he stresses about every case. That's what he does, but he handles business. He's not in jeopardy of any nervous breakdowns if that's what you're thinking."

"I'm curious; by any chance, have you seen any news reports about this triple homicide case he's working?"

Natalie thought about it for a moment. "No."

"You don't find it strange that something so big hasn't made it to the headlines?"

"Honestly, I'm not one who faithfully watches the news. It's too depressing." The last time Natalie had watched the news was Friday evening when she checked to make sure her husband hadn't been killed or injured in a fatal car crash when he didn't come home on time. There was nothing on about the homicides then, but that wasn't abnormal. Sometimes there was a lag between new cases and news reports. The twins were making a mess and Natalie had not brought a spare change of clothes or their diaper bag with her as she'd anticipated going home immediately after taking Nate to school. Her patience with Cheryl's twenty questions was wearing thin. "I'm going to have to get going so I can get them home and cleaned up. Is there anything else I can help you with?"

"Natalie, I have to tell you something that will be very difficult for you to hear. I want to remind you that we are in a public place and your children are with you." Cheryl looked at the twins. "For their sakes, I suggest that you control your reaction."

Natalie couldn't explain why she was getting upset. Was it Cheryl's tone, her demeanor, or both? As much as possible, Natalie tried to overlook the sometimes terse way that those in law enforcement spoke. She understood that, when talking to those suspected of crimes, one wouldn't necessarily pepper his/her speech with courtesy, but Cheryl's harsh tone and her smug demeanor were out of line. Even Troy knew better than to speak to Natalie in certain ways; and Cheryl was about to learn. "This was a bad idea. I don't know if it's me or if we're not gellin' right now, but something's off. We can try this again another day with a little advance notice." Natalie was about to grab her children's plate when Cheryl's next words halted her actions. "What did you say?"

"You heard me correctly. I said that Troy and I have been having an affair. We dated a long time ago when he was in college. We reconnected a couple of years ago when working on the Bible Butcher case, and we've been involved ever since."

Natalie had never considered herself to be a violent person. Besides the time she punched Corey Daniels in second grade for cutting in front of her in line and then saying "yo mama" when she told him to go to the back, she'd never been in a fight. That wasn't her style. Back in the day she did everything she could to avoid physical altercations with wives and girlfriends of her former lovers. She would talk a lot of trash, but when it came to risking getting her face scratched up and her hair pulled out over a man, it wasn't worth it. Yet, it currently took every ounce of Holy Ghost power Natalie had not to snatch Miss Weavalicious by the hair and knock that stupid look off her face. "I don't know what kind of game you're playing, but the gig is over. I know my husband very well. He loves me and our children too much to jeopardize our family for you." Natalie's insides burned with fire. She wished she could storm out of there. Not so easy to do with little ones who were joyfully making a mess with their food.

"Yes, he does love the children, but his trust in you has been shaken. I mean, your twins are beautiful, but let's not forget how you tried to prevent them from coming into the world."

"What are you talking about?"

"The birth control pills," Cheryl said nonchalantly. "I remember how upset Troy was when you lied to him, saying that you'd stop taking pills when you had not."

Natalie went from zero to sixty in three-point-five at the thought of her husband sharing intimate details about their relationship with his colleague. Still, it would take more than Cheryl's "confession" to get Natalie to believe that the man whom she loved and married had been unfaithful.

"And then there was that incident at work. It's unfortunate that it took such an embarrassing situation to force you into being the stay-at-home wife and mother that Troy had wanted all along. He's a great provider and it really hurt him that you didn't trust him to provide for you."

"What do you want, Cheryl? You're too smug to be remorseful, so there's obviously another reason why you wanted to meet. I don't know what went on with you and Troy, but if you think I'm going to throw away my marriage based on your word of a supposed affair, you don't know me at all. Matter of fact, let's call Troy and see what he has to say about this." With hands trembling from anger, Natalie searched for her cell phone, which she realized she'd left in the car. She called Cheryl's bluff by still pretending to look. "For your sake, you better hope that he's working a case because if Troy knew you were here trying to break up his family, he'd have your head."

"Before you make that call, I have proof." Cheryl pulled a manila envelope from her bag. "I dare you to search the news sites and see if there's been a recent triple homicide. Troy lied to you Friday. He didn't come home because of a case; he stayed out all night because he was with me." She slid the envelope to Natalie. "See for yourself."

Natalie wanted to take a fork and shove it into Cheryl's esophagus. Maybe then she'd finally shut up! Tears tried to find their way out, but Natalie wouldn't let them. She would not give this woman the satisfaction of seeing her cry. If, what Cheryl was saying was true, Natalie wouldn't give either of them the pleasure. The pain of her new reality was starting to sink in as she began giving more credence to Cheryl's confession. She sat, staring at the envelope, refusing to open it.

"I'm the reason that Troy didn't appreciate that pretty red outfit you put on for him Saturday night. He couldn't get me out of his mind. I'm sorry I had to be the one to break the news to you. Troy didn't know how to do it." When Cheryl's cell phone chimed, she lit up. "What do you know? It's Troy asking to meet with me." Cheryl turned the phone so she could see. Natalie's stomach, which was already knotted into a tumor, got even tighter. Sure enough, her husband's name and number appeared on Cheryl's screen with a message that read, *"Sorry 4 such l8 notice. Need 2 c u. Can u meet at the Dublin Entrepreneurial Center?"*

"Well, I guess that's my cue to leave." Cheryl reached into Ebony's plate and grabbed a tiny pit of her pancake making a smacking noise as she brought her finger out of her mouth. "*Mmm*...this is really good. I should have ordered some for myself. Oh, well, maybe next time. I have to go. My man is waiting for me. He may be your husband now, but he'll belong to me eventually." With a sickeningly sweet smile, she winked as though they had exchanged beauty tips and left.

Natalie managed to keep from falling apart while she got her babies together at the restaurant. She'd given up her job...her independence...her *life* to be Mrs. Troy Jermaine Evans and this is how he repaid her? "*...he'll be mine eventually.*" People thought the former socialite, Betty Broderick, had been crazy when she shot and killed her husband and his new wife—the woman with whom he'd had an affair and divorced Betty after sixteen years and four children to marry. The case made national news in the late '80s when Natalie was in her early teens. It was crazy how the details of such a case came flooding back to her memory as she now found herself having sympathy for the former Mrs. Broderick who had obviously been hurt beyond repair in order to be driven to homicide.

The twins screamed at the top of their lungs when Natalie took their plates away from them. All eyes were on her. Though it was only her imagination, Natalie sensed that everyone could see how empty and raw she felt inside like her pain had been exposed. They were looking at her, secretly laughing at the fact that Cheryl and Troy's relationship had done to her marriage what she had done to so many others. *This is what you get when you trust men. What goes around comes around. You thought your marriage was so good and Troy is just like everyone else. He didn't want to be with you Saturday because he left to be with her*, were some of the things that went through her mind. How could she have been so stupid! How could Troy do this to her? To their family?

"Do you need some help, ma'am?" an older lady said to her.

Natalie wasn't keen on strangers around her children, but she gladly accepted the woman's assistance to her car, making sure to take the envelope with her. Its contents had disturbed her much more than the elderly lady seeing the filthy back seat of her car. Natalie didn't have to open it to know what was inside. She didn't leave it there simply because she didn't want anyone else to know either. She wasn't sure why she cared. It was Troy's reputation, not hers. At least for now, he was still her husband.

Chapter 7: The Magic Word

Cheryl had delivered a blow that Natalie hadn't seen coming. As she left SuperChef's, she drove aimlessly, unsure of what to make of her emotions as they toggled between the likes of homicidal Betty Broderick and the love-blinded Dottie Sandusky who, to this day, stood by her convicted child-molesting husband. Two cheating men. Two very different circumstances. One choice for Natalie to make—to believe in Troy and their marriage despite the damage he'd ultimately done to it or to give up and let go.

She called Troy, but hung up without leaving a message when he didn't answer. She'd rather scream and yell at him in person rather than appear to be a raving lunatic by doing so on his voice-mail. It's funny how he had time to text Cheryl, but not to answer a phone call from her. Natalie searched her mind for a scripture, desperate for anything that could guide her. At first nothing came to her. Then she thought of the words of the psalmist, "*weeping may endure for the night, but joy comes in the morning.*" As much as she was hurting, it would be a *long* time before morning came.

Natalie's pain was numbing. She cried without tears…screamed without sound…bled profusely without being cut open. How could Troy do this to her? She'd known a lot of cheating men in her day and Troy didn't fit the profile. Then, again, perhaps he did. He had a job with varying hours, a wife who foolishly believed that he was working when he came home all hours of the night, and sometimes, he expressed his love so openly that Natalie felt it was too good to be true. Obviously, it was. Cheating husbands often overshowered their wives with affection to keep them from suspecting infidelity!

Natalie needed to be alone right now in order to get her thoughts together, but there were two little ones in the back depending on her. She'd give her life for them and Nate and yet she didn't have the mental or emotional strength to care for the twins at the moment. Natalie needed time to herself and she reached out to another stay-at-home mom and friend for help.

"Hey, Natalie, what's up?" Lisa answered sounding short of breath.

"Did I catch you at a bad time?"

"No. Girl, I'm glad you called. It gave me an excuse to put Chalene on pause. She was kicking my butt." Lisa was no doubt referring to Chalene Johnson, an author, entrepreneur, and creator of Turbo Fire and other workout DVDs, and by far, both Lisa's and Natalie's favorite video instructor. Each spoke of Chalene like she was a personal friend, saying things like, "Chalene and I are about to work out" as if the fitness instructor would actually appear next to them in person. "What's on your agenda today? Do you want to hook up with the kids?" Lisa's question wasn't abnormal. She and Natalie sometimes planned outings together for their little ones and even took turns babysitting for each other occasionally when the moms needed a break.

"I'm sorry to call at such short notice. I need a favor. Is there any way you can keep Ean and Ebony for me today? I'll see if Aneetra will be able to pick them up later. It's been a rough morning and I'm at my wits' end."

It must have been the desperation in Natalie's voice because

Lisa quickly responded "yes," asking if they were on their way now.

"No. I have to go home first. I need to clean them up and pack their diaper bag. I should be there in about an hour."

"I'll tell you what…I'll come get them from you. I can probably be there in the next thirty or forty minutes. Chandler's already dressed. Let me jump in the shower and I'll be there soon."

Natalie tried to tell Lisa it wasn't necessary, but her friend insisted, saying that it would be easier on them all since she had a few errands to run near Natalie's house anyhow. Natalie wasn't sure if Lisa was being truthful or simply going the extra mile to accommodate her. In the end, it proved to be the best option for Natalie. After she got home, she quickly cleaned the twins and put them in their playpen, and then got their diaper bag together. Natalie, in a daze, sat at the kitchen island waiting for Lisa while staring at the manila envelope, frozen by the fear of its contents and reliving those horrific few moments with Cheryl.

"Troy and I have been having an affair."

"Your husband and I have been involved ever since we reconnected on that case a couple of years ago."

"His trust in you has been shaken."

"And then there was that incident at work."

"Troy lied to you Friday. He didn't come home because of a case; he stayed out all night because he was with me."

Natalie picked up the envelope and twirled it around. She could still hear Cheryl's wicked laugh. It was all that Natalie could do to keep it together. According to Cheryl, the contents of the envelope contained undeniable proof of her affair with Troy. *"See for yourself."* Did Natalie really need to see it in order to believe it? What about the text message Troy had sent Cheryl? Wasn't that proof enough? Did she really have to torture herself more with what was inside the envelope? Before she could think about her actions any further, Natalie ripped it open and her already shattered heart was crushed even more. Inside were dozens of images of Cheryl and Troy naked in bed. There was no denying it was him. She'd recognize those dark chocolate brown cheeks anywhere.

Natalie threw the photos aside, knocking a glass off the island. It fell to the floor into tiny shards. It startled the twins and they started crying. Natalie couldn't even muster the strength to see about them and so they all sat in tears—the twins in their playpen in the living room doorway and Natalie in the kitchen. They were still crying when Lisa came.

"Are you okay?" Lisa asked when she answered the front door.

Natalie couldn't speak. She shook her head no and when Lisa embraced her, she cried harder. This was awkward for Natalie for several reasons. For starters, Natalie was a few inches taller than Lisa so it was uncomfortable to bend down on her shoulder. Plus, Lisa's long, dark hair was down and made its way into Natalie's mouth and it had more of a Chalene sweat workout smell than it did shampoo. Lisa, herself, didn't stink, but obviously her hair had not gotten the water attention that her body had gotten. Those things were all superficial, but what really made this moment unusual was that Natalie was not the one to cry in anyone's arms. Though she and Lisa had a budding friendship, Natalie wasn't one to let people see her in such a broken state. Very few had been able to witness her vulnerability. Troy was one of them.

Ebony and Ean had stopped crying, thanks to Lisa's little one who filled in for Nate by entertaining them and making them laugh. The screams had been replaced with joyful shrills. When Natalie finally got herself together, she let go of Lisa. "Thank you," she said after finding her voice.

"Do you want to talk?" Lisa wasn't oblivious to the broken glass. She may have even seen the pictures as well, but at that point, Natalie didn't care.

"No." Had Lisa asked if she *needed* to talk, Natalie's answer should have been different. Talking might have done her good, at least that's what the therapist she'd seen as a teen after having Corrine would have suggested. Natalie had been used to isolating herself during the most tumultuous times in her life and old habits were hard to break, so even if Lisa had said the magic word, Natalie would have likely responded the same. She wanted to be alone even if she didn't need to be. "You taking them for a few hours while I get my head on straight is more help than you will ever know."

Lisa didn't press the issue of talking. She simply helped get the twins situated and in the car and gave Natalie a long hug. "About what time will Aneetra be coming?"

Shoot! Natalie had forgotten to call her. "I don't know. I'm sure it won't be until after she gets off of work around four or four-thirty. If that's too long, please let me know."

"Oh, that's not why I was asking. I only wanted to make sure I would be there. She doesn't have to come at all if she doesn't want to. I'm willing to keep them for as long as you need me to do so. What about Nate? I take it he's at school?"

"Yes. Aneetra will get him, too," Natalie said by faith.

"Okay. Well, don't hesitate to call me if anything changes. I'm here for you."

"Thank you so much."

She gave Natalie a long hug. "No thanks needed."

As soon as they drove away, Natalie sent Aneetra a text.

"Sumthn has come up. Can u get Nate from school & the twins from Lisa's when u get off?"

"Sure. No prob. Is everything ok?"

"Things r crazy. Plz pray for me."

Instead of responding, Aneetra called. Natalie didn't answer. As much as Natalie trusted Aneetra and cherished their friendship, she wasn't ready to talk. But, Aneetra called again.

"I can't talk right now, Nee." She tried hard to fight back the tears that forced their way out anyhow.

"Oh, honey." Unlike Lisa, Aneetra was a little more persistent in her pursuit to know the matter. "Please tell me what's wrong?"

Natalie responded with more tears.

"Do you need me to come be with you?"

"No. I'm okay," she lied. Maybe Natalie did need her best friend; she felt like she was on the verge of insanity. Those images were branded in her mind. Aneetra would understand how she felt after all Aneetra's marriage had been through. Lisa would have, too, but Natalie couldn't get a grasp on her own feelings well enough to share them with anyone else.

"You *are not* okay. Say the word and I'm there."

Natalie was silent as moments passed.

"Okay. I get that you need to be alone right now. Before we hang up, I want to pray with you." Natalie closed her eyes and listened to the heartfelt words that Aneetra sent to Heaven on her behalf. In the midst of her pain, it temporarily brought joy to Natalie's heart to hear Aneetra pray so fervently for her. Aneetra asked for comfort, wisdom, and peace. The woman prayed so hard that she had to be calling down fire and brimstone from the sky. Natalie could have sworn she heard lightning. "In the mighty and most precious Name of Jesus, I pray, Amen."

Natalie thanked Aneetra for everything. Like Lisa had done, Aneetra responded that no thanks was needed. She also offered to do whatever she could to help Natalie, including taking off of work tomorrow to keep the kids. "Thank you, but that won't be necessary."

When they got off the phone, Natalie thought about calling Troy again. What would she say? That she was calling to end his clandestine meeting with his mistress? She didn't feel like hearing him try to lie his way out of this. This was the end of her marriage, she was sure. What she wasn't sure about is what life would look like without Troy.

Chapter 8: A Heartbeat's Moment

Troy was in the parking lot of the FBI office by seven as he waited until it opened at 8:15. He felt bad about leaving Natalie to take the babies with her when she took Nate to school. He knew it was more convenient for her when he stayed until she got back, but he wanted to be the first one through the FBI doors this morning. Cheryl's harassment was about to end, even if it meant temporarily inconveniencing his wife.

Being that this was Troy's first time coming to the federal office, he was a little taken aback by how secluded it was. It sat on the far west side of Nationwide Boulevard in a brick building that, in his mind, looked mysteriously important. Visitor parking wasn't free. There were a couple of pay-to-park meters that civilians used to purchase tickets for the spaces that were unassigned. Troy paid for his ticket and waited.

At first Troy got nervous as he watched agents pull into the lot and go inside. Maybe it wasn't such a good idea to sit out here. What if he saw Cheryl? Or worse, what if she saw him? Who knew what kind of story she would concoct in rebuttal to his accusations. He really had no proof because he'd deleted all the text messages she'd sent prior to the weekend to prevent Natalie from ever seeing them. Her most recent ones weren't incriminating in the least bit.

The closer it got to 8:15, the more uncomfortable the thought of Cheryl spotting him made Troy feel. He was on her turf and had to ensure that she would be nowhere around, so he decided to send her a text.

"Sorry 4 such l8 notice. Need 2 c u. Can u meet at the Dublin Entrepreneurial Center?"

Her response didn't come until several minutes later. *"Y there??? Let's meet at my house instead. ☺ I'm on my way home now."*

For good measure, she sent her address again, which he already had from the message she'd sent over the weekend. His plan for sending her to the northwestern suburb had been to make sure she was as far away from this office as possible. He knew she'd likely jump at the chance to meet him and he'd been banking on the flexibility of her job to allow her to do so. Apparently, his manipulative tactics had been in vain because Cheryl gave no indication that she was coming into work this morning. Had he known that, he would have left well enough alone. He didn't bother to reply. Instead, he felt a little more at ease, believing that after this visit to her place of employment, Cheryl's harassment of him would be nipped in the bud for good. Ignoring a call from Natalie, he got out of his car and went inside the building.

Having never been to this office or any FBI office, for that matter, Troy had a reality check when he walked in to find the lobby void of a receptionist or other personnel to greet him. There where two glass stairwells on either side, but it was clear that one could not access them without proper ID. He went to the elevator and made his way up to the third floor as indicated on the wall placard. He walked out the elevator and again, there was no one to greet him—nothing but plain painted walls and a door to the left with an intercom button and built-in camera.

"How can I help you?" came the voice after Troy pushed the button.

This was not the scenario he'd planned and he quickly used his law enforcement status so that he didn't seem like just another civilian. He'd even worn a suit this morning to appear more professional. "I'm Detective Troy Evans with the Columbus PD." He held his badge up to the camera. "I have sensitive information I need to share with someone about one of your agents.

"What kind of information?"

Really? Did this person think he would spill the beans in front of a camera without knowing who was on the other end? "Please, may I speak to someone in person? It's regarding Agent Cheryl Hunter." Knowing that she wasn't in the office made him more comfortable stating her name.

Several moments passed before there was any response. Next thing Troy knew, he was being approached in the hall by an agent who didn't seem pleased to start his Monday morning off with a visit from CPD. The guy was tall, like he-should-have-been-a-professional-basketball-player tall. He looked down at Troy with impatience. "What information do you have about Ms. Hunter that's so urgent?"

"Is there somewhere we can go to talk?"

"This is it. Now, what can I do for you?"

With no other options before him, Troy laid out the harassment he'd endured the last couple of years from Cheryl, leaving out the Friday night kidnapping and possible sexual assault after deciding that it sounded too strange. "I'm not trying to get her fired, but I do want her to leave me alone. Could you or one of her superiors have a talk with her, please?"

"I'm afraid that won't be possible. Cheryl Hunter is no longer with us. She was discharged over a year ago."

The news was almost strong enough to knock the wind out of him. "Why?"

"I'm not at liberty to say. If everything you've said is true, you need to file a police report. Your boys should be able to handle this one." He gave Troy a reassuring pat on the shoulder and walked away, disappearing around the corner.

Troy went back to his truck dumfounded. He'd been certain that coming here would be the leverage he needed against Cheryl. Knowing that she was unemployed, or at least no longer an agent, made her more dangerous than he'd anticipated. He was going to have to file a report for sure. First, he needed to come clean with Natalie and he planned to have a long talk with his wife tonight after the kids went to bed. It wasn't a conversation he was looking forward to having, but it was necessary.

When he got to the office, Troy started going over notes for his open cases. It was futile as he couldn't seem to concentrate. The guy didn't say that Cheryl had resigned; he'd said *discharged.* There was a big difference between those two words and the latter disturbed him. His thoughts were interrupted by a text.

"Is everything ok?"

"Yeah," Troy replied, certain that the brevity would indicate that he was running short on patience with Robert's inquiries. How ironic that Robert's text came at a time when Cheryl was preoccupying his mind.

"K. CheckN bcuz Lisa said Natalie was really upset this morn."

Within a heartbeat's moment, Troy's mind was off Cheryl and on to his wife. Had Natalie been so mad at him for leaving early that she had to share it with Lisa? He shook his head. *Women.* Then, remembering that she'd called him when he was on his way into the FBI office, he tried calling her back. "Hey, babe. I'm sorry I took off so early this morning. I had to take care of some things. I hope you're not mad at me. Robert said something about you being upset and I wanted to talk to you and apologize. Please call me. I love you."

Troy waited for what seemed like an hour when in actuality it had only been five minutes and called back. No answer. His mind began doing acrobatics, coming up with all kinds of scenarios, wondering if something had happened to Nate or the twins. He dialed his son's pre-school.

"Nate is doing fine, Mr. Evans," said Ms. Fritz, the school administrator. "Your wife called to request an extended stay and said that Aneetra Bennett would be picking him up today. Is that still correct?"

"Uh, yes," Troy replied, even though he didn't have a full understanding of what was going on. If anyone knew, it would be Aneetra and he wasted no time reaching out to her.

"Hey, Troy, what's up?"

"That's what I'm calling to ask you." He shared the text message from Robert.

"Oh."

"'Oh,' what does that mean? What's going on with Natalie and why am I the last to know?"

"I don't even know. I got a text from her asking if I would get the kids after work. I called her and though she was clearly upset, she didn't want to talk."

"Why didn't you call me?"

"I figured you already knew. Plus, you know I'm not the one to go behind Natalie's back and play private investigator. I know she'll reach out to me when she's ready."

That was an obvious dig at Troy for his actions when he and Natalie were dating and she ran off without telling him. At the time, he hadn't met Aneetra yet, but he did find her telephone number in Natalie's caller ID and dialed it, snooping for information. "I'm only trying to figure out what's wrong."

"If you don't know, then you need to get home and see about her. She sounded bad, Troy. I don't think I've ever heard her that upset before."

Troy was out of his office and headed home within seconds of his call to Aneetra. Several times he'd tried reaching out to Natalie. Still, no answer.

Chapter 9: First Instinct

"Natalie!" Troy rushed in the house calling her name. It wasn't until he heard a crunch underneath his feet that he saw the broken glass and strewn pictures. He picked up one of the photographs and that's when he put two and two together. Immediately, rage occupied every fiber of his being. He leapt up the stairs at record speed and found his wife in the bed, staring at the ceiling. It was obvious that she'd finished a hefty cry fest. "Oh, honey, I'm so sorry."

"Get off of me!" she hissed, jumping to her feet. "How could you do this to me, Troy? How could you do this to *us?*"

He managed to keep his voice calm despite the boiling temperature inside of him. His rage wasn't with Natalie. It was with Cheryl. "All I can say is that it's not what you think. I swear this is a setup."

"So that's not you?" She pointed to the image he didn't realize he still held in his hand.

He quickly threw it to the side. "Yes, but—"

"But what? I'm supposed to believe that you were butt-naked with this chick in a picture, but it's not what I think?"

"It's me, but—"

"Let me guess…you were both working on the triple homicide case and needed to comfort each other, right?"

Sarcastic wouldn't adequately describe Natalie's tone. It was beyond sarcasm as her eyes pierced him in a way that Troy had never seen before. They'd had their moments, but nothing like this. Hurt and hatred ran neck-in-neck behind her words and glare, with hatred increasingly taking the lead. "Honey, I can explain."

"Save it! I've heard enough about your affair from your girlfriend. She told me that you lied about the case."

"She's not my girlfriend."

"Oh, my bad, your mistress…or better, yet, your future wife because that's what she seems to think. What about the girl at the gym, are you messing around with her, too?"

"Who, Shay? *Naw!*" Troy was offended by the accusation. He understood her suspicions about Cheryl, but Shay??? *Really…*

"Well, she sure did give me a play-by-play account of everything you did at the gym on Friday. At this point, I wouldn't be surprised if Cheryl's not the only one."

"Will you calm down and listen, *please?* I'm not messing around with anyone. *It's not what you think!*" He didn't mean to yell. His anger was misdirected. He wasn't mad at Natalie. It was Cheryl whom he would've liked to see skinned alive and burned at the stake. This whole thing had gotten out of control. Robert had been right. Troy should have told Natalie everything from the beginning.

"You got a lot of nerve raising your voice at me because your girlfriend, or whatever you want to call her, busted you." Troy, with a lowered voice, tried to explain, but it was useless. Natalie grilled him with one accusation after another. *How long have y'all been having an affair? If you're not sleeping with her, then why didn't you tell me that y'all used to date? How long were y'all together?* It's not like Troy got a chance to fully explain anything. Natalie wouldn't let him get a word in edgewise. He managed to say that he wasn't having an affair with her. *"I'm supposed to believe that you're not having an affair with the woman you obviously felt the need to share our personal business with!"*

"I haven't shared our business with her! I try as hard as possible *not* to talk to her. She's been stalking me ever since she helped with the Bible Butcher case. I didn't know what to do."

"Oh, you don't talk to her? *Really?*" The way she cocked her head to the side and put her hand on her hip, Troy knew he was about to get hit with a huge blow, but he had no idea what was coming. "Tell me, detective, how is it that Cheryl, the lady whom you don't share our personal business with, knew about us getting into it about the birth control pills?"

Right then and there he swore under his breath. It was an occasional bad habit that Troy was still trying to break and one that he'd inherited honestly from his mother. "Natalie—"

"Don't 'Natalie' me! That's not the only thing your girlfriend told me about us. She knows about the arguments we had when you wanted me to stop working and she knows what happened at my job. She even knows that I got rejected by you Saturday night and that I was wearing red! How could you do this to me, to *us?* I thought what we had was real." Natalie slumped onto the ottoman and bawled. Troy's heart ripped into pieces. Natalie was the love of his life and to see her broken was more than he could bear. He was beginning to understand the depth of the web of distrust he had woven by not disclosing everything up front. He thought he had been protecting her, when all the while he was falling into the intricate trap that Cheryl had created for him—one that could very well destroy his marriage.

Troy knelt beside her. "Honey, I can't deny that I told her about the birth control pills or that I didn't tell you that we dated in the past. I'm sorry. It was stupid. *I* was stupid. It was when we first got into it and I was mad and—"

"So the first thing you do is go and run your mouth about me to another woman?"

"*No.* It wasn't anything like that. I don't know how to explain it." Troy began telling Natalie everything he should have said years ago, beginning from the first time Cheryl started to harass him. "I thought she was harmless at first and would lose interest. I didn't want to tell you and have you worried about nothing. I wouldn't return her calls or texts, but she kept finding other ways to insert herself into our lives. It wasn't until you called her when I was still in Texas that she knew I hadn't said anything to you and she used that against me. I could never find the right time to tell you."

"What happened Friday? Why did you lie to me about the triple homicide? Why did you stay gone all night Saturday, rejecting me when clearly I was making advances toward you? And—"

Troy cut in before the questions could continue. She wasn't yelling now. That was a good sign. He gave her his account of Friday evening to the best of his recollection. "That is me in the pictures, but I swear to you that I didn't consciously do anything with her. In every picture, my eyes are closed. She drugged me." He then went on to explain why he did not have sex with her on Saturday night and why he chose to stay at a motel instead. "I promise I was going to tell you. I don't know how she found out about the lingerie. I haven't spoken to her." Troy looked and saw Nate's toy still on their dresser. "The car!" He got up and threw it to the ground, stomping it to pieces.

"What are you doing?"

"I think there's some kind of listening device in here."

"What!"

"Think about it, babe. We don't know who sent this to him and the only way Cheryl can know details that I never disclosed to her is by spying on us somehow. Remember, I was holding the car the other night when I came upstairs and you were dressed up. I know it sounds crazy, but that has to be it. No one we know has admitted to sending the car—not Corrine, Aneetra, or any of our family members. There's no possible way she could know about what you wore Saturday unless she was listening, and the only way she could have done that is with this car."

Natalie was eerily quiet for several moments as if she were soaking his words in like a sponge. Troy's anxiety level began to decrease as he now felt confident that he was able to explain his side of things to her. He also wondered, to be on the safe side, if they should throw out the souvenir blankets the twins had received. Natalie wiped the few remnant drops from her eyes and took a deep breath. "How stupid do you think I am? It's one thing for you to mess around on me and then have the decency to come clean once you're busted. But, that's apparently too much like right because you'd rather make up this story about her spying on us and stalking and drugging you, and I'm supposed to be crazy enough to believe it. You're like a freakin' giant compared to her!" Natalie was now very much in control of her emotions and her words. They were as sharp as daggers, piercing through Troy's heart. "I trusted you. I've trusted you more than anyone I've ever trusted in my entire life and you made a fool out of me. You left me this morning so you could meet up with her."

"No, I didn't. I left to go to the FBI office." He then added the information about what had happened when he spoke to the agent.

"Just stop, Troy! Stop lying to me and yourself. I saw the message you sent to her this morning asking her to meet you."

That was it…the nail in the coffin.

"If she was harassing you as you say, why would you ask to meet her anywhere?"

Troy tried to explain his logic. "Don't you think that if I was meeting her for some sexual rendezvous, I would've asked to meet at a hotel and not the Dublin Entrepreneurial Center? C'mon, Natalie. Think about it."

"I have. I've done nothing but think about it all morning. I was on the verge of believing we could work through this if you would have come in here telling the truth. I'm sure, after all the damage I've done to other women's marriages back in the day, I probably had this coming. What goes around, comes around; I get that. I also see that you're not the person I thought you were. The Troy I married would at least be honest, even after making a huge mistake." She got up, pushing him out of the way.

"Baby—"

"*Shut up!*" The race between hurt and hate was over. Hate won by a landslide. "I'm done with you and our marriage. Neither has been what I thought."

"Where are you going?" He followed her down the stairs, ignoring the vibration of his cell phone.

"I bet you think I'm totally dependent on you, that I'm not going to be able to make it without you or your paycheck. We'll see about that." She grabbed her keys and purse and attempted to leave.

He blocked her. "Why is your first instinct to always run away whenever there's an issue? You did it when we were dating and any time we've had an argument. You're doing it now!"

"This isn't an *issue!* This is a matter of distrust. You've made a complete mockery of our wedding vows."

"Babe, please don't leave."

"It's in your best interest to get out of my way. The way I feel right now, I will be a widow before ever getting the chance to become an ex-wife."

Chapter 10: Be Fruitful and Multiply

Troy was heartbroken as he watched his wife speed away, enraged by Cheryl's latest antics. To escalate matters, when Troy checked his cell phone, he discovered a text from her.

"Hey, honey! I've been waiting 4u? I talked 2 your wife this morn abt us. I know u will b upset, but it's time that she knew. We shudnt keep r love a secret. It's fate. I love u."

Messing with him was one thing, but dragging Natalie into this sickness of hers was a game that Cheryl did not want to play. Troy wasted no time getting into his truck and burning rubber to get to her address. The argument with Natalie replayed in his head. Simply imagining the pain she must have been feeling was more than he could handle. Troy was aware that one of Natalie's biggest fears was that he would cheat on her. He'd never given her any reason to think that. It was her own insecurity and Cheryl had hit his wife where she hurt most.

He pulled into Cheryl's driveway so fast that he almost sideswiped a maroon car parked on the street and nearly rear-ended Cheryl's sedan. Troy jumped out of his truck and banged on the door of her ranch-style home, shouting at the top of his lungs for her to answer. When she did, he barged in and lost all self-control. Troy, who had never before been physically violent with a woman and loathed men who put their hands on them, found himself with a tight chokehold around Cheryl's neck as he lifted her tiny frame against the wall. He could have literally strangled her to death that very moment. Had it not been for the images of his family that popped in his head, he probably would have, but the visions were enough to remind him of why he needed to keep his freedom. He let go and she dropped to the ground, gasping for air.

For the first time, he took in the surroundings. He'd knocked over a lamp and he felt the burning sensation on his face and neck from gouges Cheryl left while trying to fight free from his grip. The pocket of his dress shirt was torn and there were also drops of blood on the floor. He wasn't sure if it was hers or his. He hadn't hit her. Or had he? Not knowing troubled his spirit. He'd grown up watching his father physically abuse his mother. Though his parents had gotten past that stage of their marriage, and Troy's relationship with his dad had been steadily improving within the last year or so, the propensity toward domestic violence was part of his father's behavior that Troy never wanted any part of. He had his family, his badge, and also his own personal character to consider. Yet, what transpired in these last few moments showed that he was capable of going against himself.

He knew his actions had scared Cheryl; they'd scared him. He loosened his tie as if that would somehow calm his heavy breathing. "Leave my family and me alone," he said sternly.

She said nothing.

"I never want to hear from you again. Next time I might not let go." He backed out the door, hopped in his vehicle, and sped away.

Troy drove around with no real destination in mind. His concern was Natalie and where she could be at the moment. He tried calling her several times. He wanted, no, he needed to hear her voice. He knew she was devastated and he wanted to be the one there wiping her tears. For the first time since they'd been married, Troy thought he would lose her. He remembered the pain of when she'd walked out of his life once when they were dating. It wasn't because of infidelity, but because he had been stupid and afraid to admit to her, or even himself, how much Natalie meant to him. He wasn't scared now. He'd tell anyone who'd listen how special she was to him. More than anything, he'd tell her.

There were a few calls that came in from the office that Troy ignored. Part of him felt bad for doing so. What if they were leads to a case? Troy loved his job and often took his cases personally. He didn't have the right mindset to help anyone at this moment when his own life was falling apart. Selfish or not, he simply couldn't do it. He didn't feel like a cop today. He felt like a failure.

Frustrated that he had no idea where to find Natalie and crushed that she wasn't answering his calls, Troy found himself pulling into the parking lot of the rehabilitation residential facility. The last time he was here, he'd been working a case and was desperate to find answers then. Now, he was desperate for another reason. The generally stoic detective, who cringed anytime one of his buddies got too emotional, was in need of a heart-to-heart. He knew he was about to share his feelings with someone who could understand. Troy took a deep breath and removed his suit jacket before going in.

Natalie stared at the white ceiling of the hotel room, fighting the negative voice telling her that Troy's infidelity was inevitable. *"You, of all people should know better. You were a whore. You slept with married men. You're getting back exactly what you deserve. Did you really think you would have a marriage that would last happily ever after?"*

She couldn't deny her past. Had she been silly enough to think that because she now believed in Jesus and tried to live her life as morally right as possible that all would be forgiven? She'd never known pain this deep, not even when she was forced to give Corrine up for adoption and learned to stuff her feelings. Natalie had been a child then. Now, as an adult, this thing with Troy hurt worse than she could ever imagine. It was partly her fault because she'd allowed herself to be vulnerable by fully loving and trusting him.

"*You should just give up,*" the voice in her head told her. "*Life isn't worth living anymore. Your husband made a fool of you.*"

*Life isn't worth living...*Natalie let that thought linger longer than it should have. Would she really sink that low over a man? There's only one other time in Natalie's life that she could recall having such thoughts and, ironically, Troy played a factor then, too. It was when they were dating and got into a bad argument about their future together. She wanted one. He didn't. Though the thought continued tormenting her, something would not allow Natalie to internalize it. Her life wasn't about her anymore. She was a mother and, no matter how bad things got for her, she wasn't going to do something foolish to herself that would hurt her children. Troy wasn't worth it. Besides, if Natalie weren't around, her babies would be left in the care of Troy and his tramp! There was no way in the world that she would let that happen.

Yeah, maybe Natalie did deserve this after all she'd done in her past. Okay, so life sucks. That's been the story of her entire life from the death of her father when she was five, the crazy circumstances of Corrine's birth, and now this situation with Troy. Corrine, Nate, Ebony, and Ean were the rays of sunshine that God had given her and she would not let them down. *I am stronger than this. No man has ever had the ability to make or break me and that won't change now*, she thought as she continuously ignored Troy's calls.

Natalie longed for the wisdom of Big Mama, her paternal grandmother, who'd passed away in her sleep from a heart attack when Nate was a baby. Big Mama would have the words to comfort. She always did. She was a smart woman who truly embodied Jesus's command to the disciples in Matthew 10:16 when He told them to be as wise as serpents and as harmless as doves. Big Mama had quick wit, knowledge, and a gentleness about her that made her loved by many. So many people showed up for her service that the procession line literally went down the street and around the corner of the Jackson, Mississippi church where her life celebration was held. Ida Mae Coleman was the matriarch, not just of Natalie's family, but in many ways of the Jackson community. To Natalie, she'd been a pillar of strength, source of wisdom, and great big bundle of love. Though Natalie often thought of both her mother and grandmother, it was Big Mama she missed most; especially during rough times, like now, when she needed her grandmother's guidance.

Big Mama had been so down-to-earth. She had a way of keeping it real and biblical all at the same time. Natalie could almost hear her grandmother encouraging her to read her Word. *"It's the sword you need to face any challenge that comes your way,"* Big Mama had once told her. Though she wasn't in much of a reading mood, Natalie heeded the instruction anyhow and opened the Bible app on her iPhone. She pulled up the scripture of the day, which was Genesis 1:28, *"And God blessed them, and God said unto them, be fruitful and multiply—"* She couldn't read anymore. Adam never cheated on Eve! Besides, Natalie had been as fruitful as she ever intended to be with Troy. She closed out of the app and went to the Internet, typing "scriptures to help when you're hurting" in the search area. She smiled when links to several psalms appeared. Psalms had been Big Mama's favorite book of the Bible. Natalie clicked on Psalm 69, one of the scriptures that showed up in her results.

It was clear that David, the writer of that particular psalm, had been going through a tough time when he drafted these words. The passage started out with him saying, "*Save me, O God, for the waters have come up to my neck. I sink in the miry depths, where there is no foothold. I have come into the deep waters; the floods engulf me.*" Engulfed…that's how Natalie felt. This situation with Troy and Cheryl was drowning her, swallowing the dreams she once had of growing old and living happily-ever-after with Troy. She continued reading, identifying with many other of David's feelings of despair. Everything was good until she got to verse 22 when David started to ask for revenge against those who'd wronged him. She found herself enjoying verses 27 and 28, a little too much. "*Charge them with crime upon crime; do not let them share in your salvation. May they be blotted out of the book of life and not be listed with the righteous.*" Praying that God would sentence Troy and Cheryl to eternal damnation was a very tempting idea, but her focus wasn't on them. It was on her. She needed to get herself together so she would be strong enough to care for her babies.

Backing out of that scripture, Natalie clicked on another one in her list, Psalm 34. It was verse 18 that struck a chord in her heart and reproduced her tears. "*The Lord is close to the broken hearted and saves those who are crushed in their spirit.*" A broken heart…a crushed spirit…both described her to a tee. Now, if only the Lord would rescue her.

Chapter 11: Drunk In Love

Prior to leading Troy to his office, Robert had instructed the receptionist to send all his calls straight to voicemail and only to notify him if Lisa called. He was turning off his cell phone. "I have my cell number on my voicemail greeting," he explained to Troy. "I don't want anyone to call and interrupt us if they don't get me on the office phone."

Troy appreciated how RJ dropped everything to lend him an ear, and Troy shared the entire ugly truth of how bad this situation with Cheryl had gotten.

"So you really think Cheryl planted some kind of listening device in Nate's toy?" Robert asked skeptically after Troy had finished his story.

"That's the only thing that makes sense. No one has admitted to sending it or the other presents, so it had to be her."

"It's a good thing you destroyed it then."

Troy held his breath, waiting to hear the "I-told-you-so" from Robert. "Go ahead and get it out the way. I'd rather you say it now and we squash it than for you to bring it up later."

"Say what now?"

"That I should have told Natalie everything from the beginning."

"Man, it's not my style to say what you should have done. That won't help with the reality of what we're dealing with now."

We're? Troy was caught off guard by his use of a plural pronoun.

"My main concern at this moment is making sure Natalie is okay. You don't think she'd do anything irrational, do you?"

Troy pondered the question for a moment. He remembered the time when they were dating and he went to her apartment and saw the pile of pills lying on her desk underneath a poem she had written. That was before Corrine was in her life...before Nate and the twins. Even if Natalie hated him, nothing could interfere with the love she had for her four children. "No," Troy finally answered, confidently.

"Good. I would ask Lisa to reach out to her, but she probably made arrangements for the kids because she needs some space. Let's give her that. Meanwhile, let's figure out what to do about Cheryl. Her drugging you is serious. Do you think you can get a restraining order?"

"I don't have any proof."

"It's a long shot, but if you're willing to give your consent, I can have one of the nurses here draw and test your blood. Depending on what she gave you, it could be long gone out of your system, but it's worth a try. My first guess is Rohypnol, but it normally takes anywhere from ten to fifteen minutes to take effect. The fact that you blacked out so quickly suggests that Cheryl used something else."

Having done a brief stint in the sex crimes unit several years ago, Troy was all too familiar with the "date rape drug." "Could she have mixed Rohypnol and another substance to combine the quick onset and the long-lasting effects?"

"It's possible. We can also test you for sexually transmitted infections if you want. It'll save you the trouble of going down to the health department or making an appointment with your physician."

Troy agreed and, within moments, he was undressed, in a hospital gown, getting blood drawn and a very uncomfortable swab done on his private.

"Hey, I'm on my way to pick up the kids. Are you at home?" Natalie had called Aneetra as she was leaving the bank parking lot. It was a few minutes before six and she wanted to make sure she fed them dinner and got them to bed on time.

"Don't worry about it. I'll bring them to you in about an hour. I think you need to have a talk with you-know-who about this situation with y'all."

"How do you know? Did Troy call you?" she asked irritably. It would be just like Mr.-Want-to-Control-Everything to call Aneetra and ask her to be peacemaker.

"No. Well, yes, he did, but not about the situation. He called this morning to ask why I was on duty, but he didn't say anything to me about the matter. When I went to retrieve the identical package, someone asked if I'd spoken to you and said that her other half told her that you-know-who came to see him. I don't know all the specifics of the conversation between them. I don't think she knows, but the one thing that was made clear is that you think there has been a violation of some kind."

Natalie could tell by the way Aneetra was talking that Nate was in her immediate vicinity. It wasn't hard for Natalie to catch on to the fact that "identical package" referred to the twins and "you-know-who" was Troy. But, "a violation" was sugarcoating it for sure.

"I don't *think* anything," Natalie fired back. "I have undeniable proof that he cheated on me. He's so stupid! Why in the world is he going around telling people? I bet he put RJ up to talking to

Lisa because he wants to manipulate me through her. It's not going to work. I'm done, Aneetra. *D-o-n-e!*"

"You know I understand how you're feeling. I do want to talk to you, and *no,* you-know-who didn't put me up to it. I want to because you're my friend and I love you. Now's not a good time for me to say anything and I'm sure you can guess why. We'll be there within an hour. I'll help you get them together and if we can, we'll talk then, okay?"

"Yeah, whatever." Natalie hung up without saying bye. Why was she taking her frustration out on Aneetra? Aneetra wasn't the one who'd cheated on her. Unlike Troy, the one thing Aneetra had been throughout their entire relationship was faithful, even during the early days when they'd first met at Dennison and Natalie was busy trying to dodge their budding friendship. Aneetra never let on that she took any of Natalie's rejections of her lunch invitations personally. She was, by all means, the best friend that Natalie ever had, even before Natalie recognized that they were friends. "I'm sorry," she called Aneetra back to repent.

"It's all right. I know you're hurting and trying to make sense of everything. We're good."

Aneetra's attitude proved all the more why she was a wonderful person. "Thanks, Nee."

"You're welcome. I'm about to hang up first this time. I'm not giving you a chance to hang up on me twice in a row."

Natalie laughed. "Bye, you crazy woman." The temporary happiness Natalie felt that moment quickly began to fade as she got closer to her home. Her heart raced with dreaded anticipation that Troy might be there. She didn't want another confrontation with him. She didn't care to speak with him at all for that matter.

It was lying in that hotel room when she'd realized that she'd forgotten her chicken wings at SuperChef's. *Ugh!!!* She likely wouldn't have been able to enjoy them anyhow. After crying and meditating on Psalm 34, Natalie spent the rest of her time at the hotel thinking about a game plan. She had withdrawn $27,000 from their joint savings account and opened a checking account solely in her name. Since Natalie was going to be on her own again, she needed to take precautions to ensure she could care for her and her children.

The $27,000 was the bulk of the money in their savings account, but it was rightfully hers. It was money she'd received from her severance pay when she was forced to quit her job. There was still several thousand left in the savings and they had a nice chunk of money in their checking account, but Natalie didn't touch either. The last thing Troy would ever be able to accuse her of was going after his money. The money she'd withdrawn had been specifically given to *her* and she would need it to get an apartment and live off of until she found another job—and to eventually order another Wings and Waffles platter when she got a chance. Natalie was determined to start her life over as *Miss* Evans. She believed that Alex, her previous supervisor, would give her a good reference, despite what had happened, especially if Aneetra went to Alex on her behalf. Alex liked Aneetra and that worked in Natalie's favor.

When Natalie opened the garage and saw that Troy's truck wasn't there, she was relieved. For a split-second she wondered where he was. *With Cheryl trying to smooth things over? Working on a real, or perhaps another fake homicide case?* She wasn't going to stress over his whereabouts. She was better than that. He could be drunk in love and sleep with whomever he wished; she couldn't care less!

If that was true, why was her heart still aching? There was a tightness in her chest and her stomach knotted as she walked in and saw the pictures of her husband on top of his mistress. Natalie sucked back her tears. She had to be stronger than that for her little ones and also for Corrine. She couldn't let her adult daughter see her fall apart over a man. She refused to give Troy the power to make or break whom she'd become. She put the pictures back in the envelope and threw them in the trash before cleaning up the broken glass from the morning.

The house felt so empty. Natalie felt like her entire marriage had been a forgery. All the memories she had of them together... the dreams she'd held close to her heart...like the glass, it had all been shattered by the revelation she'd received earlier. There were so many questions. Questions she wasn't sure that she wanted answered. *Did Troy ever really love her? Had Troy ever had Cheryl in their home? Was she the only one he'd been unfaithful with?* "What does it matter?" she said aloud, wiping a tear before it fell. The reality of her marriage now was that it wasn't what she'd thought it had been. No matter what, it would never be the same.

When Natalie finished in the kitchen, she went upstairs and saw the broken pieces from Nate's toy car as a result of Troy's theatrics earlier. Of all the crazy stories that cheating husbands came up with, a bugged toy car had to top the list. The fact that it was still in this house was proof enough to Natalie that he'd been lying. The Troy she knew would never leave remnants of an unwanted listening device in their home. The Troy she knew? More like the Troy she *thought* she knew.

Natalie cleaned up the mess within moments of the doorbell ringing. That was fast. Aneetra had come much sooner than the hour she'd said. Natalie went to the door, ready to shower her babies with hugs and kisses, but was surprised to find their neighbor instead. "Hi, Natalie." Charla stood wringing her hands as her left eye wandered in a direction of its own. "My mom told me to come and ask if we can borrow a piece of bread."

Natalie looked over Charla's shoulder looking for Ann to come running behind her. Ann lived directly across from Natalie and Troy along with her adult daughter, Charla, who suffered from a rare compulsive eating disorder. Strangers who came in contact with Charla would not be able to tell from an initial encounter that she also had slight mental disability because she spoke clear and fast. "I don't believe she sent you, Charla. There isn't much she can do with a single slice of bread."

"I'm for real this time, Miss Natalie. She's making me a sandwich and she only has one piece of bread and she needs two pieces for my sandwich." Charla held up two fingers to emphasize her point.

"No. If Ann needs anything, I'm sure she'll call. You need to go back home."

"I can't. I'll starve if you don't give us a piece of bread. Just because you're having a bad day, it doesn't mean that you should make me starve."

"I'm not having a bad day, Charla. I'm also not giving you any bread. Now go home!"

"Liar, liar, pants on fire. You're having a bad day. A really bad day. So is Mr. Troy. You both seemed angry this morning. Let me come in and we can talk about it over cheese and crackers."

Natalie checked her pockets for her cell phone so she could call Ann. *Darnnit!* She'd left it upstairs. On a good day, she could deal patiently with Charla's manipulative antics. At this moment, with all she's going through, Natalie cursed the day when she ever met the Harrows.

Ann and Charla had moved into the neighborhood shortly before the twins were born. Not the let's-be-friends-with-our-neighbors type, the extent of Natalie's contact with them was a wave whenever their paths crossed. That was until one day last spring when Natalie was on mater-

nity leave. She was out walking Ean and Ebony in their stroller while Nate tagged along on his bicycle. As they made their way back home, Nate wasn't quite ready for his bike ride to end, so Natalie told him that he could ride for a few more minutes. While watching him, she rocked the twins back and forth in their stroller to keep them calm and began eating a protein bar.

Ann and Charla had been outside doing gardening work and Natalie waved at them simply to be polite because Ann was staring. The woman always stared. Though Natalie hadn't known Charla's name at the time, Troy had told her Ann's name. He'd met Ann previously when he was out jogging and filled Natalie in on the details of their brief conversation. That particular day, when Natalie was munching on her bar, Charla bolted across the street toward her after Ann had stepped into the house. "My mom's trying to starve me to death. Can I have a bite, please?" She'd asked having the nerve to open her mouth and lean causing some of her micro-braids to fall into her face.

Charla's face was elongated with a thin upper lip, almond-shaped eyes, and a prominent nose, but her overall appearance didn't appear to be that of someone who was suffering from starvation. In fact, Natalie thought that Charla could benefit from a brisk walk or two around the neighborhood. She was a little on the obese side. Her request was so bizarre that Natalie stood still without giving a response.

"Please, ma'am. She's locked all the cabinets and refrigerators in our house and I'm so hungry." Charla was on the verge of tears. Natalie figured she had to be pretty desperate to approach a stranger for food. Natalie handed Charla the rest of the protein bar and watched her devour it within seconds."Ooh, can I have this too?" Charla snatched the pack of fruit snacks Natalie had on top of the stroller for Nate.

There were a lot of questions going through Natalie's mind such as Charla's age. She looked young...like maybe she was in her late teens or early twenties, but surely someone that old wouldn't be forced to live in a home where she was denied access to food. Thus, Natalie assumed that Charla was a teenager and perhaps being abused in some manner. There had to be some validity to her story because Charla had eaten everything like she hadn't had a decent meal in weeks. She licked her fingers for remnants, not caring that dirt from doing gardening work was also getting in her mouth. Natalie was about to gather her children and go inside to call Troy and notify him of things when the other lady with braids, Ann, came running across the street. "Charla! I left you alone for a few minutes and you're bothering our neighbor for food. Go inside and clean up. You are not having anything else until it's time for dinner!"

Seeing Ann go off made Natalie believe that this was indeed a case of child abuse. She wished she'd had more to give Charla, but Natalie was determined to help her by reporting the incident to Troy and letting him take it to the proper officials. Not knowing what other harm Ann was capable of, Natalie's first priority was to get her babies safely inside their home. "Nate, we're going inside," she said, ignoring his unhappy moans about her request.

"Please wait," begged Ann. "I know you are probably wondering what the heck is going on, but whatever my daughter told you is a lie. She suffers from Prader-Willi Syndrome, also known as PWS. It's a disorder in which people want to eat constantly because they never feel full." As she'd done with Charla, Natalie stood staring, not knowing what to say. "I swear to you that I'm not making this up. I have literature on the disease that I can bring over. Or, better yet, read this." Ann pulled out her cell phone and opened a webpage to show Natalie who scanned the material because her curiosity about this mother-daughter duo had taken over.

Prader-Willi (PRAH-dur-VIL-e) syndrome is a rare disorder present at birth that results in a number of physical, mental, and behavioral problems...constant sense of hunger...may be stubborn, angry, controlling or manipulative...specialized care and supervision throughout their lives.

"I monitor what she eats because, if I don't, she could literally eat herself to death."

"I'm sorry. I didn't know."

"It's okay. I'm the one who should be apologizing. I'm Ann, by the way. I don't know if my daughter introduced herself, but her name is Charla."

"I'm Natalie. Welcome to the neighborhood. I apologize that I haven't said this before."

"Not a problem. It's nice to hear all the same. Who are these lovely little people?" Ann asked.

Natalie introduced the babies and Nate.

"It's nice to officially meet you all. I met your husband once before. His name is Troy, right?"

"Yes."

"He seems like a nice guy. He gave me the name and location of the gym where he works out and I'm going to check it out as soon as I get settled. You look great for recently having twins. Tell me your secret. Are you a member of the gym as well?"

Natalie wanted to tell Ann that the swimsuit edition of her body told a different story than what Ann could see. "Thanks. No, I'm not a member of the gym. I have a lot of exercise DVDs and games. I do those, or when it's nice like today, I like to go for walks. My husband works a lot and his schedule is often unpredictable, so I wouldn't have time to go to a gym even if I wanted to."

"Is he a cop?"

"Yes. A homicide detective. Why do you ask?"

"I thought he had that law enforcement look about him. I started to ask him, but we didn't talk long and plus, I didn't want to come across

as the nosey neighbor who asks twenty questions. I hope you don't mind me asking you. I'm trying to make small talk and get over the embarrassment of my daughter taking your food."

"It's okay. I learned something new today. I'd never heard of that condition before. What's it called again, praterwilly?"

"Prader-Willi, like Prada, but with an 'er' sound and though it's spelled with a 'w,' it's pronounced with a 'v.' Most people say PWS for short. In addition, Charla also has mild retardation. Well, nowadays, it's called slight intellectual disability to be politically correct. It's common for people with PWS to have intellectual disability. Their reasoning and problem-solving skills are below par. Some people even have problems with articulating words, but we got Charla into speech therapy early on and, as you can tell, she speaks extremely well. In Charla's case, her logic is way off, but her communication is not. It's easy for her to make people believe that she's being mistreated. I assure you that's not the case."

"I believe you," Natalie responded with certainty.

"It's hard sometimes because I'm by myself now. My husband is no longer with us." For the next fifteen minutes or so, Ann shared with Natalie her struggles of caring for Charla, whom Natalie learned was actually twenty. Ann admitted to having locks on the refrigerator and cabinets for Charla's benefit. She also had to keep the exterior security alarm activated at all times when they were inside the house to prevent Charla from sneaking out and looking through people's trash for scraps.

Ann, who was only thirty-six, had had Charla as a teen and had been married twice. Charla's biological father had died from a drug overdose when Charla was four. Ann married her second husband when Charla was six and both she and Charla took his last name. They'd moved from Cleveland to the Gahanna suburb of Columbus to get a fresh start after Mr. Harrow's recent death. Ann didn't say how he'd passed and Natalie didn't ask. She also didn't ask any details about the man she saw over there on a few occasions. Ann, however, did inform Natalie about some other specifics about her life. Natalie learned that Ann worked from home as an IT specialist, had no other children, both parents were deceased, and had one older sister. "Most people with Charla's disorder live in group homes, but that will be my last resort. When I need a break, I drive to Cleveland and leave her with my sister for a while. There's also a local facility I use from-time-to-time when my friend comes to town." Ann's voice trailed off at the tail end of her sentence, like she was a bit embarrassed about the disclosure of having a "friend." It was a little too soon after Mr. Harrow's death, in Natalie's opinion, but not being one to judge, she kept her thoughts to herself. "But, as long as I have breath in my body and the activity of my limbs, Charla will live with me. I'm all she has."

"I'm sure you're doing a good job." Natalie was trying to find a way to end the conversation. Nate, who was only four at the time, helped her out when he started holding his private and saying he had to pee. She, again, told Ann that it was nice meeting her and quickly made her way into the house with her children.

Since that time, it wasn't unusual for Ann and Natalie to engage in small talk whenever they saw each other outside. It was usually Ann who initiated it, often asking questions about Natalie, Troy, and their family. At first Natalie thought Ann was way too nosey, but then began to see her inquisitiveness as loneliness. Since their initial introduction, Ann had joined the gym where Troy was a member.

Natalie still wasn't the type to be overly sociable with neighbors, but she normally didn't mind when Ann stopped her to talk. She seemed liked a nice woman whose entire life had been dedicated to caring for Charla since she was sixteen. Natalie could only imagine the high level of stress she experienced as a two-time widow dealing with Charla's disorder. Ann had warned Natalie that Charla would do and say anything to get food and she'd been right. This latest tactic of asking to borrow a slice of bread was proof and Natalie's patience, in general, was at an all-time low.

"Charla, I'm not giving you anything else. *Go home!*"

"I bet you'll give it to me if I tell you a secret. I saw a lady at your house today."

"I'm so sorry." Ann came running up the driveway. "I have a friend over and we got so caught up in our conversation that I didn't realize she'd slipped out. I need to change the alarm code again." Ann's attire wasn't necessarily intact which led Natalie to believe that she and her gentleman friend had been doing more than talking. This was a different one than the man who used to come by when the Harrows first moved into the neighborhood. The new guy was older; someone she'd met at the gym who Troy said had a reputation for being a player. "Charla, apologize to Miss Natalie right now for coming over and disturbing her," Ann demanded.

Like a puppy scolded for misbehavior, Charla's head drooped. "I'm sorry."

I saw a lady... "Charla, I want to clarify something real quick. You said there was someone at my house earlier?"

From the way Ann quickly cut in, she obviously sensed that Natalie was attempting to squeeze her daughter for information. "Charla's imagination can run wild sometimes. I'm sure she was mistaken. C'mon, Charla, let's get back home and leave Miss Natalie alone." As they were walking back across the street, Natalie could hear Ann chastising Charla for sticking her nose in other people's business.

*I saw a lady...*Natalie couldn't allow herself to get emotionally worked up again. Aneetra had pulled up with the kids. Seeing her babies reminded her that her time with Troy hadn't been in vain.

Without him, there would be no them and that helped her keep things in perspective in regards to their relationship.

Ean and Ebony were both cranky. Natalie could tell immediately that they either had not had a nap or had a very short one. Nate talked nonstop about his recent visit to Magic Mountain, which is where Aneetra took them after she picked them up. When Natalie commended her for bravely taking on such an adventure after having put in a full day's work, Aneetra admitted that she bribed her daughters to help.

"Where are they now?"

"Still there. Marcus dropped them off and is on his way to pick them up because everyone couldn't fit in my car."

"Mommy, is Daddy downstairs? I wanna show him my yo-yo."

"No. He's not here. Let's get ready for bed and you can show him tomorrow, okay?"

Nate started to whine, an indication that he, too, was tired. Still, he was getting too old for this. "Nathaniel, stop it!" Rarely did she ever call him by his full name and when she did, he understood that his grace was running thin. "You're a big boy and big boys don't whine when they don't get their way. Your dad isn't here; you'll show him tomorrow, okay?"

"'Kay." He still chose to have a pout face that Natalie ignored.

Aneetra helped Natalie get the kids bathed and in bed. They gathered in a circle to pray and Natalie felt a twinge in her heart when Nate prayed that his daddy would come home so he could show him his toy. It was then she realized that Nate would take the breakup hardest. He'd only known life with the two of them being together. His world was about to change more than either of theirs. "God bless my sissy and my friends. In Jesus's name I pray, amen."

After tucking him in and laying the little ones in their crib, Natalie joined Aneetra downstairs at the island. "So, do you want to talk?"

"What's there to say? My husband cheated on me. I'm sure you know how I feel."

"I do."

"At least in your case, Marcus came clean when he was confronted. Troy had to go all Clinton-Lewinsky on me, claiming that he 'did not have sexual relations with that woman.'" When Aneetra laughed, Natalie was also forced to find humor in her bad impersonation of former President Bill Clinton and the statement he'd made about Monica Lewinsky during the investigation to impeach him. The fun lasted only a second. "Troy lied…but as the saying goes, a picture is worth a thousand words." Natalie filled her best friend in on the horrid details of her encounter with Cheryl that morning. She then retrieved the envelope from the trash and pulled out the pictures before Aneetra had a chance to object. "I know those are Troy's butt cheeks."

"I'll take your word for it." Aneetra kindly slid the pictures back Natalie's way. "What does he have to say about all of this?"

"He claims that she drugged him." As Natalie began to relay Troy's lame excuse about the events of that weekend, she separated anger from hurt, making sure that only the former came through and not the tears. "Like I said, at least Marcus told you the truth. You've seen Cheryl before, haven't you?"

"No. Not that I recall."

"Well she's petite, like my neighbor, Ann. There's no way Cheryl could force Troy to do anything. Besides, right before you came, Charla told me that she saw some woman over here today. I bet you it was Cheryl."

"No offense, but Charla isn't the most reliable witness. I'm inclined to believe Troy. I'm not saying that *nothing* happened between them. I think their emotions may have temporarily gotten out of control, but if Troy says he didn't have an affair with her, I believe him. I don't know how you and Troy roll behind closed doors, but I'm pretty sure the brotha wouldn't have someone stand around and snap photographs, especially if he was cheating on you. Someone else has to be involved."

Natalie did not want to have to apologize to Aneetra a second time, so she took a deep breath to calm her nerves before speaking. "Not necessarily. Cameras can be set to automatically take pictures. We can do that with our cell phones. I don't care if there was a third party involved or not; all I know is that Troy's story is completely absurd!"

"I agree. It sounds crazy. So crazy that it could be true. If there's anything I believe about Troy, it's that he loves you, Nat. I couldn't see him doing anything to jeopardize what you have."

"Yeah, I felt the same way about Marcus and we see how well that worked out." As soon as Natalie spat out the words, she regretted them. Immediately, Aneetra started gathering her things to leave. "I'm sorry. I shouldn't have said that."

"Let's not talk about it. I understand you're upset and rightfully so. I can't be your verbal punching bag right now. I love you and I'm praying for you." She blew a kiss to Natalie with her hands and left.

Chapter 12: Laugh Fest

At Robert's urging, Troy stopped trying to contact his wife. Doing so was likely irritating her more than anything. Natalie needed her space and as much as it pained him, he would give it to her. Troy spent hours hanging out in Robert's office, even falling asleep on the couch after getting the invasive procedure done at the lab. The entire day, Troy ignored every call that rang through as there was only one person with whom he wished to speak. The sworn officer couldn't, in good conscience, throw his cases totally to the wayside. He had taken an oath and there were heartbroken families dependent on him for answers. Thus, he reached out to a fellow detective to make sure things were covered in case there was a break in any of his cases.

Thankfully, his tests for HIV and Trichomoniasis came back clean. It would take twenty-four hours to a few days before he got the results for other STIs. Overall, Troy felt fine, at least in terms of being drugged. He hadn't had a headache since Saturday evening. Still, it would be good to know for sure what Cheryl had given him and if there were any additional side effects he could experience.

Troy felt like a bum hanging around Robert's workplace though Robert didn't seem to mind. Robert went about his daily routine while Troy lay back on the sofa not knowing what to do about anything. He was in no mental or emotional condition to be on his own and he didn't want to go home. Not until he knew Natalie was there. If she saw his truck, she might be tempted to take off again and he wasn't going to let that happen. Somehow Robert convinced Troy to follow him home and he had dinner with Robert, Lisa, and their little one. Aneetra had already picked up the twins by the time Troy had gotten there and Lisa wasn't sure if she was taking them straight home or elsewhere. It was clear by watching Lisa and Robert interact that dinner together wasn't a special event they were doing because he was present. It was their routine. Troy couldn't recall the last time he'd actually sat down at the table and had dinner with his family, excluding the times when they ordered pizza or picked up fast food and ate on the go. The nature of his job didn't allow it. "How much do you know about my situation?" Troy asked Lisa.

"Nothing really except that you and Natalie are obviously having a tough time."

Troy gave her an abbreviated version of the recent events. "I'm not trying to pry, but can you give me some insight on how to repair things with Natalie based on what you and Robert went through? He and I have been talking, but I would like to have a female perspective."

Lisa seemed more than happy to oblige his request. "Well, you know that RJ and I were divorced for what, about five or six years?" She turned to him for verification.

"Something like that. I try not to dwell on those days."

"Yeah, it's a blur to me as well. Anyhow, my point is that we were apart for a while and although he made it clear that he wanted to get back with me, I was stubborn. I'm not sure there was anything he could have done differently. It was on me and unfortunately, it took a tragedy to bring us back together." She paused for a second. "I say all of that to say don't give up fighting for your marriage. It's worth it in the end."

Troy had no intentions of giving up, and he stated as much.

"Good. I want to talk to Natalie, but I don't want to press her. I can tell from our Wise Wives meetings that she's a private person. She and Aneetra don't talk much during our sessions, so I don't want to overstep my boundaries. I know she has Aneetra to lean on, so I'm using the most powerful weapon I have, which is prayer. I'm praying that her heart doesn't become hardened as a result of this situation."

"Thanks. I appreciate it. Please pray with me that Natalie will eventually see the truth."

"She will," added Lisa. "I already believe it. There's a proverb, I can't remember which one, but in the NIV, it says that the truth endures forever and a lying tongue is only for a moment. I'm paraphrasing, of course, but you get the point."

Proverbs 12:19. Troy was almost sure of it as he'd come across that scripture numerous times during his readings of that book.

Robert furrowed his brows. "Honey, I hate to see you misquoting the Word. Are you sure that scripture says endures and not *endureth?*" The two of them busted out laughing at some kind of inside joke that Troy obviously wasn't privy to with Lisa telling Robert that he was "wrong for that," all while cracking up.

Troy found himself chuckling as well, but only because their reactions amused him. "*O*-kay. Does someone want to fill me in?"

"My bad, man. I was making fun of Eric Freeman; you remember him, don't you?"

Troy nodded. How could he forget? Eric had been smack dab in the middle of one of Troy's biggest cases a couple of years ago.

"You don't have to say any more. I'm all too familiar with the idiosyncrasies of Pastor Eric Joshua Freeman of the Tabernacle of Jesus." Troy said the latter part of his sentence using his best impersonation voice.

The Hamptons got a kick out of it. "See, God's going to get y'all for talking about that man," Lisa, still laughing, warned.

After the laugh fest, Troy and the Hamptons talked a little more. Lisa filled him in on all the funny things that Ean and Ebony had done while in her care. She'd gotten a chance to witness their eerie synchronization firsthand and always found it amusing. By 9:30, Troy had worn out his welcome and thanked them for their hospitality. Robert walked him out to his truck.

"It's going to be all right, man. It may be rough for a little while, but ultimately, I believe everything will be okay and you and Natalie will be stronger as a result of this."

"Man, I hope so. I appreciate you being there for me, Robert."

"Not a problem. You know," Robert looked at him wryly, "It's mostly older people and strangers who call me Robert. My friends call me RJ."

Troy smirked. "All right. I'll keep that in mind." The two men shook hands and Troy hopped in his Navigator whose alarm was still acting crazy. It had been several hours since he'd last tried Natalie, so he called her again. *Insanity is doing the same thing over and over again and expecting different results,* he thought as his call went into his wife's voicemail. Wanting to be sure that someone had at least spoken to her, he called Aneetra.

"I'm starting to think you have my number on speed dial because this is the most you've ever called me since we've known each other."

"Hey, Aneetra. I don't mean to harass you—"

"You're not harassing me, I was only playing. What's up?"

"Have you spoken with Natalie?"

"Yep. I literally just left your house. I'm driving down the street now."

"Good. So she's home. How is she?"

"Angry and hurt."

Troy had been hoping she would have cooled down by now. "This is a big mess. I don't know what to do, Aneetra."

"And I don't know what to tell you."

"I didn't have an affair with Cheryl."

"I believe you, but I'm not the one who matters. I think Natalie will come to that same conclusion in time."

"I hope so." Aneetra did her best to provide words of encouragement and Troy thanked her before ending the call. He felt so defeated. If only he could go back to that Friday two summers ago when he and Cheryl met at Starbucks on High Street and her sexual innuendos made him feel uncomfortable. He would have never met her there if he'd known how much of a problem she'd become. He'd gone only with the intentions of talking about the case they were working on, but things took a detour when she began taking a trip down memory lane. Immediately, Troy left and he'd rejected all of her advances since then. Like cancer, she started out at a small lump and then infected other areas of his life. If he never saw Cheryl Hunter again, it would be too soon.

Instead of pulling in the garage next to Natalie's vehicle like he would have normally done, Troy purposely parked his truck on the outside of the garage door, on the side where he knew Natalie's car would be. He wasn't going to give her a chance to run away from him this time.

He walked in the front door and found her at the kitchen island in tears, staring at the pictures of him and Cheryl. "Hi" didn't seem like an appropriate greeting at the moment. He stood, not knowing what to say, wanting to rush to her and hold her, but not wanting to be pushed away. Natalie was the first to speak.

"Where have you been?"

"With Robert."

"What happened to your shirt? And what are all those marks on your face?"

Troy looked down and saw the ripped pocket of his dress shirt and the encounter with Cheryl came flooding back to him. All of a sudden, the wounds on his flesh felt fresh. "I allowed my temper to get the best of me."

"So you were with Robert *all* day?"

"Pretty much. I went to his job and stayed there until he got off, and then I followed him home where I've been ever since."

"Cheryl didn't come by the house to visit you any time today?"

"*No!* Where'd you get that?"

"Charla." Natalie told him about her encounter with their neighbor earlier.

Are you seriously questioning me about something Charla said? Troy wanted to say. Instead he opted for, "Call over to the Hamptons'. I'm sure they'll both verify what I've said. I have not spent the day with Cheryl nor have I been having an affair with her."

"I really want to believe you; I don't know how. You told me about the Shay girl at the gym liking you, but you didn't tell me about your history with Cheryl. That has me inclined to think that you kept Cheryl a secret for a reason. I'm scared…I don't want to be like those women who stand by their husbands only to look stupid in the end. How can you explain these pictures?"

He moved toward her slowly. "I can't. All I know is that I love you and I have never willingly done anything with Cheryl or anyone else that violates our marriage." He waited for her response. When he didn't get one, he continued. "I admit that I should have told you about her harassing me. I thought it would eventually stop and I didn't want to worry you unnecessarily. It's apparent to me now that Cheryl is out to destroy my life. I don't know why and I'm not even sure I care. If I lose you as a result of this, she will have succeeded." Troy reached out to Natalie and was relieved when she came into his arms. Her body wasn't totally relaxed, but holding her was more than he thought he'd get. He pushed her back slightly and lifted her chin. "I promise that I didn't cheat on you. I love you too much to hurt you like that," he said, wiping her tears.

Seeing the pain in her eyes, ripped Troy to the core. He knew how fragile her emotions could be. She put on a front of having a tough shell in front of others. Even when she tried to do it with him, her eyes would give her away. Beautiful, big, and brown eyes, that spoke volumes when her words got lost. "I'm sorry," he whispered, still holding her face. When she closed her eyes and arched up to him, he did not let the moment pass. He met her lips with his. The tenderness of her mouth ignited him. He pulled her in close, fervently kissing away the saltiness left by her tears. She, too, must've felt the passion because she wrapped her arms around his neck. He was seconds away from scooping her into his arms and taking her to their bedroom where the culmination of their love awaited when the doorbell rang followed by a demanding knock.

Troy, slightly irritated by the interruption, quickly sobered his hormones, remembering that he was awaiting test results. He would have gladly ignored the door and savored the emotional reconnection he and Natalie were experiencing. She, however, reacted differently. Natalie snapped back into a defensive position as if she regretted letting her guard down. "I'd better get that."

"Babe, let it go," he pleaded, gently holding on to her arm. "We need this. It's probably Charla again and you know she doesn't want anything."

Natalie denied his request. "I can't!" She shook her head. "This is too soon. I need time."

Troy watched her walking toward the door feeling dejected. He held on to the kitchen island for strength, nearly hating whoever it was for the intrusion.

"Hello, ma'am, I'm Detective Nugent. I need to speak with your husband. By any chance, is he available?"

Troy, overhearing the introduction, rushed to the door. There was no love lost between him and Donald Nugent as the two had personalities like oil and water. Troy wasn't sure how anyone got along with him. Nugent had been on the force for well over twenty years. He was a stocky guy who seemed more drawn to law enforcement because of the power he had as a result of the badge rather than a love for justice and helping others. He wore a gold class ring imprinted with the year he graduated from high school on the side and the word "Bruins" at the top right above a small purple stone. Troy was willing to bet that Nugent was a jerk back then as well. Two uniformed officers stood quietly behind him, dangling their hands from their holsters. "What can I do for you?"

Nugent, standing at the front door all smug with his arms crossed, made Troy want to smack him simply for the heck of it. "Well, since you asked, you can answer a few questions about your encounter with Cheryl Hunter this morning."

That name alone was enough to anger Troy. "Don't tell me that she called y'all because I went to her house. If she pressed charges on me, then—"

"You went to see her!"

Oh crap! Troy hadn't had a chance to share the details of this morning with Natalie. "Honey, it's not what you think. I only went there to tell her to leave us alone. I know it was stupid, but I was angry and didn't know what else to do at the time."

"You told me you were with RJ all day."

"I was. I went to Cheryl's first and then I went to his job."

Natalie looked at him with an even deeper level of disgust than she had that morning. "You expect me to believe that you weren't having an affair with her and yet you know where she lives. I'm done!" She turned away and stormed up the stairs.

Instinctively, Troy started to shut the door and run after her, but Nugent kept it from closing. "Not so fast. I still have some questions for you about Ms. Hunter. You can answer them here and risk upsetting the missus even more, or you can come with us down to the station."

Troy looked back, glancing up the stairs one last time. He and Natalie had been so close to bonding again, if only for the moment.

"Well, what's it gonna be?"

Reluctantly, Troy agreed to go to the station with the condition that he would drive himself. He hated to leave Natalie, but the quicker he settled this mess with Cheryl, the sooner he'd be able to get back to his wife and console her. He grabbed his keys and followed Nugent and the other officers to the station. As he was backing out and looking through his rearview mirror, he noticed a hole in the blinds quickly close across the street at the Harrows. *Great!* Just what he needed...his mentally challenged neighbor or her mama to make up something else!

Chapter 13: Catch 22

At the station, Troy followed Nugent into the interrogation room where Nugent read him his rights with a smirk.

"We could've skipped the formalities," Troy responded impatiently. He wanted to get this over and go back home. "I don't know what Cheryl told you, but I know it's nowhere near the truth. She started a whole bunch of drama with my wife and me. I'm tired of it and after this, I'm pressing harassment charges."

"Is it true that you went to Miss Hunter's home earlier?"

"Yeah."

"And what happened when you went there?"

"I told her that she needed to leave my family alone. She's been harassing me with phone calls and text messages, and then this morning, she told my wife that we've been having an affair."

Troy noticed the ever so slight tension lines in Nugent's face. "So you and Cheryl Hunter have not been having an affair?"

"*No!*"

Nugent smirked and, again, Troy wanted to smack him just because. "I have witness reports that you were seen banging on Miss Hunter's door this morning. Is that true?"

"Yeah. Like I said, I went there to tell her to leave us alone. I was angry."

"What time did you visit Miss Hunter's residence?"

"I don't know. Sometime between nine and ten, I guess. I wasn't really paying attention."

"And what happened when you arrived?"

"*I told you.* I told her to leave my family alone and I left."

"Did things get physical between you and Miss Hunter by any chance? I'm curious to know what happened to your shirt, and you have some prominent marks on your face. You mind telling me how you got those?"

Flashbacks of his hands around her neck brought an embarrassed flush through his veins. This question was a catch 22. If Troy said yes, he'd go on record admitting to assault. If he said no, he could potentially make matters worse, especially if there was any evidence that he'd laid the slightest hand on Cheryl. To his knowledge, he hadn't hit her, but he couldn't be sure. "Look, Nugent. I know how this game works. Instead of asking me all these questions trying to find a way to trip me up, tell me what this is about. What accusations has Cheryl trumped up against me?"

"Let me play something for you. This is a nine-one-one call that came in at nine thirty-seven this morning. I think you'll find it interesting."

"Nine-one-one, what's your emergency?"

"He's trying to kill me," a woman whispered in the midst of someone yelling and hitting things in the background.

"I'm having a hard time hearing you. Please speak up."

"He's trying to kill me!" She spoke more frantically while noise continued with the man screaming profanities at her.

"Who's trying to kill you?"

"Troy...Detective Troy Evans. He's upset because I told his wife about our affair. Please hurry. I'm scared!"

Nugent stopped the recording.

"That's not me!" Troy vehemently protested.

"By your own admission, you were at her house this morning during this time frame and you were upset with her. Are you now changing your statement?"

"No, I'm not. I know that's not me. Cheryl opened the door for me. Why would she do that if she was scared I would kill her? I'm telling you, she's crazy. She's trying to set me up. Friday evening, she drugged me and took me to a motel. She did it so she could take pictures that made it look like we slept together, and then she showed my wife, claiming that we are involved."

"You expect me to believe that someone as tiny as her drugged you and forced you to go to a motel against your will. C'mon, Troy. I know better than that. You were upset with her this morning for telling your wife that the two of you were having an affair, weren't you?"

"*We didn't have an affair!* That's what I'm trying to tell you. She made all of this up!"

"You were at her house, right?"

"Yes, but not when that call was made."

"Officers showed up at Cheryl's address within ten minutes. Guess what they found? Evidence of a struggle. Her front door was broken, glass was shattered on the floor, and there was blood. Furthermore, Miss Hunter, was nowhere to be found."

"Okay. And?" Again, Troy didn't want to elaborate.

"Will you consent to giving us a blood sample to compare with what we found at her house?"

"Of course, if you have a warrant, but I'm guessing you don't, which is why you are asking so nicely, right?"

"Are you saying that the person in the background of the nine-one-one call isn't you? What about this?"

Troy's stomach dropped to the pit of his feet when Nugent played a recording of the angry and deeply disturbing message Troy had left for Cheryl Saturday evening after leaving his wife standing in her lingerie. In it, he called her out of her name several times and said, "I could kill you for this."

"What did you mean by that?" inquired Nugent.

"Nothing. I was upset and sometimes people say things they don't mean when they're angry." Deep down, Troy had meant every word in that recording. "You of all people should know how it is to run off at the mouth and say something stupid, especially to an attractive woman."

Troy found some twisted pleasure in watching Nugent turn red. Back in the early 2000s, there had been a sexual harassment accusation against Nugent by one female personnel worker who said that he consistently made crude and inappropriate comments to her. There was an investigation, but nothing came of it because of the lack of evidence supporting her claims. Plus, she had some other personal issues that made her allegations questionable. Nevertheless, the whole thing was embarrassing to the department, and Nugent's second marriage couldn't withstand the strain.

"You think you're funny, don't you, Evans? I'll be the one laughing when you're behind bars with inmates who can't wait to get their hands on a fresh piece of former cop meat. I'm sure a nice-looking, well-built guy like yourself is the kind of eye candy those men have been waiting for."

"If I didn't know any better, I'd think you might want a piece of me yourself," Troy replied cynically.

"I'm getting tired of this comedy act you're portraying. There's nothing humorous about playing with women's emotions. You broke her heart before and you were going to do it again this time after you finished having your fun, except she wasn't going away quietly. Shut up and tell me what you've done with Cheryl!"

"Nothing."

"The evidence says you did?"

"You're using that term rather loosely, don't you think?"

"You left a threatening message on her voicemail, witnesses put you at her house this morning, and you are heard screaming at her during a terrifying nine-one-one call. To top it all off, you're the last person who admits to seeing her today. Call me crazy, but that all sounds like evidence to me."

Troy returned the sneer that Nugent gave him. "Am I under arrest?"

"Not yet."

"In that case, we're done here."

Natalie lay in bed, but couldn't sleep a wink. Troy had left with the other officers and she hadn't a clue what was going on or why they were questioning him about Cheryl. Troy had seen her this morning. Worse, he'd gone to her house! All of this *after* Natalie had confronted him about their affair. That was the part that Troy had conveniently left out when she'd asked him where he'd been all day.

"*With Robert.*" That had been his explanation and she foolishly was going to believe him. In the time that they had known Lisa and RJ, to her knowledge, Troy had never hung out with RJ except for the times Natalie dragged him to the Wise Wives meetings to do so. Now, all of a sudden, RJ had become his alibi.

Her suspicions could be verified with a simple phone call or text to the Hamptons, but it was after 11:00 and Natalie wouldn't contact them for something this trivial. Besides, she had no doubt that Troy had seen RJ, and perhaps Lisa, at some point during the day. She was sure that he'd spent just enough time with them to make his story legit. The fact was that after she left him this morning, he went straight to Cheryl. *I saw a lady*...And sometime during the day, he and Cheryl were here.

As Natalie lay in the bed, a feeling of disgust came over her. Had Cheryl been in her bed? *Their bed?* Natalie was so hurt that tears no longer were an option. Needing to feel valued by someone, Natalie reached out to her eldest daughter with a text. "*143*," she wrote. It stood for "I love you." She wasn't sure how the text linguistics got those three words from those three numbers, but ever since Corrine had educated her on its meaning, Natalie used that special code only with her daughter. She grinned when, a few minutes later, Corrine replied, "*1432*."

Seconds later, Natalie was startled by an unexpected call from Aneetra. Natalie welcomed the interruption and took the opportunity to rectify the rift from earlier. "Hey, Nee. I'm sorry about what I said."

"Yeah, okay, whatever, I forgive you and it's squashed. Are you watching the news?"

"No. Why?"

"There's a story on about Cheryl I think you need to see."

Cheryl was the last person in the world she wanted to know more about, but the urgency in Aneetra's voice made Natalie curious. Luckily, the cable box was already set on a news station and when Natalie turned on the television, she caught the tail end of the story. Thanks to digital cable, she was able to rewind it to the beginning.

"Police are investigating the mysterious disappearance of former FBI agent Cheryl Hunter. Earlier today, Hunter made an emergency nine-

one-one call claiming that her boyfriend was trying to kill her for revealing details of their affair to his wife. We have learned that Hunter was dating a Columbus police detective, but officials are not releasing his name because he's not been charged with any crime at this point. Officers responded to the nine-one-one call within minutes. When they got to Hunter's home, she was missing and there were clear signs that a struggle had taken place. Officers have taken the detective in for questioning, but he has not been charged. We learned that Cheryl Hunter had been an FBI agent for over twenty years until last year when her employment was terminated for reasons the agency has not disclosed. If you know anything about the disappearance of former FBI agent Cheryl Hunter, please call the Columbus Police at 614-555-TIPS. You can remain anonymous. We'll be sure to keep you posted as more details emerge."

"They think Troy did something to her." Natalie, finally putting things together, told Aneetra about the officers that had come to their home. "He admitted to being at her house this morning. Nee, he had scratches on his face and his shirt was ripped! Oh, my gosh, what's happening to my family!" Immediately she started to get choked up.

"Calm down. I'm on my way."

Natalie wanted to thank Aneetra for her kindness and unmatched friendship, but she couldn't speak. Her tears had taken over.

Chapter 14: A Little Faith

Troy left the station feeling empty and even a little scared. He'd never been in any kind of trouble. He was certain that he would ultimately be cleared of whatever it was that Cheryl was trying to set him up for, but he wasn't sure what the entire ordeal would cost him. His marriage? His job? He could handle the latter much more than the former. Losing his family would mean losing everything.

Troy wandered around the city for what seemed like hours. He wanted to go home and yet knew he wouldn't be welcomed. Natalie had not tried to contact him once since he'd left. He'd been so close to comforting her and now he had to start over from zero. Actually, he likely had to work his way up from being in the negative. Zero would be relief right.

Though it was well after midnight, Troy reached out via text to Richard and he called back within seconds. "I'm sorry to bother you so late. I hope I didn't wake you."

"No. I was up going over my trial notes. What's wrong? Are the kids okay?"

"Yeah, they're fine. I'm not." Troy gave him the synoptic version of all that had taken place with Cheryl over the last two years, but described, in extended detail, the events that had recently transpired. Troy, knowing how much Richard disdained adultery, made sure to stress that he had never done anything inappropriate with

Cheryl. Richard had been married once, a long time ago, before meeting and dating Natalie's mom. Troy didn't know him then, but the story he'd heard from Natalie was that Richard's ex-wife had been a chronic adulterer.

"Nugent's a prick. You should have never spoken to him without an attorney," Richard scolded.

"I know. I wasn't thinking. I had no idea that Cheryl would pull this stunt. She's trying to make it seem like I did something to her."

"You did the right thing by not answering the question regarding whether or not things got physical between the two of you. Let's hope this all ends soon, but if not, you need legal representation. Obviously, I can't represent you, but I know an excellent defense attorney who makes me scared to go up against him in court. His name is Lawrence Murphy. He's a good guy who doesn't take a case unless he believes the client is innocent." Richard gave Troy Mr. Murphy's information. "I'll call him first thing in the morning to tell him about you. Make sure you contact him as well."

"Will do. Thank you."

"How's Natalie taking all of this?"

"Not good. She's not convinced of my innocence regarding the affair."

"Give her time. She'll get there. For what it's worth, I believe you."

"Thanks, man. That means a lot."

When Troy hung up the phone, he contemplated making one more phone call, knowing it would involve a good old-fashioned tongue-lashing once he told her everything. It wasn't necessary that he inform her, but since she normally called Natalie more than him, he certainly didn't want her hearing his wife's version of things. Either way, Troy knew he would get cussed out. "Might as well get this over with," he said aloud, bracing himself for the inevitable. His call was answered on the first ring.

"Do you want me to call the station and see if I can find out any information about what's going on with Troy?" Aneetra offered. It was nearly one o'clock in the morning and the two were laid up in Natalie and Troy's bed like teenage girls at a sleepover except there were no movies or popcorn to go with the occasion, only fear and tears.

Natalie shook her head no. She was married to a cop. She knew interrogations could last forever. "Troy will call when he can." So many unanswered questions ran through her mind. "Do you think he did something to her for real? Even if we're not together, I don't want him to be locked up," she bawled.

"Shh. Don't start thinking the worst. You're stressing yourself out. For all we know, it could be another officer she pulled this stunt with as well. Besides, the news reported that no one has been charged with anything, so Troy's obviously not going to be locked up."

"They were here to talk to him about her, *not* to involve his help with finding her. When I asked him about his scratches and shirt, he admitted that he'd lost his temper. I know he was mad because Cheryl told me about them."

"Okay, but you still can't be so melodramatic. One minute you're spitting fire because you think he had an affair; the next you're crying a river because you're afraid he'll be in jail. I know this isn't easy, but don't let your emotions take over. Personally, I think that if Troy went over there, it wasn't to confront her for telling you about their affair; it was because she was lying. Natalie, that man loves you. If he says that he didn't mess around with her, I'd be willing to bet money that he's telling the truth."

"But the pictures—"

"I don't care about those pictures. We live in a digital age. Anything can be made to look like something. Shoot, with the right tools, someone could show a picture of me with flat abs, a Kim Kardashian booty, and hair as long as silky as yours."

"I appreciate what you're trying to do, Nee, but let's face it. Karma is coming back to bite me for all the wives I've done wrong."

"Oh, see, now I know you're trippin' because last time I checked, you believed in the grace given to us by Jesus, not karma. That's a bunch of crap."

"The Bible does say that we reap what we sow. I'm being real and accepting the fact that I did some shady stuff back in the day that is now coming back to haunt me. It was bound to happen."

Aneetra gave Natalie a look like she wanted to smack her. "Girl, you have lost your mind to be thinking that way. God hasn't been sitting around waiting to orchestrate circumstances so you can get back things that you've done in the past. You've repented and have been forgiven. He's over it; you're the only one still hanging on to it. I don't know what Bible you're reading, but mine says that He throws our sins into the sea of forgetfulness. That's grace, sweetheart; not karma."

Natalie was not in the mood for Bible study. She knew about grace and forgiveness. She also was aware that when something walked like a duck and quacked like a duck, one should call it a duck and not a chicken. "Okay, whatever. The fact of the matter is that Troy hasn't denied it's him in the pictures."

"That's because he's probably as confused as you are. Look, all I'm saying is relax a little. I believe God will bring clarity to this whole thing. Quit all that karma talk and have a little faith, will you?"

Faith? Did Natalie even have that anymore? If so, what was she believing—that God would take care of her and the kids if she and Troy split or if he went to jail? She hadn't a clue what to believe when it came to her marriage. She wanted to believe in it, but there was too much evidence pointing against it. When her cell phone rang, she'd hoped it would be Troy only because she wanted to know what was happening. However, from the sound of the personalized ringtone, she knew it was her mother-in-law, Diane.

"You want me to answer it?"

"Yes, please," she responded to Aneetra, buying some time to get her emotions together. Natalie and Diane spoke regularly, at least once at week. It hadn't always been like this, but ever since Natalie transitioned from a working mom to a full-time caregiver, Diane had started calling more than she used to. Occasionally, Diane would say something to irk Natalie's nerves and, as a result, Natalie would avoid talking to her for a week or two, but that didn't happen too often as each had started to become aware of the other's limits. Their conversations generally involved the kids and usually took place during the daytime. Diane never called this late unless something was wrong and Natalie tried to brace herself for whatever it was that her mother-in-law had to share.

"No, this is Aneetra. Natalie's right here. Hold one sec." Aneetra turned to Natalie, covering the cell phone speaker with her hand. "You good?"

Natalie wasn't sure if she had the capacity to handle any more bad news, but she shook her head anyway and grabbed the phone. "Hey, Di, is everything okay?"

"No! Why didn't you tell me about Troy and this FBI lady?"

On one hand, Natalie was relieved that Diane wasn't calling to report a family catastrophe. On the other, she was immediately irritated by her mother-in-law's tone. Already this seemed a like conversation that would ultimately result in a two-week phone strike. "I didn't know anything until this morning and quite frankly, I didn't feel like talking about it."

"Well, I guess I can understand that. I just got off the phone with Troy. He's upset about what happened, obviously, but I told him that he needed to be there with you. He should be on his way home. How are you doin'?"

"I've been better. So, I take it that he's admitted everything to you?"

"If by 'admitted,' you mean he confessed to an affair, then no, but he told me how much trouble that woman has caused for y'all." Not one to tame her tongue or sugarcoat her feelings, Diane went on to profanely express how angry she was about the entire situation, how she wanted to beat both Troy and Cheryl—him for being so stupid and not saying anything about what he'd been going through, her for trying to be a home-wrecker. "I know you're pissed right now, but you need to get over how you feel and open your eyes to what's really goin' on. Troy didn't cheat on you with that woman. That heffa is tryin' to break y'all up. Don't be foolish and fall into her trap by pushin' him away."

Foolish!?! "How do you know what Troy has and has not done when you're all the way in Texas? I bet if you'd seen the pictures of the two of them naked in bed together, you wouldn't be so sure."

"She drugged him! He told you that."

Whatever! Troy could fool Aneetra and his mama with that story, but Natalie would not believe it. Not for a second! "Even *if* that's true, what would be her purpose for wanting to break us up if Troy wasn't messing around with her?"

"They were together in the past. Maybe he put somethin' on her so good that she never got over him. If Troy takes after his daddy—"

"Di, *puh-leaze* don't go there!" Natalie's words were so abrupt that Aneetra gave her a "what-did-she-say" look to which Natalie responded by rolling her eyes and mouthing the word "crazy"!

"All I'm sayin' is that you never know what goes on in the minds of these whores, but you should know your man. Troy loves you,

Natalie. You and my grandbabies are his world. He would never risk what he has with you for even one minute of pleasure with that girl. I'm willin' to bet my life on that."

Natalie wanted so much to believe Diane, but the images of Troy's black butt cheeks smiling for the camera as he lay between Cheryl's legs made it difficult. *I saw a lady*...

"I know my son and, if he was guilty of any of this, Troy would have never called me because he knows I would have cussed him up one way and down the other. He's grown, but I know the last thing Troy wants to hear is my mouth. He would have avoided me like a fat girl does veggies."

Aneetra, who had leaned her ear closer to the phone, apparently overheard Diane's weird analogy and covered her mouth to contain a chuckle. Natalie wasn't in a laughing mood. Besides, it wasn't like Diane could exactly be classified in the thin category. She had a small upper torso, but her hips kept her shopping in plus-sized sections. "I'm going downstairs to get some water," Aneetra whispered.

"When Troy told me what happened, I did fuss at him for keepin' all of this a secret for so long, but I didn't get on him too bad 'cuz I didn't want to kick him while he's down. You have to stand by him and believe in him, Natalie, no matter what it looks like. Troy may be many things, but one thing he's not, is a liar. If he says he didn't have an affair with that woman, then you, of all people, should take him at his word. You know how much Troy hated Reed for his actions. Troy never wanted to be anything like his father used to be. I can't see him doin' that to you."

Natalie allowed her mother-in-law's words to rest on her heart like morning dew falling on grass. For a split-second, she felt at peace. But, like the parable Jesus explained in Matthew 12 of the sower and the seed that fell on stony ground that could not grow because it had no root, ultimately, such were Diane's words. Natalie's heart was hardened as fear of being humiliated took over. She was in pain now, but she could only imagine how much worse the situation would hurt if she was like Hillary Clinton who stood by former President Clinton when he was accused of inappropriate behavior with Monica Lewinsky, only to learn that the accusations had been true in the end. Natalie had not been an angel in her pre-Jesus days, and it didn't surprise her that someone would sleep with her husband like she'd slept with many others.

Diane had warned her not to be foolish, but Natalie already had. She'd been foolish enough to think that she could live her married life happily-ever-after when she hadn't respected the union of others. She believed in grace, no doubt. Corrine, Ean, Ebony and Nate were proof that grace existed. Had it not been for them, Natalie's life situations would have all been in vain. This situation with Cheryl was karma whether Aneetra liked the word or not. Natalie believed it would be possible for her and Troy to work through his affair. Aneetra and Marcus had made it; so had Lisa and RJ. Even her in-laws' marriage had defied all odds. If there was any chance that Natalie's marriage could survive, Troy had to first be honest with himself and her, and he wasn't. That made her realize that her marriage would ultimately end in demise. "Di, I appreciate your love and concern, but I really can't talk about this right now."

"Okay, but please do me a favor and don't give up on him so easily, Natalie. Have faith in him and in God to work this all out for your good and His glory."

Stunned by her mother-in-law's final words, Natalie held the phone even after Diane hung up. *"Have faith in him and in God to work this all out for your good and His glory."* Such a statement was not the norm for the sailor-like-cursing sixty-something-year-old whose Bible likely contained more cobwebs than a barn in the middle of the field that had been abandoned for decades. What was even more eerie was Aneetra had said something similar prior to Diane's phone call.

Natalie's emotions were all over the place. Confusion...anger... guilt. Why was everyone so insistent that Troy was telling the truth? Troy was not perfect! Why couldn't her loved ones accept that she had a right to believe differently? Why was she so afraid to believe him? She thought about Diane and what she knew about her mother-in-law's commitment to Troy's father. Diane and Reed had a rocky marriage until a couple of years ago. Troy's dad had cheated multiple times, been abusive, and even fathered a child outside of their union. When Reed had been accused of murder, Diane's belief in him didn't waver, not even for a second, despite the evidence pointing in his direction. Yet, here Natalie was, ready to throw her husband to the wolves because of one woman's word—and some pictures—that Troy had had an affair. *"Have faith in him and in God to work this all out for your good and His glory."*

Natalie pondered on the meaning of faith—to believe in what one cannot see. There was a fine line between faith and foolishness. Natalie had vowed that no man would ever make a fool of her. She'd already given up her heart, her independence, and her career for Troy. Was she expected to throw away common sense as well?

Not wanting to be alone in the room with her thoughts anymore, Natalie decided to join Aneetra downstairs. She'd been gone a while and Natalie suspected it was because Aneetra had wanted to give her privacy during her phone conversation with Diane. It certainly didn't take twenty minutes to get a drink of water. Natalie didn't know what to think when she walked in the kitchen to find Aneetra holding a picture of Troy and Cheryl up to the light.

"Come here. You need to see this."

"No thanks. I've seen enough. I'm trying to figure out what disturbs me more—the fact that you're staring at that photo, in general, or that you dug it out the trash to stare at it."

"Oh, hush. Trust that this is quite uncomfortable for me as well. Seriously, though, you need to take a look at something." Aneetra used a free hand to motion for Natalie to hurry.

"What," Natalie said after she'd moseyed over.

"Look right here. You can see the reflection of someone in the headboard."

Natalie snatched the picture to investigate further.

"You know what this means, don't you?" Aneetra's sly grin had "I-told-you-so" all over it. "This photograph was staged."

Chapter 15: A New Day

As he turned down the street into his neighborhood, Troy wasn't certain what to expect when he walked in the house. When he left, Natalie had been livid upon hearing from Nugent that he'd gone by Cheryl's. Ironically, it wasn't something that he was purposely trying to keep from her. They were having such a tender moment that he didn't want to ruin it by bringing up her name. Cheryl had now pulled a disappearing act to make it seem like he'd done something to her only added to his anger. He prayed he would never see her again; he wasn't sure he'd have sense enough to let go this time.

Troy was surprised to see Aneetra's car in his driveway so late. He was glad that she was there for Natalie. Plus, it didn't hurt that Aneetra believed him. She was Natalie's best friend and as down-to-earth as a friend could be. Aneetra was a good person on the outside and at her core. Troy knew that and he was certain Natalie did as well by the way she valued her friendship with Aneetra. If anyone could possibly sway Natalie's opinion in his favor, Aneetra would be the one.

Unlike earlier, Troy decided to park in his normal spot instead of on the outside behind Natalie's car. Aneetra's car was there anyhow. He walked through the garage door into the kitchen and wasn't quite sure what to make of Natalie and Aneetra at the island with a magnifying glass, staring at a picture of him and Cheryl.

"Hey, Troy," Aneetra spoke nonchalantly as if she and Natalie were putting together a jigsaw puzzle.

Natalie ran and put her arms around him. "Are you okay?"

"Yeah. Cheryl's gone missing and they wanted to talk to me because of what happened earlier." It felt so good to have her in his arms that Troy didn't want to let her go.

"What did happen?" Natalie's reddened eyes looked both worn and weary. She'd been crying.

"I'll tell you, but first can someone let me know what's going on here?"

"There's been a break in the case." Aneetra explained the new revelation and he rushed to see for himself. Sure enough, there was the reflection of someone's image in the background. "Do you have any idea who that is?"

Troy squinted at the picture like doing so would bring clarity. "No. I'm pretty sure it's a male because of the baseball cap."

"Here, use this." Aneetra handed him the magnifying glass, but it didn't help. Troy laid both it and the picture on the island. He could tell that the images themselves were still painful for Natalie. He would get down to the bottom of things, just not tonight.

"Come here." Troy motioned to his wife who came to him and buried her head into his chest. "I'm sorry that you have to go through this."

"No...," she cried, "I'm sorry. I should have believed you. I'm a horrible wife."

Troy and Aneetra looked at each other with a "here-she-goes-with-the-drama" expression. Natalie could be so hard on herself. Troy observed her insecurities whenever things went wrong with the kids or she and Corrine had a falling-out, and he was sure that Aneetra could testify to having witnessed it at other times. "No, you're not. You're a wonderful wife. I didn't make it easy for you to believe me by keeping so much from you."

"I was scared. I thought this was perhaps the big payback from my past."

"*Baaabe.*" Troy took a step back so he could hold Natalie by her shoulders and look her into her eyes. They'd had a similar conversation before and he sincerely hoped they wouldn't have to have it again. It was getting old. "I love you. I don't understand why you think I'm out to hurt you, or even worse, that God is. Yeah, I know things happen," he said before she had the chance, "But God is merciful, Natalie. Everything you've done in the past has been forgiven. God isn't waiting for me to cheat on you so He can say, 'Ha, that's what you get!' He doesn't hold our past against us."

"That's the same thing I was saying to her earlier. She never listens to me," Aneetra teased.

Natalie playfully stuck her tongue out at Aneetra. Childish? Yeah, but Troy couldn't be happier. After the day he'd had, he was glad to have his high-maintenance wife display any kind of emotions other than hatred toward him. "I'm sorry." Natalie turned back to him.

"Me, too, babe." For several moments, the two of them went back and forth with the "I love yous" and "I'm sorrys" between kisses until Aneetra had had enough.

"All right, lovebirds. I see that three's a crowd. I need to get out of here anyhow and hopefully get a few hours of sleep before having to get up for work."

Both Natalie and Troy thanked Aneetra for her friendship. After Aneetra left, the couple went upstairs where they continued to talk.

"Your mom called."

"It figures. I told her to leave you alone, but you know my mama. I hope she didn't upset you. She went off on me."

"She told me that she didn't come down too hard on you."

"Yeah, okay. You know my mama, right?"

Natalie laughed and filled him in on some of the things that his mother had said to her. "I felt like crap when comparing myself to how she stood by your dad through murder accusations."

Not wanting her to get back on her self-pity soapbox or having to repeat the God-has-forgiven-you-for-your-past speech, Troy quickly cut in. "Natalie Renee Coleman—"

"*Coleman?*"

He knew saying her maiden name would grab her attention. "You are the only Missus Evans there will ever be. I love you and the only way you're going to get rid of me is if you kill me."

"Okay, now *you're* talking crazy. I would never kill you."

"That's not what you implied earlier. You threatened my life with your widow before ex-wife comment. You had me sort of scared. That's why the officers were here. They came to ensure my safety. By the way, I filed a protection order against you while I was at the station. Technically, you're a little too close to me right now. You need to back up."

The cackling sound of Natalie's "whatever!" response was music to his ears. He'd give anything to keep that smile on her face. "I love you, Missus Evans."

"I love you, too, Mr. Coleman," she said simply to be ornery.

Last night was good for us! Troy thought to himself as he awakened Tuesday morning with his wife lying snugly in his arms. Last night, after the playful banter, things got more serious. They talked. Natalie wanted to know everything that had happened over the weekend until the time he left the station. Troy told her about leaving the gym, waking up in the hotel, the paranoia he felt at the Commons and why he'd lashed out at Richard, how he wanted to make love to her Saturday night, but was concerned about her safety, going to Cheryl's, going to see Robert, the tests, and everything else. He included his conversations with his mother and Richard, until the very moment he pulled into the driveway and saw Aneetra's car. That took time. Natalie also asked him about his history with Cheryl, and he gave her all the gritty details, starting from the very beginning.

"We met at a party," he'd explained. "I didn't expect to communicate with her again after our initial hookup, but we did. I think we sort of got comfortable with each other because we had a lot in common."

"Like what?"

"Well, for starters, we were both interested in law enforcement, which was motivated by our passion for justice. You know I always carried some guilt because of what happened with Elana." The disappearance of Troy's best friend's eight-year-old sister when Troy and Elvin were eleven had haunted him for over three decades. Elvin, along with Troy, was supposed to be looking after Elana that morning while their mother went out. Elana had been getting on the boys' nerves and they picked on her until she ran out of the house crying. Hours later, when Elvin and Elana's mom returned home, Elana was nowhere to be found. It wasn't until thirty years later when her body was discovered that Troy was finally able to help find answers regarding Elana's mysterious disappearance, though, in the end, the quest for justice brought the family more pain.

"Cheryl's drive resulted from the things that had happened in her childhood. When she was nine, someone broke into her home and murdered her parents and two younger brothers. Cheryl hid with her baby sister in the dryer. Obviously, I wasn't there, but the way Cheryl told the story, she was so happy to have a baby sister that her parents let her name her. When we were dating, Cheryl talked a lot about finding Chyanne. She said that she used to get up in the middle of the night, get her baby sister out of the crib, and sneak downstairs to the laundry room to play with her so their parents couldn't hear. That's where they were the night when her family was killed. Afterwards, she and Chyanne were placed in different foster homes. My guess is that the baby got adopted eventually, but I know Cheryl was raised in a group home. It bothered her a great deal to lose her family. To my knowledge, no one has ever been held accountable for their murders."

"That's sad. Did she and her sister ever reconnect?"

"Nope. It was something Cheryl had hoped for, though. She always said that she wanted to find Chyanne one day. We were both drawn into law enforcement because of things that had happened in our past. I became a cop because of Elana; she joined the FBI because of what happened to her family."

"Humph. I wonder why she's gone to such great lengths to make it look like you guys were involved or that you've done something to her. Did you do something to anger her when y'all were together, or did you give her any kind of false hope that there would be a chance for the two of you when y'all reconnected while working on the Bible Butcher case?"

"The answer to both of your questions is no. If I did do something to her back in the day that's caused her to have a grudge for over twenty years, I haven't a clue as to what. When it became clear to me that she wanted more than I was willing to give her, I ended our relationship." He recapped the night of their breakup to his wife.

"Why won't you tell me you love me?"

"Because that won't be enough. You'll want more."

"We've been dating for over a year now and you can't even say you love me. Elvin and Nicole haven't been together as long as we have and already he's proposed to her."

"We are not them! I don't want to get married because my best friend is."

"But you will spend seventy-five dollars on a stupid stuffed animal to keep up with him."

"I am not ready."

"Do you love me?"

He looked down at her petite frame, wishing he had never allowed their contact to extend beyond their one-night stand. But, she'd called him the next day and before he knew it, they were dating. She was a nice person whom he'd had a lot of fun and great sex with, but she wasn't someone he wanted to spend the rest of his life with. "I can't give you the answer you want."

"So what are you saying?"

"This is obviously an issue that won't go away. Maybe it's best that we end things."

Cheryl went into a hysterical rage, screaming how much she loved him and wanted to be with him forever. She punched him repeatedly until he'd finally grabbed her arms and held her to his chest. To be so small, she hit hard. He felt horrible, but he refused to lie and play with her heart, or any woman's for that matter, by admitting to feelings he did not have. He apologized profusely for hurting her. She kicked him out of her apartment.

"That was the last I'd ever seen or heard from her until she helped with the case a couple years ago, and I certainly didn't give her any hopes that we could rekindle the past then."

"What stuffed animal was she referring to?"

"I won it at Cedar Point at one of the carnival games. If it weren't for my stupid ego, I wouldn't have gotten the stupid thing."

They'd been at the amusement park since it opened and ten hours later, they were all roller coastered out. Not yet in the mood to make the two-hour drive back to Columbus, the couples decided to play some games. They spent about an hour or so in the arcade where the testosterone competition between Elvin and Troy had begun. It spilled over into the carnival games where each friend tried to one up the other. They were at their last game, and had planned to get on the road whenever the other was ready to quit. They'd both wasted money, but they were neck-to-neck on wins at the carnival games until El got lucky.

The object of the game was to throw a ring on top of the bottle. If successful, the prize was a giant stuffed animal of choice. Troy had thrown his last ring and of course, it didn't make it. Elvin flung his and it bounced from bottle to bottle and somehow miraculously landed around the neck of one.

"We have a winner!" the game attendant announced.

Nicole beamed. She had already picked out the one she wanted in the event that her boyfriend won. Elvin gloated. He was "the man." They were headed back to Columbus and he'd won the ultimate prize for his girl. Cheryl was leaving with nothing but a few cheap souvenirs. Troy was not listening to this all the way back home. "Eh, man, hook me up again," he said to the game host. Ring after ring, Troy tossed only to be disappointed when he'd run out of turns and had to fork over another five dollars to play again. Seventy-five dollars later, Cheryl had a bear.

She jumped into his arms, hugging and kissing him like he'd just asked her to marry him or something. Troy hadn't realized how badly Cheryl wanted one of the stuffed animals and he was glad that he had been able to make her happy. More importantly, he was glad that Elvin wouldn't have one up on him.

"I won mine first," El whispered as they were walking to the parking lot.

"Yeah, but Cheryl's looks better."

"It wasn't too long after that day when we broke up."

"Do you think it's possible that you did love her, but were afraid to admit it, similar to how things happened with us?"

Troy had to take a deep breath before responding to his wife's inquiry. The argument he and Cheryl had had about his feelings, or lack thereof, was eerily similar to one that had transpired between him and Natalie when they were dating. However, there was no comparison between the two women when it came to which of them had actually captured his heart. Natalie had needed the reassurance and he'd wanted to give her such. Gently, Troy lifted her head so her eyes met his and held her face so it would be impossible for her to turn away if she tried. "Babe, I have never been in love with any woman besides you." He'd admitted his foolishness in almost letting Natalie get away from him. "When Cheryl and I broke up, I went on about my life like she'd never existed. When you and I split, I fell apart. There wasn't a day that went by that I didn't think about you. When we got back together, I swore it would be for keeps. I'm not letting you go, Natalie. And no one from my past or in the future will be able to take me away from you."

With those words, Natalie had leaned into his chest and the two of them eventually ended up in bed. It wasn't about sex. As a matter of fact, Troy was still waiting on his test results, so making love wasn't an option. Rather, they lay together and Troy took pleasure in holding her tightly until they both drifted off to sleep. That, in and of itself, was more than Troy thought would happen when he returned from his interrogation. He woke up this morning with a new sense of thanksgiving and appreciation in his heart.

From now on, he would try to be more open with Natalie about everything.

Troy smiled as he watched his wife lay in his arms. He had to pee, but held it for as long as he could simply because he didn't want the moment to end. When it got to the point that he couldn't wait anymore, Troy tried to gently finagle his arm from underneath Natalie as not to wake her.

"I'm not sleeping." She startled him when she spoke and lifted her head so he could break free. He was surprised. It was only a few minutes after seven and they had been up until well after three.

"What were you doing?"

"Thinking."

"Uh oh, let me go to the bathroom first. I have a feeling this could take a while." Troy hurried to take care of business. When he came out, Natalie went in to do the same. They met again under the comforter and Troy asked, "What were you thinking about?"

"Everything that happened yesterday. I don't want to rehash the details. I'm very thankful that today is a new day."

The chime of Troy's cell phone alarmed them both. Troy was concerned that it could possibly be Cheryl with some sick, twisted text message and he suspected Natalie may have thought the same. He checked it breathing a sigh of relief when it wasn't from Cheryl.

"Saw the news last nite. U good? How's Natalie?"

"Who's that?"

"RJ," he answered while responding, *"Yeah, all is well. We r both good. WorkN thru this 2gether. Will talk 2u l8r."*

"I've never heard you call him that before?"

"Call him what?"

"RJ. You normally call him Robert."

Humph. Troy thought he'd said Robert. "I'm liable to call anybody anything with only two minutes of sleep under my belt."

"I know, right. I want to go back to sleep, but as soon as I do, I know one of the kids will get up and it'll be time to report for mommy duty."

"Go ahead. I'll take care of them."

"That's sweet, honey, but I know you have business to handle."

By "business," Troy knew Natalie had meant getting down to the bottom of Cheryl's latest charade so he could clear his name and get back to work. He'd been placed on paid administrative leave until further notice. His first course of action probably needed to be contacting Richard's attorney friend for advice.

Troy and Natalie continued to lie in bed for another half hour or so. Neither said a word. They simply held each other, enjoying the moment until their solitude was interrupted, not by one of their children as had been anticipated, but by loud banging on the door.

Not again! Troy thought to himself as he jumped up and looked out his bedroom window.

"Who is it?"

"I don't know. I thought it might be Nugent, but I don't see a vehicle. Stay here. I'll be back." He slipped on some sweats and grabbed his personal firearm for good measure. With Cheryl on the loose, one could never be too sure. "Coming!" he yelled as the knocking continued and he raced down the stairs to meet their persistent early morning visitor. After seeing who it was through the peephole, Troy secured his weapon in the back of his sweats and greeted their guest with irritation. "Charla, does the doorbell not work?" he asked sarcastically and pressed it to prove a point. "It's okay to ring the bell and wait for someone to come to it instead of nearly breaking the door down."

"I'm so, so sorry, Mr. Troy. Please don't be mad. I'm here because I need to borrow some lunchmeat? My mom's making me a sandwich and she ran out of meat."

Charla spat her words out so fast that it took a second for Troy's brain to comprehend. "Yesterday she didn't have bread and today no meat. Interesting."

"She forgot she didn't have meat. She told me to come over and get it, or she said if you have bread, you can make the sandwich for me; she doesn't mind."

"It's way too early in the morning for this. Goodbye, Charla."

"No, wait." She put her foot in the doorway. Troy could have easily overpowered her, but he didn't' want to hurt her. "There were a lot of people here yesterday. Police and more people. Did Miss Natalie die?"

"No! Why would you ask such a thing?"

Charla shrugged. "I didn't see her after you left with the police. Her lady friend came with the kids, she left and came back and then you came, but I didn't see Miss Natalie."

Common sense should have indicated to Charla that the "lady friend," also known as Aneetra, would not have left Nate and the twins home alone. Then again, common sense wasn't one of Charla's strong points.

"Not to worry, Charla. I'm alive and well." Natalie descended the stairs in a short, silk house robe. Troy hadn't gotten a good look at her hair earlier. Its disheveled appearance turned him on. That's how her hair sometimes looked after they made love. Boy, Troy was anxious for those test results! "There was a lot of commotion around here yesterday, but it's because it was a busy day for us," Natalie explained. "Thank you for checking to make sure everything's okay. You should probably get home so you don't upset your mom again."

"I like you, Miss Natalie, and I don't want you to die. Can we borrow some peanut butter?"

Troy was done. He let Natalie stand in the doorway talking to Charla. He decided to put away those manufactured pictures of Cheryl and him in case Nate came downstairs. It made sense that someone helped Cheryl with this setup. Cheryl was strong with muscular arms, but she was small, and Troy had wondered how she managed to drug him and get him inside the motel on her own. As Natalie coaxed Charla into going back home, Troy thought of something that Natalie had said to him last night. "Charla, wait!" He ran to the end of the driveway to catch her.

"You got some lunchmeat for me?"

"No, but I do have a question. Natalie said that you saw a lady at our house yesterday."

Charla started violently shaking her head from side-to-side. "My mom said to stay out of people's business." Charla pointed her finger and changed her voice trying to imitate that of her mother's. "'Don't stick your nose where it don't belong! That's not our business.'" She snapped out of her trance and looked at Troy. "It's not my business."

"Listen, Charla, it's very important that you tell me what you saw because I'm a police officer and that lady could have been here to do bad things. I'm here to keep us all safe. So, *please*, tell me what you saw."

"Can I have a piece of bread?"

"Yes," Troy relented, thinking he'd get the information from her and then send her on her way, but it was Charla who maintained control.

"Give it to me and I'll tell you." She held out her hand.

"It's in the house." Troy looked back at Natalie who was standing in the doorway looking at them. He knew that neither she nor Ann would approve of what he was about to do. "Wait right here."

Troy moved out of Natalie's eyesight and entered the code to open the garage door from the outside. Neither he nor Natalie bothered to use their car alarms when parked at home—his barely worked anyway—and he'd be willing to bet that there were remnants of food in the back of hers. Sure enough, there was a half-eaten cereal bar wedged in the crack of the seat. There was no telling how long it had been in there, but he knew Charla wouldn't care. Troy quickly got it and out of the garage before Natalie came to see what he was doing.

"Come here." He motioned to Charla.

She ran to him salivating. She tried to snatch the bar from him when she saw it.

"No! Not until you tell me about the lady." Troy moved it out of her reach like one would a dog being trained to do tricks. Charla zeroed in on the bar with one eye while the other circled in every which way. Troy felt bad about exploiting her condition in order to gain information. This wasn't his finest moment as a detective or a person, but Cheryl had threatened the security of his family and he'd do anything to stop her.

Like someone who had been offered a plea deal in exchange for testimony, Charla rambled off everything she could think of. Troy learned that "the lady," whom he already knew was Cheryl, had been driven by someone else in a purple car with dark windows. Troy wondered if it was the man who had helped her set him up in the motel photographs. According to Charla, they stopped in front of his home, Cheryl got out and put something in his mailbox and then they drove off.

"Can I have it now?"

Oh crap! Troy looked up and saw Ann running across the street in her robe. "Here comes your mom," he whispered.

Charla lunged and snatched the bar so fast that Troy barely had time to let go before she shoved it in her mouth.

"Charla, what are you—" When Ann saw the empty wrapper in her daughter's hand and observed Charla still chewing, she scowled. "Where'd you get this?"

Immediately, Charla threw him under the bus. "Mr. Troy gave it to me. I told him about the lady, Mommy. He's a police officer and he's gonna keep us safe because she could have been doing bad things."

The anger Ann had at Charla for sneaking out of the house was quickly directed to Troy. "*You gave her food in exchange for information!*"

"It was only a cereal bar. I—"

Ann didn't pause long enough to hear an explanation, not that he had a reasonable one to give. Instead, she went off on him. Troy was more shocked than offended. He'd been cussed out before on many occasions by his mother, most recently as of last night. What surprised him about Ann was that he didn't know she had it in her. In the year or so that the Harrows had lived across from them, Ann had always seemed like a docile, stressed-out, single mother who was doing all she could to keep her adult daughter with a child-like mentality out of an institution. Today, Ann's light-skinned face was as red as burning embers and she displayed the rage of a mama bear protecting her cub, calling him all kinds of profane names. Her behavior was so over-the-top that Charla started crying.

"All my fault. I'm sorry…all my fault."

"No, Charla. It's *my* fault. Your mom's right. I shouldn't have manipulated you with food. I was wrong and I'm sorry," Troy said to both of them.

"Yeah, you're sorry, all right. You're a sorry excuse for a human being." Ann still had hold of Charla's arm and stormed away, but not before calling Troy the unedited version of a butthole.

Troy waited until the Harrows were inside their house and then went to check his mailbox. Inside, mixed with mail from over the weekend and yesterday, was an unmarked white envelope.

Chapter 16: Truth Seekers

After Troy and Charla moved out of Natalie's eyesight, she had to go tend to their twins and she missed the whole incident with Ann. Troy filled her in when he came inside and also showed her the contents of the envelope.

"I don't get it. Why would Cheryl leave a picture of a teddy bear in our mailbox?" inquired Natalie. "What does it have to do with anything?"

"It's the one I told you about last night that I won for her at Cedar Point. Cheryl obviously knows the police think I've done something to her, so she's playing games with me. The time I met her at Starbucks when we were working that case, she told me she still had it, but I didn't give it much thought. Shortly after Cedar Point, Elvin and Nicole got engaged," Troy explained to Natalie. "Cheryl wanted the same, but I already told you how things went down with us."

"Can't you take this picture to the detective as proof that she's not missing and is harassing you?"

"This picture doesn't prove anything except that she clearly thinks she's in control."

Later that day, Troy received a text from Richard stating that he'd contacted his attorney friend and that Lawrence would like to meet him that afternoon. Richard had taken the liberty to set the time for the meeting and told Troy that he only needed to call

Lawrence if the time wasn't good. Natalie stayed at home with the kids and Troy made her promise not to go out anywhere while he was away. The one good thing about being relieved of his duties was that he had the capability to keep an eye on his family night and day. He wouldn't let them out of his eyesight unless absolutely necessary…not until Cheryl was caught.

Troy pulled up to the northeastern Westerville address he'd been given to a small, brick office that sat next between a real estate company on one side and an upscale hair salon on the other. A few doors down from the salon was a sandwich shop. "Mr. Evans?" The receptionist greeted him upon entering the building. Troy nodded to confirm. "Have a seat and I'll let Lawrence know you're here." She dialed a few numbers on the phone. "Where's your—Yes, tell him that his one o'clock is here. Okay." She turned her attention back to Troy. "He'll be out to get you in a few moments. He's wrapping up a conference call."

"Okay. Thanks." Troy surveyed the office. It was much bigger on the inside than it had looked. Troy was surprised at how plain the decorations in the waiting room were. The walls were virtually bare except for one large plaque with the words "The truth will set you free." Though the plaque itself had no biblical reference, Troy knew it was in reference to John 8:32. Troy pondered on it for a moment. He'd learned from his experience with the serial killer, dubbed the Bible Butcher, that scripture was often taken out of context. That nutso thought the first part of Romans 6:23, *"For the wages of sin is death,"* was license to murder people for their transgressions. Troy frequently heard people refer to John 8:32 for one reason or another, but he wanted to take the time and read the passage for himself, so he pulled up the entire chapter on his cell phone while waiting for Mr. Murphy.

The chapter began with the scribes and Pharisees bringing a woman to Jesus who had been caught in the act of adultery. They were testing Him to see if He would command her to be stoned as the Jewish law required. Instead of answering them, Jesus stooped down and began to write on the ground. When they wouldn't relent, He finally said that whoever was without sin should be the first one to cast a stone at the woman. All of her accusers left and when she was alone with Jesus. He told her that He didn't condemn her and that she should go and sin no more.

The passage then addressed Jesus's dialogue with Jews who did not comprehend the meaning of the things He said, such as Him being the light of the world, and that if they didn't believe in Him, they would die in their sins. This went on all the way until verse 30, when Jesus addressed those who were believers.

[31]Even as he spoke, many believed in him.[31] To the Jews who had believed him, Jesus said, "If you hold to my teaching, you are really my disciples. [32]Then you will know the truth, and the truth will set you free."

The chapter continued, but Troy stopped reading for a moment. He wanted to figure out how verse 32 could apply to his life and current situation. Was there some truth he was missing that could set him free from this web in which he found himself entangled? Of course, had he been honest with Natalie in the first place, none of this would even have been an issue. Now that it was, getting to the truth of the matter of why Cheryl held such a grudge against him and wanted to destroy his life wasn't such an easy feat. Who was helping her? Perhaps he…

"Troy?" Startled, he looked up to a hand extending in his direction. "I'm Lawrence. Nice to meet you. Come on back to my office so we can talk and see how I can help with your situation."

Troy was taken aback by Lawrence Murphy's young age. Since

Richard was in his sixties, Troy assumed the defense attorney would be the same, but, dressed in a pair of khakis and a polo, Lawrence was a couple of decades younger than Richard. In fact, Lawrence looked much younger than Troy. He had a head full of blond hair and his face was as clean and smooth as a baby's bottom. He looked like a slightly older version of Justin Bieber when his first album was released. There's no way Richard could have been intimidated by this guy. The ink on his law degree couldn't even have dried yet.

"Stop it!" the receptionist scolded and then looked at Troy. "Mr. Evans, please forgive my son. He's studying law and interning with my husband for the summer. His name is Lawrence *Junior*; we call him Larry. Soon we might call him unemployed if he doesn't act more professionally, especially around new clients."

"They take everything so serious around here." Larry shook his head disappointedly to Troy. "My dad just got off of a two-hour conference call and needed to take five real quick. He asked me to come take you back to his office. I didn't mean any harm; just trying to lighten things up a bit."

"You're cool, man." Troy wasn't offended; he was relieved. "It's okay," he said to Mrs. Murphy who continued to give Larry a disapproving look.

Back in Lawrence's office, Troy found Larry to be dutiful. He gave Troy a paper to read and sign, which basically stated that any information Troy shared would be protected by attorney-client privilege with the exception of Troy admitting to a future crime. That, by law, would have to be disclosed. Troy understood all the terms and he signed with confidence.

Troy found Larry to be extremely philosophical. The younger Murphy revealed that he was beginning law school in the fall and hoped to come back to work alongside his father after he graduated. "That is, if he will have me. My father and I have different ideas when it comes to the law. He's too stuffy and believes that everything has to be done by the book. I think the book sometimes has a few pages in it that don't apply, so I'm willing to take my chances and tear them out if it means that truth will prevail in the end. You know what I mean?"

Not really, but Troy nodded anyhow.

"Sorry to keep you waiting," the elder Murphy said as he came in. "I'm Lawrence. You've already met my son, Larry, who I'm told likes to give people the false impression that it's his name on the front of the building." Like his wife had done, Lawrence gave Larry a look of disapproval. This Lawrence embodied the image that Troy had imagined. He was closer to Richard's age and unlike Larry, Lawrence had on a pin-striped suit, buttoned all the way up to his neck, and a bow-tie. He had a serious look about him. No smile; not even a hint of a lighthearted bone in his body.

"I'm Troy. Thanks for meeting with me."

"Not a problem. Richard is a good friend of mine. I'm doing this as a favor to him. He's told me a little about your situation, but I want to hear it from you. Do you have any questions about the form Larry had you sign?"

"No."

"Okay. Good. If you don't mind, Larry's going to sit in with us; the lad has a thing or two to learn about law."

Lad? Who says that? Troy thought to himself, beginning to understand why Larry had used the word "stuffy" to describe his father. "I don't mind," he responded and began his story with the morning Cheryl went missing, including all the details of his talk with the FBI agent and admitting his own actions of becoming physical with her. He'd even brought those embarrassing photographs with him to show that he was being set up.

Unlike Larry who nodded affirmatively while Troy was talking,

Lawrence was motionless, giving no indication one way or the other whether or not he believed Troy. When Troy had finished his account of yesterday's events, Lawrence had two questions for him: "Did you have an affair with Cheryl?" and "Did you have anything to do with her disappearance?" Troy emphatically answered no to both. Lawrence then revealed that Richard had stopped by that morning and paid the initial deposit for Troy to retain him as an attorney. "I know you weren't aware of this," Lawrence responded to the look of shock that must have been apparent on Troy's face. "I wasn't sure I would take your case because I wanted a chance to speak to you first. I told Richard as much, but he was persistent and convinced of your innocence. He and I serve on opposite ends of the justice spectrum, but we do have one thing in common…we are both truth seekers. Hopefully, this thing with your ex will blow over and she'll come out of hiding. If not and the boys in blue take things a step further, then I'm here for you."

"Wow. I don't know what to say. Thank you."

"How about you not say anything to anyone, especially the police. Under no circumstances are you to speak with them again outside of my presence, and no matter what, stay away from her house." Lawrence looked at his watch. "I have to run. I have a personal appointment I need to get to. Larry will see to it that we have all of your contact information and you have ours. Good luck, Mr. Evans. Hopefully, you won't be needing my services."

Chapter 17: Brunhilda

In the days following Troy's meeting with Mr. Murphy, things had been pretty quiet. Troy stayed around the house and helped Natalie with the kids. Last night, they hooked up with Aneetra and her family, along with the Hamptons and Corrine, and all went to watch the Red, White, and Boom fireworks display.

Troy hadn't been at the gym since the incident with Cheryl last week. That's where she had gotten inside of his vehicle and there was no way she could have done that unless someone had given her access to his keys…keys that had been secured inside the gym lockers. *Will…* Will had lied about being at the gym that day. At first, Troy thought it was because of Will's illegal side job. However, after studying the shadowy figure in the photograph and being certain that the darkened image on the perpetrator's arm was a tattoo of some kind, Troy began to believe that Will was possibly involved. His suspicions were magnified when Troy tried to call Will back under the pretense of wanting to know more about the "shady stuff" at the gym, only to have his calls go straight to voicemail. After several attempts, Troy called the gym and spoke with Shay.

"I don't know where he at. He sent me a text askin' me to cover for him 'dis week 'cuz he was goin' out of town. I did it 'cuz we cool like 'dat, but I don't appreciate him leavin' me wit' all his responsibilities. He could have at least had the decency to call or came by and seent me in person instead of sendin' me a text," she complained. "If someone from corporate comes, he's scuh-*rood!*"

Troy found it interesting that Will hadn't been to the gym and yet when they'd last seen each other Saturday at the Commons, Will had indicated that he would be there this week.

"When you comin' back? Ain't been no real eye candy in here for a couple of days."

Troy ignored her question. "Shay, let me ask you something… did Will come to the gym last Friday?"

"Why you askin'?"

"I saw his car in the parking lot when I was leaving. I also saw him over the weekend at the Commons and when I said something about it, he said he wasn't there."

"Well, I ain't spose to say nuttin', but you and me is cool like 'dat, so Imma tell you 'da truth. He was here," she whispered. "He didn't want no one to know 'cuz he was workin' on sumthin'. I don't know what, but he said if anybody asked, to say I drove his car to work 'dat day. I told him nobody would believe it 'cuz he ain't neva let nobody behind 'da wheel, but you can't tell him nuttin'. 'Dat was my last time talkin' wit' him 'til he sent me 'dat text. I tried to ask him 'bout 'dis trip he said he was takin', but he didn't respond."

"Have you ever heard him mention someone named Cheryl Hunter?"

"No, who 'dat?" Her tone became angry. "Is 'dis some chick he spose to be messin' wit? I know we ain't got no commitment to each other or nuttin' like 'dat, but on 'da real, he ain't gon' have me here workin' for him like a Hebrew slave while he's off wit' somebody else. Uh-uh, huh-nee, he got me messed up. I will call corporate in a minute and tell on his a—"

"Calm down!" Troy was sure that Shay was swerving those freakishly long nails and neck at the same time that very moment. "I don't even know that they know each other. I was asking because..." He contemplated how much he should reveal. He didn't really know Shay that well, definitely not in the manner that Will knew her. The one thing he knew for sure was that she was fond of him and if there was a connection between Cheryl and Will, Shay could be of help to him. Troy decided to take a chance and give her an abridged version of what was going on. "Long story short, Cheryl Hunter doesn't like me and someone at the gym is helping her set me up."

"You think it's Will?"

Troy contemplated on how much to reveal knowing the relationship dynamics between Shay and Will. If he told her too much, she could tell Will and blow any lead Troy had in the case. Ultimately, that disclosure might actually work in his favor. Shay had a crush on him and he was willing to exploit it to his advantage. First Charla, now Shay...there seemed to be no boundaries Troy wouldn't cross in order to protect his family. "I can't say for sure that it's Will helping her, but I know it's a man. Someone helped Cheryl drug me and set me up so it would look like I was cheating on my wife. Will is the only one who makes sense right now, especially now that I know he's missing in action. Cheryl is, too."

"I don't know, Troy..." Shay sounded skeptical. "That don't sound like nuttin' Will would do. Yeah, he got his li'l hustle goin' on the side, but 'dis is a bit much. I can see him goin' off somewhere to be wit' somebody, but I can't imagine Will goin' to 'dis length for a woman. He likes you and speaks very highly of you. To drug you and make it look like you and 'dis Cheryl chick were havin' an affair seems too far out of Will's character."

"I know it does. I can't say for sure that it was Will, but it definitely had to be one of the dudes around there. Will you do me a favor?"

"*Anything...*," Shay said a little too suggestively.

"Keep your eyes and ears open." He gave her a description of Cheryl. "If you see anyone like that around there or if you hear someone mention her name, let me know. Also, let me know if you hear from Will, but *please* don't tell him anything I told you," Troy said with a smirk. He knew Shay would not be able to refrain from questioning Will, especially about leaving her to do his job while he was possibly with Cheryl.

"Don't worry, Southie, I gotchu."

"Please just call me Troy."

She gave a playful sigh. "My bad. You gon' give me your number, *Troy*, so I can call or text you if sumthin' happens."

He did so, knowing that was likely the highlight of Shay's day. After he got off the phone with her, he immediately informed Natalie of what he had done as not to keep his dealings with Shay a secret. Natalie wasn't crazy about his investigative techniques and asked him, *again*, if there was anything about his interactions with Shay that she needed to know. After being reassured that he was in no way, shape, or form attracted to Shay and hearing his thought process about why he involved her, Natalie ultimately agreed that Shay might be helpful. Like Shay, Natalie wasn't buying the whole Will and Cheryl conspiracy thing, but she understood how he'd come to that conclusion. Troy promised Natalie that he wouldn't respond to any messages from Shay that weren't directly related to his inquiry about Will and Cheryl so there could be no misunderstandings about his intentions. If the gym manager and Troy's former girlfriend were in this together, Shay could help flush them out.

Troy set up a surveillance system outside of his home, in the event that Cheryl and her accomplice came back around. If so, her actions would be caught on tape and he'd take it to Nugent, and the whole crazy ordeal would finally be over. He was getting sick and tired of hearing the news reports about her mysterious disappearance. He hadn't been called back in for questioning again, but the fact that he was still "relieved" of his duties until further notice was clear indication that a cloud of suspicion continued to hang over him. Convinced that ultimately, Cheryl's antics would be uncovered, he decided to focus most of his time and energy on rebuilding his relationship with Natalie.

Troy's mom had called nearly every day to see how things were between them. She meant well, but she was working both his and Natalie's nerves. Troy regretted reaching out to her that night he was asked to come in for questioning, and finally started to ignore her phone calls. He told Natalie she should do the same, but she didn't want to seem rude. Natalie's answer to his mom had been the same every time, "God was good" and that they "were working things out." Troy wasn't sure if Natalie truly felt that way or if she was telling his mom what she wanted to hear. Either way, Troy would take it.

They had been getting along well that week for the most part. Natalie was still hurt as was evident by the additional questions she'd asked about him and Cheryl. "Did you kiss her?" "Did you think about kissing her?" "Did you talk about doing things to her?" were some of the repeated questions she asked, wording them various ways as if his answers would change. One day she seemed to believe him wholeheartedly and then the next day she had questions again. Truthfully, he was getting frustrated with the interrogations and thought Natalie was overreacting, but Troy understood from talking to RJ that this was part of the process. RJ agreed that surveillance cameras were a good safety precaution. So far, the only suspicious activity he saw was a black Acura that had driven by slowly several times on two different occasions. It didn't match the description of the car Charla gave and Troy couldn't get a clear look at the driver who, by all indications, was male. Since there was no female passenger accompanying him, Troy didn't worry too much about the incidents.

Troy's STI results came back clean. Unfortunately, there was nothing in his toxicology report that helped identify what Cheryl had used to sedate him. Based on Troy's account of what happened, RJ was pretty certain that Troy had been given one, possibly two, benzodiazepines. His best guest was Lorazepam and Rohypnol. Lorazepam because of it was fast-acting; Rohypnol because it was long-lasting. Troy had to face the truth that he would probably never know for sure. He was thankful that there didn't seem to be any permanent side effects and that he could finally make love to his wife.

Exactly one week after being set up by Cheryl at the motel, Troy decided he would do something special for Natalie that Friday evening to help ease her mind of whatever lingering insecurities she still had. He enlisted Natalie's younger look-a-like for help. "Hey, Corrine, I need a favor."

"What's up?"

"Are you free tonight? I want to take Natalie out and wanted to know if you could come stay the night with the kids."

"Yeah. What time do you need me?"

"Would six be too soon?"

"Naw. That's cool. Did the kids like the fireworks last night?"

"I know Nate did. That's all he's been talking about today. He had fun."

"I did, too. I'll think of something to do with them tonight at the house. I take it you and Natalie are not coming home since you asked me to stay over?"

"That's the plan."

"Y'all celebrating your anniversary already?"

"No. That's next weekend." Realizing that Corrine didn't know anything about the situation with Cheryl or the damage that had been done to his marriage, Troy responded that he was doing this as a pre-anniversary celebration, "simply because I love her."

"Aw, that's so cute. I'll be there at six."

"I need you to do something else." He explained the rest of his spur-of-the-moment idea, giving her his credit card number.

"All right. I'll hook you up."

"Thanks, Corrine! I owe you one." Troy hung up and called Skyler's to make reservations for a private dining room. Owned by a local wealthy businessman, Skyler's was one of the most upscale restaurants in the city. It was located in downtown Columbus and overlooked the Scioto River. Troy had never been there, but he'd heard others talk about how nice it was. The night he proposed to Natalie, his intentions had been to take her there, but he learned that she'd been banned from the establishment due to trying to skip out on the bill when a previous date had bailed on her. Instead of taking her to Skyler's to propose, Troy had come up with another plan. But, tonight he wanted to do something special for his wife and there was no place in Columbus like Skyler's. He made reservations there anyhow, despite Natalie's restrictions. Her situation had happened so long ago that he was sure no one would remember.

Unfortunately, all the private dining rooms were booked, so Troy made general reservations. When he informed Natalie of his plans, she was skeptical at first, but quickly got over it. She did fuss a little about him not giving her enough time to get dressed. In the end, she came down the stairs looking like a princess in a long, black spaghetti-strapped dress that proudly displayed her curves. He imagined the words "do me" written all over it. There were two things Troy was certain of: he would be the envy of every other man in the place; and he would happily oblige the dress's request at the end of the night.

"You look gorgeous," Troy said as he extended his hand to help her down the final few steps and relieved her of her overnight bag. He, himself, had on a suit that was starting to feel warm now that his internal temperature arose at the sight of his wife.

"Wow, Natalie. You are so beautiful."

"Yeah, you are bootiful!" Nate mockingly echoed Corrine's sentiments. He knew how to pronounce the word. He was being silly.

Natalie laughed lightheartedly. "Thank you guys. I had a hard time finding something to wear since I still have this baby weight. The dress doesn't look too tight, does it?" Thankfully, she was asking Corrine because Natalie had to know better than to solicit his opinion.

"No. It's fine." Corrine chuckled when Troy gave her an overexaggerated wink and a thumbs-up behind Natalie's back.

"What?" Natalie turned to see what he had done.

"Nothing," he said in a sing-song manner. "Let's go, babe, or we'll be late." Before leaving, Troy gave Corrine firm instructions about keeping the exterior alarm on at all times. "There's been reports of a prowler in the neighborhood," he said regarding Cheryl. "Call me immediately if you see or hear anything strange."

"Yes, sir."

As he escorted his wife in the passenger side of his truck, he looked across the street and noticed a big gape in the front blinds at the Harrows' house. He waved and immediately they shut. Between the security alarm, the surveillance system, and the Harrows, Troy was confident that Corrine and kids would be safe.

Dinner could have not gone more perfectly. The atmosphere in Skyler's was romantic. Equipped with soothing sounds of classical music and an attentive server dressed in black slacks, a white shirt, and a tie, Troy felt good about his decision to come here. No one, not even the owner who had been there upon their arrival, questioned whether or not Natalie had a right to be there. Both men and women did a double-take upon seeing her. The men, because they wished for a moment they could trade places with Troy; the women, because they secretly wanted to hurt her for drawing their other halves' attention away from them. At least that was Troy's perception. He proudly walked alongside of Natalie as they were led to their table.

The meal was great, the conversation good, and the mood was sensual. There was no question that they would tear into each other the minute they got to the hotel room. The entire evening, there had been no mention of Cheryl or any of the craziness of that week. It was as if it had never happened. They talked about their upcoming wedding anniversary and reflected on that day they got married nearly six years ago.

"I was so nervous. I know I probably hurt Earl's arm by holding it so tight." Earl was one of Natalie's uncles and the person who walked her down the aisle. "I was afraid I would trip. Oh, my gosh, can you imagine? That would have been so embarrassing. I would have run out of the church."

"I'm sure you would have fallen gracefully…right into my arms. Then I would have carried you out and we would've skipped the reception and went right to the honeymoon for some baby-making practice."

She shook her head amusingly. "Whatever. You are crazy, you know that?"

"Crazy in love." Completely out of character, Troy started singing the "uh oh" part of the chorus to Beyoncé's "Crazy in Love" song. He even put his back into it a little as he subtly did the moves.

The delightfulness of hearing his wife laugh made embarrassing himself worth it. "Okay, *okay!* I get the point. Please stop. You're going to get us kicked out of here."

Seconds later, when the waiter came with the check and said, "I can take this for you anytime, Mr. Evans," Natalie gave him a "see, I told you" look. Troy winked at her as he gave the man his debit card. Skyler's was the type of place where one didn't know how much the meal would cost until the bill came. Based on the $125.97 total, he and Natalie had eaten well. "I'll be right back, sir."

"Where are we staying tonight?"

"I thought you might like to stay at the Hilton in Polaris." Polaris was an area on the far north side of town that had been built up quite a bit over the last decade or so. It was equipped with all the amenities and attractions his high-fashioned wife would enjoy. "Tomorrow afternoon, we have an appointment for a couples' massage and then we can hang out and maybe go to the mall until Corrine summons us home." The idea of going shopping with Natalie was painful. She could spend all day there and either buy nothing or more than needed. Not his thing. Her eyes grew big, but not because he'd mentioned going shopping as he'd thought.

"*You're* getting a massage! Wait...you requested a female, didn't you?"

"You know it." Troy was still a typical hardcore man's man. The idea of having a dude's hands caressing his body didn't sit well with him, even for therapeutic reasons. "We both have females."

"That's not fair. How come you get to have a female, but I can't have a male?"

All she needed to do was find a mirror and her question would be answered. "When you and Aneetra go, you can have whomever you want, but when I'm in the room, that ain't happening, Mrs. Evans. There's no way I could relax while another man touches all over you. Um, did you see how you looked in that dress?"

"Okay. I see how you are. That's why I hope you get a big burly woman named Brunhilda with an Adam's apple."

Troy cracked up. Unfortunately, the waiter came and interrupted them before he could think of a clever comeback. "I'm sorry, sir. This card was declined. Is there another I can try?"

"That's weird. It should have gone through. Here, try this one." Troy gave him his credit card instead and soon the guy was returning with the same results. In all, Troy had given him four cards—the debit card from their account, two separate Visas and his only-use-in-case-of-an-emergency MasterCard. All were declined. Natalie hadn't brought any cards with her; only her ID.

"Troy, what's going on?" Natalie looked terrified. Troy could only imagine the déjà vu thoughts going through her mind from her last encounter here.

"I don't know." He pulled up the app on his cell phone to transfer money from their savings to their checking account. What he saw made his heart sink.

Chapter 18: Superwoman

The ride back home was not pleasant. Instead of joining forces and being upset with Cheryl for this latest incident, Troy and Natalie turned their anger on each other.

"Are you sure that you didn't sleep with her?"

"Yes, I'm sure! *Why do you keep asking me the same questions! I didn't do anything inappropriate with Cheryl!*"

"Well, she's definitely a woman scorned for some reason. I admit that the pictures were fake, but it's hard for me to believe that she'd be that stuck on you after all the years of y'all not being together. Something happened to make her mad. I can't help but wonder if you're still keeping a secret."

"Don't talk to me about secrets. We've been having conversations all week and not once did you mention taking the money out of our savings account."

"Yeah, well, if I hadn't done that, we'd be flat broke right now and no way to pay RJ back for coming to bail us out."

She had a point there, but Troy was too bullheaded to concede. They had some other investments that he prayed hadn't been infiltrated. When he'd checked their accounts online, everything had a zero balance and all of their credit cards, except the MasterCard, had been closed. Its three thousand dollar limit had been maxed out, all within the last thirty days.

Not knowing what to do, the couple dismissed the idea of calling

Corrine. If Cheryl was anywhere in their neighborhood, it would be difficult and dangerous for Corrine to load three sleepy kids and their car seats into a sports car in which they wouldn't all fit safely anyway. Natalie's call to Aneetra went straight to voicemail and thus, RJ had been Troy's last resort. He quickly came to their rescue. After the bill fiasco, the mood had been ruined and neither Troy nor Natalie thought about going to the hotel. Not surprisingly, Corrine, who happened to be in the kitchen at the refrigerator when they walked in, was startled to see them home so soon. She nearly dropped the orange juice container. "Whew! Y'all scared me. What are you doing here?"

"Troy's girlfriend stole all our money!" Natalie hissed and stomped up the stairs.

"I don't have a girlfriend." His rebuttal was more to Corrine than Natalie because his stepdaughter had a "what-in-the-blank" look of confusion on her face. "Did you have any problems making the reservations earlier?"

"Yeah, I did. It wouldn't go through, so I used my card."

"Why didn't you tell me?"

"It wasn't that big of deal," she said defensively. "I figured I'd copied down a number wrong or something. I was planning to get the money back from you later. What's going on, Troy?"

Troy and Natalie tried hard to keep the kids out of their issues. Though Corrine was technically an adult, she was still Natalie's daughter, but since Natalie had opened the door to much speculation in Corrine's mind by telling her he had a girlfriend, Troy wanted to set the record straight. Thus, he gave her an extremely condensed version of the week's events. "Her latest stunt was stealing our money."

"Wow." Corrine looked at him for several minutes. "I don't know what to say."

"Join the club."

"Can't you call the police?"

"And say what? That the woman I'm suspected of having kidnapped and possibly harmed has stolen my money? It's not going to get me anywhere."

"It's identity theft, isn't it? She can go to jail for that."

He would love to have seen Cheryl in jail; better yet, the morgue. "Yeah, but it has to be proven."

To Troy's knowledge, this was the first time Corrine had ever witnessed a fight between him and Natalie. She sat silently for a few moments. Eventually, she said, "I'm going to go so y'all can have some privacy and talk. Tell Natalie I'll call her later." Before leaving, Corrine did something that she rarely did with Troy; she gave him a hug. "I hope everything works out."

He was touched by the gesture. "Thanks." After his stepdaughter left, Troy decided he wasn't chasing Natalie this time. He was so angry that he wasn't wasting another breath trying to convince her that he didn't do anything with Cheryl. Instead, Troy went down to his man cave, plopped on the couch, and fired up the Xbox.

Natalie buried her head in the pillows, expecting Troy and/or Corrine to come up at any moment. She was relieved when neither did. When the door slammed, she hadn't been sure if it had been Corrine or Troy who'd left, but an incoming text brought clarity and a half smile. *"Idk what's going on, but 143."*

"1432," Natalie replied. It was thoughts of Corrine, Nate, Ebony, and Ean, that, once again, kept her from falling apart. She lay thinking of them until she drifted off to sleep.

Saturday morning, Aneetra called to apologize for missing Natalie's call. Her battery had died. After Natalie explained what had happened at Skyler's, Aneetra, who was already out and with her girls, offered to come by and sit with the kids while she and Troy went to the bank to handle business. That was a huge help. They closed their accounts and opened new ones together with the money from Natalie's severance that she had withdrawn earlier in the week. The ink wasn't even dry on her paperwork and already she closed her personal account to once again combine finances with Troy. She prayed she wasn't being foolish! Additionally, they filed reports about the credit cards, and Troy disputed all the charges on the MasterCard, which included several astronomical charges from the gym for personal training services. The money that was in their joint checking and savings accounts had been wiped clean, but luckily, none of their other investment funds had been touched. They took safety precautions anyway.

The ride to and from the bank was eerily silent. The tension between her and Troy was noticeable and thick. Aneetra tried to remind Natalie that her anger toward Troy was misdirected. *Whatever!* Natalie wasn't trying to be preached to at that moment. Not even her pastor's sermon the next morning about unconditional love did much to sway her. She'd never stopped loving Troy. And though she still teetered back and forth between believing his story and not, it didn't stop her from being mad at him for the mess they were currently in. She believed her anger was justified.

With the exception of going to the bank together, Natalie and Troy distanced themselves from each other the entire weekend. He stayed in the basement and she was upstairs with the kids. Troy didn't even bother to go to church with them Sunday. Natalie returned home from service to find him missing in action. He came home about an hour later with no explanation of where he had been, and she didn't bother to ask. She wasn't going to worry herself with the whereabouts of her husband who was giving her the silent treatment like she had done something to him!

On Monday morning, Natalie took Nate to pre-school. Troy had been gracious enough to come from the basement when it was time for Natalie to leave and say that Ebony and Ean could stay there with him. She'd gotten them up and dressed since she had no idea what his mentality would be. Had he come up even a half hour earlier, she wouldn't have had to wake the twins, but she kept her sarcastic comments about him waiting until the last minute to herself. When Natalie and Nate left, the twins were eating breakfast and Troy was at the table with them reading a book. *Seriously!?!* Their lives had been turned upside down and all of a sudden, he decided to become a reader! That man was losing it, she was sure.

Natalie was on her way back home when Diane called. She had evaded her mother-in-law's calls over the weekend; she didn't feel like talking. Like a cold sore, Diane was determined to make her presence known. "Hey, Di." She tried her best to sound "normal."

"Hey! I've been tryin' to get in touch with y'all all weekend. How's everything?"

"Okay."

"*Okay?* You don't sound like you did last week when you were doin' all that talk about God bein' so good. Did sumthin' else happen?"

"I only answered the phone so I didn't seem rude. I'm not in the mood to talk." Heck, she didn't even want to *think* about Troy, let alone discuss him. "Call your son and let him fill you in."

"Girl, you know Troy ain't gon' tell me nothin'. I ain't hangin' up this phone 'til you do."

It won't stop me from hanging up on you! Natalie thought as she refrained from saying a single word.

"Natalie, *please*… I'm not askin' to be nosey or all up in y'all's business for the heck of it. I'm concerned about y'all. I know you love each other and I love the both of you. I talk to you more than I do either of my children, and my daughter lives in town. I'm sorry if I'm gettin' on your nerves, I—" Diane tried to mask it by coughing, but Natalie still heard the crack in her voice. "I don't want to see y'all's marriage fall apart 'cuz of this."

Natalie had no doubts about Diane's sincerity, but she wished the woman could leave well enough alone. "Di, I'm not trying to be mean. It's hard. I've never been in this situation and I have mixed emotions about everything." Reluctantly, Natalie relented to Diane's wishes and shared the most recent events, including her own secretive actions. "He wants to have an attitude with me because I took money from *my* severance out of the bank, but he should be thankful. Had I left it in there, Cheryl would have touched that, too, and we'd be flat broke."

"Natalie, I understand you're upset but—"

"I don't want to hear any buts," she said defensively. "You wanted to know what's going on. I've told you. I'm tired of people telling me how I need to feel. I'm not superwoman! I have right to be upset. Let me feel what I feel and deal with it on my own."

"I'm not askin' you to be superwoman. All I'm saying is—"

"Di, I have to go!" Natalie said in a panic as she pulled into her driveway. The cops were standing at her front door talking to Troy. "What's going on now?"

"I have to go back to the station," Troy answered without making eye contact with her.

"*Why?* What happened?"

"They found Cheryl… she's dead."

Chapter 19: Manic Monday

Natalie tried not to fret as Troy followed the officers to the station for questioning. Troy assured her that he wasn't under arrest and would be home before she knew it. His lawyer, some Murphy guy, was meeting him there. Thankfully, Troy had fed the twins and they were content for the moment in their playpen. Natalie hated keeping them locked up in that thing like caged birds. Normally, she didn't use it unless absolutely necessary when she was cooking, cleaning, or as a timeout if they were out of control. They sometimes took naps in it as well. However, Natalie allowed the playpen and Nick Jr. to do her mommy work for a while. She was unable to tend to their needs and work through her ever-fluctuating emotions about Cheryl at the same time.

"*She's dead.*" Troy's statement echoed in her mind. Considering that he was being questioned, it was pretty evident to Natalie that Cheryl's death hadn't been a result of natural causes. Natalie was concerned about the impact that an implication would have on him. Regarding Cheryl being dead, Natalie ashamedly felt relieved that the woman would be out of their lives for good now.

Lord, forgive me, she thought as she sent Aneetra a text updating her on the morning's events and requesting prayer. She also called Diane back who, since Natalie hung up on her, had called both the home phone and Natalie's cell like a bill collector. When she informed her mother-in-law of what had happened, Diane's solution was to see if there was some way one of their family members could help. "He already has an attorney. Plus, I don't think Troy wants everyone knowing what's going on."

"I ain't said nothin' to nobody except for his dad, and you know Reed ain't about to call and get in y'all's business. I just wish there was somethin' I could do."

"You can pray," Natalie suggested.

"I'm tryin', baby. I'm tryin' harder than ever before. I can only hope the Lord ain't turned a deaf ear to me 'cuz I ain't been no saint."

"He hasn't." Natalie was touched by her mother-in-law's sincerity. She believed it would only be a matter of time before Diane finally made a commitment to Christ. All this God and prayer talk was evidence that maybe Diane was starting to come around. It was much better than the superstition theories Natalie had been holding her breath for. Her mother-in-law was the queen bee when it came to believing in that stuff and it drove Natalie crazy. "*... [L]ast time I checked, you believed in the grace given to us by Jesus, not karma.*" Aneetra's words from last week came back to haunt her. Perhaps Natalie's own beliefs had been temporarily misdirected. Before she and Diane hung up, Di made Natalie promise to call her the minute she heard from Troy. "Will do." After getting off the phone with Diane, Natalie decided to follow her own advice and pray. She did believe in grace and by it, she and Troy would get through this storm in their marriage. Instead of stressing over this manic Monday morning, she hoped that having a little talk with Jesus was going to make everything all right.

Troy had on a pair of gray sweats that had a large Velcro pocket on the right pants side, near his knee. That's where he'd kept the diary since last night until this morning when he put it in the center console of his truck on his way to the station. Troy was nervous with the thing out of his sight. He tried not to think about it as he sat across from Nugent once again, only this time Lawrence Murphy was by his side.

"For the record, I would like to ask if my client is under arrest."

"No."

"Okay. Then it's our understanding that Detective Evans is here of his own free will as a courtesy to the department on which he serves. If, at any time, I feel your questions are out of line, he will be instructed not to answer and this interrogation will cease."

Nugent ignored Lawrence and went straight in for Troy after reading him his rights. "Why don't you start by telling me where you were yesterday?"

"At home with my wife."

"All day?"

"Pretty much."

"I don't know what 'pretty much' means? It's a yes-or-no question."

Troy refused to answer definitively because he had left the house yesterday…twice. The first time had been to take Corrine the money that she'd put on her credit card to make the reservations on Friday and also to hook up with RJ to pay him back for dinner Friday evening. The second time he'd left had been late Sunday night. After he was sure Natalie had gone to sleep, Troy sneaked out of the house and went to Cheryl's looking for evidence.

"I don't think it's a good idea," RJ had said to him when Troy told him about the plan earlier that afternoon.

"You're probably right. I keep thinking that there has to be some clues

in her house regarding her whereabouts. She can't pull this disappearing act forever. She'll have to come out of hiding soon, and maybe I can find something that will draw her out. She nearly destroyed my marriage, framed me for abducting her, and now she's wiped our bank accounts clean…it has to stop!"

"I understand your frustration, but if one of her neighbors catches you, it's a wrap. Breaking and entering won't be a good look, man."

"I know…I don't know what else to do." Troy had temporarily abandoned the idea of going to Cheryl's after his talk with RJ. The more he stewed in the basement while Natalie paraded around the house like he was nonexistent, the angrier he became. Friday night would have been perfect if it weren't for Cheryl. She had gone too far and he would see to it that she went no further.

"I think I'm goN 2do it," he said to RJ in a text.

"Do what? Go over Cheryl's??? NOT A GOOD IDEA! Does your wife know?"

Troy never addressed the question. Natalie didn't know and he wasn't sure he would tell her. Her emotions were too unstable at the moment. Troy wanted answers and when he uncovered them, she'd be the first that he informed. Sunday night Troy waited until he was sure she'd fallen asleep. It was about 11:30 p.m. when he left. Troy sent one last text to RJ as he was on his way out of the door. "Pray for me." He wondered if it was right to ask for prayer knowing he was about to do something wrong. Troy knew he needed divine covering. He didn't know if asking for it under such circumstances was proper protocol.

As Troy rode over to the west side, he devised his strategy. He would park a few blocks away from Cheryl's house, but not on the street in front of anyone else's. The last thing he needed was for someone to see a strange vehicle in front of their house and call the police. Instead, he'd leave his car in the church parking lot that was within walking distance of Cheryl's place.

Wearing a baseball cap, T-shirt, and gray sweat pants, Troy headed toward his ex's. He'd thought about wearing a hoodie and then thought twice in the event that there was a neighborhood watch person who found him suspicious. That individual's suspicions, Troy concluded, would be well founded because he had no legitimate reason to be in this area.

With his heart pounding and his conscience willing him to turn around and go back home, Troy ran to the back of Cheryl's house where he was thankful for the tall trees that shielded him from any possible onlookers. He took the glass cutter from his pocket and craftily carved though a window until he had the ability to unlock it and slip through. Once inside, the alarm chirped. Troy held his breath. Luckily, it was disarmed and only signaled the opening of the door. Troy had been so focused on gaining entry that he hadn't considered the possibility of Cheryl having a security system. Relieved that authorities had not been summoned, Troy pulled out his flashlight and began his search. He had no idea specifically what to look for, but he was looking for something…anything that would put an end to this mess.

The living room was in disarray. Troy didn't remember it being like that when he was here. Then, again, he didn't remember much from his last visit except stopping short of taking her life. Part of him wondered if the living room had purposely been tossed to give the appearance that a struggle had taken place between them and give credence to the disappearance theory. Nothing unusual stood out. Whatever he found would be scraps because CPD had already done a thorough search of the area. Crime scene tape was all over the place. Cheryl had done a great job at staging!

A Sears family portrait of nine-year-old Cheryl holding a baby while standing in the middle of her parents and brothers hung crookedly on the wall. Next to it was a multi-photograph frame that included various pictures of Cheryl with people, including one of him and her at a party back in the day, and a wedding photo of Cheryl and her husband. Troy stared at Cheryl's wedding photo, recalling the details she had given him about her marriage. "I got married about a year after we split," she had said to Troy that time they'd met at Starbucks. Cheryl also revealed that he'd cheated on her and died in a car accident. "I loved the idea of being married more than I loved him. He was a rebound. After that I focused on my career and now I sort of regret not having kids. I love my job, but I think I could have been happy just being a wife and mother."

Cheryl's husband had been a tall, white bald man. He looked vaguely familiar, but Troy couldn't figure out why. Besides their height, Troy saw nothing that he and her deceased spouse had in common. She had gone from him, a dark-skinned man, to a white skinhead-looking dude. Troy had nothing against interracial relationships. In fact, if they didn't exist, neither would his wife. Troy simply found that extremity ironic. He'd been open to dating all nations and creeds in his younger days. Tall, short, light, dark, it didn't matter…all the women looked the same when the lights went out. At least that was his mentality back then. He never held it against Natalie that she'd slept with a lot of men before him. He hadn't been conservative with his goods either. Yet, God had kept both him and his wife from contracting any diseases. That was grace.

Troy made his way to Cheryl's room. It was still intact, nothing like the mess left in the living room. Yet, Troy could tell that his people had done a thorough job combing through the place. He wasn't sure what he hoped to find that they hadn't until he reminded himself that he and his comrades had come with two different objectives. They had been looking for evidence regarding her abduction; he was looking to uncover her charade.

Troy began ripping through every drawer and box in sight without any regard to putting things back in place. He didn't care if there was evidence that someone had gone through her things. He just didn't want the evidence to reveal that he had gone through them. Thanks to his gloves and shoe covers, no one would be the wiser. He hadn't a clue what he was looking for, but he searched every nook and cranny hoping to find something, anything that could shed light on her whereabouts.

In one section of her room, Cheryl had all of her stuffed animals. Like she had told him once before, the bear he'd won for her was sitting next to her first Cabbage Patch doll. Cheryl had read way too much into his actions at Cedar Point. Troy now resented that bear and without thinking about the absurdity of his actions, he pulled at it until its head popped off. Stuffing flew everywhere as Troy tore it into shreds. Subconsciously, perhaps he was destroying Cheryl like she was trying to do to him. When Troy was satisfied that he'd mutilated the animal until it was unrecognizable, he continued with his search.

Tucked away in the far back corner of her closet was Cheryl's high school yearbook. Troy wouldn't have given it much thought had he not seen the word "Bruins" engraved on it. He'd seen that word before! He started flipping through the pages and that's when it all became evident to him. Nugent and Cheryl had attended Briggs High School together, located on the city's southwest side. They were called the Briggs Bruins and the symbol was a purple "B" with a bear print on the left. From the pictures of the two of them together and Nugent's note in her yearbook, there was no mistaking the fact that Cheryl and Nugent had had some kind of close relationship.

To Cheryl, thanks for all the laughs and good times. You are a special person and I hope one day, you'll like me as much as I do you. Good luck with everything. I'll be here whenever you call. If you don't call, I'll stalk you. —Don

Troy wasn't sure what all of this meant. It did explain how Nugent had known about his and Cheryl's past relationship when Nugent questioned him about her "disappearance." Troy backed away from the closet and sat at the top of Cheryl's bed as things were sinking in. That's when

he sat on what could have been the most damaging piece of evidence against him if those working the case had found it first.

"*Well?*" The sound of Nugent's voice brought him back to the present interrogation. "Perhaps you didn't understand the question. Were you at home all day yesterday?" he pressed.

"Detective, I want to remind you that, unless my client is under arrest, he's not obligated to answer any of your questions. Perhaps you should move on," Murphy interjected, giving Troy a sideway glance.

"When's the last time you've been by Cheryl Hunter's home?"

"I last saw Cheryl a week ago. You know that."

Nugent smirked. "You're being very evasive, Evans. Could this be the reason why?" He threw several pictures of Cheryl's dead body on the table. "She was found last night at Alum Creek. She'd been sedated and then stabbed fourteen times. Someone really wanted to make sure she was dead." Troy stared at the pictures, wanting to feel sorry for Cheryl like he would any other victim of homicide. Yet, all he felt was relief. Cheryl was finally out of his life. "When's the last time you've been to Delaware?"

Delaware, Ohio, a city about thirty minutes north of Columbus via Route 23, was home of the Alum Creek State Park, and apparently the location where Cheryl's dead body had been discovered. Troy could not be sure of the last time he was in Delaware, but he was certain that it hadn't been any time recently and he told Nugent as much.

"You see this?" Nugent pulled out another picture of Cheryl, a blowup that zeroed in on her neck where a shoe imprint was clearly visible. "Stabbing her wasn't enough. The sadistic perp crushed her larynx after she was already dead."

"What does this have to do with me?"

"I would think you would feel some sense of remorse for someone you loved at one time."

"I would only feel remorse if I'd done something to her. I have never been in love with her."

"Troy…" Lawrence shook his head in disapproval.

"I bet the person who did this didn't love her either."

"Maybe. Or, perhaps it was a crime of passion. Maybe she never got around to liking the fat football jock from high school who declared in her yearbook that, if she didn't call him, he'd stalk her. I would hate for him to be the one investigating her case because that would surely be a conflict of interest, don't you think?" Troy wasn't sure whether Nugent and Cheryl had ever been romantically involved after high school, but two divorces and an interdepartmental scandal obviously didn't sway Nugent's commitment toward her. He still cared for her and that helped Troy understand why Nugent had been taking this case so personally.

Like the last time Troy was being questioned, he managed to ruffle Nugent's feathers. He'd upped the ante this time as Nugent's face turned as bright as the apple depicted in the Snow White fairytales. *"Did you leave your house anytime yesterday?"*

"Detective, that's enough. Your questions are becoming repetitive and quite frankly, it's making me nauseous. Obviously, there is no evidence linking my client to this crime and I think he's done his due diligence by *volunteering* to assist you with this investigation. I'll ask again to make sure there's no misunderstanding: is my client under arrest?"

"No," Nugent snarled.

"Okay, we're done here."

"We're not done, Evans. I'll be visiting you real soon with paperwork. Don't go too far."

Once they were outside the building, Lawrence said to Troy, "My office...*now!*"

"What are you hiding?" Lawrence wasted no time ripping into Troy in front of Larry who watched confounded.

"Nothing."

"Don't play games with me. I'll give Richard his money back and turn you loose quicker than you can blink. The way you were dodging that detective's questions regarding your whereabouts yesterday, I know you're hiding something. Spit it out or find yourself a new attorney."

Lawrence was good. Troy didn't have to see him in court to know that. The word of Richard Griggs, one of the best district attorneys in the city, carried a lot of weight. Plus, Troy had seen the way Lawrence blocked Nugent's line of questioning during the interrogation. Troy couldn't afford to lose him. He confessed. "Last night, after my wife went to sleep, I went over to Cheryl's."

"You did what! I specifically told you not to go to her house and I'm quite certain that I spoke English. What were you thinking?"

"I wasn't. I was frustrated because of what happened Friday night when my wife and I went out." Troy realized that he had been so mad that he hadn't informed his attorney of the events at Skyler's and took the opportunity to fill him in now. "I don't believe for a second that she was ever missing. I went there hoping to find clues to her whereabouts."

"Was Cheryl there?"

"No."

"Of course not because she was being murdered and now you don't have an alibi for the time of her death!" Lawrence loosened his tie while contemplating his next words. "Who knew you were going over there?"

"No one." That was kind of the truth. Troy had sent RJ a text stating that he was *thinking* about it, but he never actually admitted to RJ that he had gone.

"Detective Nugent knows."

"How? It was after midnight. I parked a few blocks from her house and I'm sure no one saw me go in or out."

"Why do you think he kept asking you if you were home all day? He was trying to get you to say yes so he could prove otherwise. C'mon, I shouldn't have to tell you this; you're a cop! You know how these things work."

"For all I know, Nugent might be involved in all of this. I found Cheryl's high school yearbook. She and Nugent went to school together. He liked her. I also found her diary and I think she was using it to set me up. It contains a lot of entries about us that aren't true. I have these things with me if you want to see them." The yearbook was in his truck; the diary was immediately returned to his pocket after leaving Nugent.

Lawrence, whose bald head had turned amber, didn't speak for several minutes. "You do realize that whatever you have in your possession has been obtained through breaking and entering, an act that is illegal according to the Ohio Revised Code!"

"I know. I was hoping to find clues as to where she was hiding. I didn't know someone was going to kill her. I bet it was the person who was helping her frame me. That could very well have been Nugent."

"Dad," Larry timidly interrupted, "He may have a point. Maybe we should take a look at the things Mr. Evans has. He can't go back to the house and return them now because I'm sure there are cops crawling all over her place. Perhaps we can use the information in it to help find her killer and clear Mr. Evans's name."

"You watch too many *Perry Mason* and *Matlock* re-runs. It's the detectives' responsibility to find the killer, not ours. If Detective Nugent is dirty or biased, there are legal steps we can take to make sure he's removed from the case. But, we will play by the book. My job is to make sure my client doesn't get charged and convicted of this crime. As long as there's nothing to tie you to Alum Creek or her murder, that shouldn't be a problem."

"Then it won't be," Troy said confidently.

"You better hope so. Get rid of the stuff you have illegally obtained and I don't want to hear another word about you going over to her place," Lawrence warned as his desk phone rang. "Yes, dear, what do you need? No, you can go ahead and send it through." He looked at Larry. "Please walk Mr. Evans out. I have a phone call to take."

Larry was all too eager to oblige. "Mom, I'm going to go grab a sandwich. You want something?" She shook her head no and waved him away. When they were outside, Larry surprised Troy by asking to see the yearbook and diary.

"I don't know if that'll be a good idea. Your dad doesn't want anything to do with those things."

"Mr. Evans, if someone is truly setting you up, then the cops will be sniffing around you hard. The last thing you want is for them to find her things in your possession. My dad told you to get rid of the items. He didn't say how," Larry leered. "Give them to me and he will never know. I promise."

Troy had to be at the end of his rope to find himself placing his trust in an ambitious Robert Shapiro wannabe. "Here." Troy gave Larry the yearbook. "I'll keep the diary," he said. There were so many false incriminating statements against him in it that Troy didn't want it to be anywhere except at the bottom of a furnace.

"Okay. Be careful with it. Meanwhile, I'll take care of things," Larry said before jogging off.

"Hey, wait! What do you mean by you'll 'take care of things.'"

"Have a good day, Mr. Evans!" Larry yelled back and disappeared into the sandwich shop. Troy started to run after him, but he knew that doing so would be futile. Larry wasn't going to give back the yearbook and Troy was all the more glad that he'd held on to the diary. Troy got into his truck and headed home, hoping that he hadn't made matters worse by adhering to the younger Murphy's request.

Chapter 20: The Last Entry

If there was one good thing that came as a result of Cheryl's death, it was that it opened lines of communication between Troy and Natalie again. Feeling grimy and in desperate need of a shower, Troy expected to come home to chaos. Instead, things were peaceful. Natalie had already picked Nate up from school and he and the twins were taking a nap. Troy found his wife sitting in the living room reading her Bible. She jumped up and threw her arms around him when he walked in.

"People need to die more often if that's how you'll greet me every time."

She didn't think his comment was funny. "I was worried about you. What happened?"

"Cheryl was stabbed to death last night and the detective brought me in for questioning. It's standard procedure, really. Nothing to be concerned about. I do have to tell you something, though." Troy sat her down on the sofa. "Last night, after you fell asleep, I went over to Cheryl's. Let me explain!" he quickly added as he saw her face distort. "She wasn't there. I went looking for clues. I was hoping to find something that would help me figure out where she was hiding."

"Well, we know she's no longer hiding. Someone killed her last night, right?"

"Yes… I feel like a monster because I'm not sad that she's dead. I know that's horrible for a man of my stature to say. I work in law enforcement, I have a family, and most importantly, I'm supposed to be a man of God."

"You're still all of those things. Even if you did something bad to her, it won't change how I feel about you."

Troy noticed the tears welling in Natalie's eyes and how much she was caressing his hand. Her right leg bounced rapidly and her breath was heavy. She was nervous. "Relax, babe. I did *not* kill Cheryl. I'm sure I could have, but I didn't, and hopefully, we'll have nothing to worry about."

"What do you mean by 'hopefully'?"

"I found this when I was at her house. It's her diary."

"Is that what you were reading this morning?"

"Yeah. It starts out legit and then it turns into fiction. Some things are true, like this." Troy turned to a page and read out loud. "'*Today, I met with the Columbus PD to provide a profile for the Bible Butcher case. My heart almost stopped when I saw Troy. Our last conversation had been over twenty years ago and here I was expected to act professional and not let on that this man had severed my heart into many broken pieces. I managed. I avoided looking at the wedding ring on his finger. I couldn't believe it when I learned that he was married and had children.*' I believe that was honest, but check out her entry from the weekend she drugged me." Natalie snatched the diary from him and instead of him reading aloud, Troy did so over her shoulder.

Last night, Troy and I were together again. His wife had been waiting for him to come home so she could go to some meeting, but Troy told me to meet him at the gym and, together, we rode to the motel in his truck. We argued because he still hadn't told Natalie about us. He promised he'd do it, but I'm getting impatient. When I told him that I would tell her, he asked if I would wait until after he spoke with a divorce attorney. He wanted to make sure he had a chance to get full custody of his children. He said Natalie is vindictive and might try to prevent him from seeing them. He called her the wicked witch of the east.

"That never happened," Troy said to Natalie. "I promise that I've never call you out of your name to her or anyone else."

"Shh!" She was annoyed by his interruption and kept reading.

I don't know what to believe anymore. I told Troy that I would give him until Monday morning to tell Natalie about our affair and, if he didn't, I would. He got really mad at me and we got into a huge argument about it. Eventually, we made up and made love. I'm still mad at him, though. If he doesn't tell Natalie by Monday morning, I swear I will.

"See what I mean? You know that those pictures of the two of us were fake. Yet, she's writing that we made love. Look at the last entry."

I'm sitting across from Nate's pre-school waiting for Natalie to arrive. Troy left a threatening voice message on my cell phone Saturday night. He threatened to kill me. I don't know what's gotten into him. When we made love Friday night, everything was fine. Then, Saturday he was going off on me. I'm scared for my life. I'm scared for Natalie's life, too. That's why I'm going to tell her about our affair. Before, I was going to do it because I thought I would have Troy to myself. Now, I'm in fear for my life and hers. After the message Troy left me threatening my life, I think it's best that I end our affair. I'm not telling Natalie to be revengeful. I'm telling her so she can know the kind of man she married and so I can apologize for the role I played in violating their vows. Troy is a dangerous man. Worse, he's a cop. He once told me that he knew how to plan the perfect murder and make it so that a body would never be found. I thought he was playing at the time, but after his threatening message on Saturday, I think he was forewarning me. Everyone thinks Troy is a perfect husband, father, and officer of the law. I know different. He's a man who thinks he can have whatever he wants, do whatever he wants without getting caught. I'm about to bring his perfect image to an end and it may very well cost me my life. If I don't write another entry after today, then it means Troy has made good on his threat from Saturday night. Gotta go…Natalie just pulled up.

Troy wasn't sure what to make of his wife's silence, so he asked, "What are you thinking?"

"I don't know what to think. I do see what you mean in terms of her making up stuff. She wrote as if she was planning to apologize to me and that couldn't be further from the truth. She took pleasure in telling me about y'all's affair."

"We didn't have an affair," he clarified.

"You know what I mean. She's good. If I didn't know better, I'd be inclined to believe everything she wrote. It's good that you found it and not the police."

"Something doesn't sit right about that either. It was too easy for me to find. Natalie, our guys are good. I know CPD has been all through her place and yet I found her diary under her bedroom pillow. It was too convenient. Whoever killed Cheryl knew that the cops would be back to search her place and I think they wanted the diary to look like it had been an oversight. It was purposely left there to incriminate me. I wasn't supposed to be the one who found it."

"Okay, now you're not making sense. Cheryl wrote the diary. She didn't stab herself."

"No, she didn't. I bet the plan was to only make it look like she'd been murdered, but then whoever was helping her flipped the script and actually killed her."

"Who would do this? Surely, you still don't think it's Will, do you?"

Troy didn't know. The connection between Nugent and Cheryl was suspicious. Before he could verbalize this thought, his cell phone rang.

"Who is that?"

"I'm not sure. I don't recognize the number." He answered anyway. "Hello."

"Troy, 'dis Shay. Will was at my house. I been tryin' to git in touch wit' him since you and me spoke last week, but he neva returned my calls. 'Den he show up ova here outta nowhere and try and git an attitude when I ask him where he been? I *almost* went off on him 'bout 'dat girl you told me 'bout, but you told me not to say nuttin', so I didn't." Troy was surprised. He was sure Shay would have spilled the beans. She was more loyal than Troy had thought. "Plus, he was actin' weird, talkin' 'bout personal trainin' sessions at 'da gym, and cryin' for no reason. He wouldn't tell me what was wrong. He only said 'dat he did sumthin' bad. I didn't ask what 'cuz the less I know, the less I can testify to, huhnee. He said he came ova to tell me bye 'cuz he's leavin' town again and 'dis time he wasn't comin' back. He said he had to go home first and 'den to 'da gym. I thought you'd wanna know."

"Yes, thank you! How long ago did he leave?"

"Like three minutes ago. I called you right away."

"Good. I'm glad you did. Thank you. I'm headed there right now."

"No problem. I said I gotchu and I meant 'dat. Imma meet you 'dere cuz I wanna see how he act when you confront him 'bout all 'dis stuff wit' 'dat girl. 'Den Imma go off on him 'bout playin' me and havin' me do his work while he out messin' around. I ain't dressed yet, but give me a few and I'll be on my way."

Troy hung up without giving a response. "What was that about?" Natalie asked.

"That was Shay." He quickly recapped what Shay had told him. "I don't know where he lives, but I hope to catch him at the gym and see, once and for all, what he has to do with all of this."

"I don't like this, Troy. Please, be careful. I love you."

"I love you, too," he pledged before running upstairs and getting his personal firearm. He didn't anticipate having to use it unless he needed to make sure Will remained on the premises until the cops arrived. Troy couldn't resist the temptation to peek in on his children who all slept peacefully. On the way out, Troy kissed Natalie and once again affirmed his feelings for her. He grabbed the diary and put it back in his pocket despite her objections that she wanted to read through it. Troy was scared that if he left it there, Natalie's mind might get all discombobulated trying to separate between fact and fiction. She was on his side again. No need to risk messing that up.

Chapter 21: Quality Check

Will's car wasn't in the lot when Troy arrived. He ran inside, looking for the day receptionist. The place was pretty empty for a mid-Monday afternoon. None of the regulars he knew were there, except for his neighbor, Ann, who ignored his head nod by rolling her eyes and giving him the finger. Clearly, she was still upset about the cereal bar thing.

Troy spotted a blonde walking from the back carrying a stack of towels. By process of elimination, he pegged her to be the front worker. "Has Will been here yet?"

"No. I haven't seen Will in over a week. Are you Shay's police friend?"

"Yeah."

"She told me y'all were meeting here. You can wait in Will's office. Let me take these downstairs to the aerobics room and I'll be right back."

Troy lingered at the front desk wrapping his mind around how he would confront Will while he waited. Having been forced to surrender his badge, he had no authority to hold Will if he tried to run. *Will doesn't know that*, he thought. Sure, it was illegal to impersonate an officer or act as one when suspended. But, if Will perceived that he still had the authority of his badge without Troy explicitly saying such, then Troy couldn't be held accountable for

Will's assumptions. He'd simply play into them until his suspicions were confirmed and then those officially on the case could take it from there. If Will was a murderer and trying to frame him, the law would ultimately be on Troy's side in the end.

"All right. Follow me." Troy walked behind the blonde—Heidi, according to her nametag—to the back where she'd come from with the towels. "I haven't seen you before. Are you a member here?'

"Yeah. I normally come in the evenings or sometimes on the weekends."

"That explains it. I'm usually never here those times, except this last week we've all been working all kinds of crazy schedules trying to help Shay hold down the fort until Will gets back. He's lucky we all like him around here because everyone is pissed. He hasn't even had the decency to call in and check on things like he normally does when he's away. Even mom is angry. She called earlier looking for him and was upset because he hadn't communicated his plans with her. I don't know what's going on with Will, but this is my last time busting my butt while he's away." Heidi motioned for him to go into a room. "Here ya go. Make yourself at home. Shay should be here soon."

"Okay, thanks." In retrospect, Troy should have told Shay to stay put when she said she would meet him here. Will might get spooked if he saw the both of them, especially considering that he'd gone to Shay's place to say good-bye. Troy tried calling the number displayed on his cell phone. "Hey, 'dis Shay. Leave a message and I'll hit you up another day." He hung up.

Left alone in Will's office, Troy seized the moment to snoop. The place was pretty customary—a large steel-framed desk, a brown leather swivel chair, a bunch of health-conscious charts and sayings on the walls. The only thing of a personal nature was a picture of his young nephew whom Will looked after like a son. Poor little guy, now his parents and uncle would all be in jail. Will was an idiot!

Not surprisingly, the file cabinets and all the drawers on the desk were locked except the center one. Troy slid it open, finding nothing of importance, only regular office supplies. Frustrated, he slammed it shut.

Troy reflected on the last time, ten days ago, when he was at the gym. He knew Will had lied about being here. What else was he missing? Troy closed his eyes, trying to visualize that day. *Take slow deep breaths*, he told himself, recalling the instructions once given to him when he'd undergone forensic memory recall, or what the rest of the world would call hypnosis. Mentally, he retraced his steps during that last visit. He remembered getting off the phone with Natalie as he pulled into the parking lot. *Was there anything strange in the parking lot?* Troy asked himself. He circled the area with his mind. *Nope.* He was also sure that Will's car hadn't been there. He went in and secured his things in the locker. He remembered seeing Charlie, Fudago, and the married couple. Fudago left prior to Troy finishing his programmed time on the elliptical. Charlie was not far behind though he first stopped to flirt with Shay. Miriam and Ted stayed a while. They were still there when Troy went to the weight room.

The weight room...that's where Troy saw the Naughty by Nature guy! He'd been eyeing Troy suspiciously the entire time and when Troy was finally ready to approach him, the dude was gone. Troy regretted not asking Shay about him. He wasn't going to wait until she got here to do it either; he ran back to the front to find Heidi.

"Hey, have you ever seen a guy around here, about my height and skin complexion, but probably like twenty years younger with a bunch of tattoos. Two of them are very distinguishable. On one arm, he has a picture of an Uzi, and on the other, the words 'Naughty by Nature.'"

"Oh, you're talking about Rio!" Heidi responded. "That's not his real name, but that's what everyone calls him. He's usually here about three or four times a week. He's a bit of a gym celebrity right now because he holds the record for the most personal training hours in one month. The trainer he was working with recently moved to L.A. and so now all of the others are competing for his business. It's funny to see the different incentives they're offering. Why do you ask about him?"

"[H]ave you ordered any personal training services?" That was one of Will's last questions to Troy. Could there be a connection? "Oh, I was curious. Like you said, he's a bit of a celebrity. Maybe I'm a groupie. You wouldn't by chance be able to access his records and get his contact information for me, would you?"

"I'm not buying the groupie thing. What do you really want?"

"Shay told you I'm a detective, right? Truth is, I'm working on a case and I need to ask Mr. Rio a few questions."

"Do you have a warrant?"

"Ah…not with me. Is it possible for you to give me the information now and I'll bring the paperwork back later? You know I'm legit because Shay told you about me."

"Yeah, but we can't release information about our clients to a third party without their written consent or a warrant. Company policy."

"Can't you make an exception this *one* time?" Troy softened his tone to a more seductive level and leaned across the counter. "I'm working on a big case and I really need Rio's information. No one has to know you gave it to me. I won't say anything if you don't."

Troy wasn't sure what bothered him most: that he'd become desperate enough to resort to such tactics to get what he wanted or the wary look he pretended not to see coming from Ann who'd walked past on her cell phone as she went out the door. He couldn't be certain, but it sounded like she was talking about him.

"Oh, my gosh! You're a mole, aren't you?" Heidi exclaimed. "Now it all makes sense. You were sent from corporate to do a quality check. Will's not really out of town, is he? This whole week has been a test to see if we employees would follow procedure when no one's looking. By the way, that sexy thing you tried was a nice touch. If I didn't already have someone willing to eventually put a ring on it, I—"

"I'm not from corporate!" Troy yelled. "I'm a detective investigating a case, like I said."

"*Riiight.* Well, detective," she used air quotes, "Like *I* said, it's against company policy to release personal details about our members. However, if you're in need of a deejay, I would strongly suggest that you check out the bulletin board. A lot of our members advertise their services there. Excuse me, will you? I have to run to the ladies room. Nice talking to you, Mr. I'm-not-from-corporate." Heidi winked and giggled as she walked away.

It took a second for it to dawn on Troy what Heidi had done. When it did, he bolted to the board where he found a bright yellow flier offering the disc jockey services of one DJ Rio! Troy tore off one of the frayed edges with the guy's number as a man burst through the front door. He and Troy made eye contact. Troy had seen this dude before. It was the same bald white man with a baseball cap who'd been staring at his family last weekend when they were at the Commons!

"Come with me!" The man charged at him.

"Who are you?"

"Listen, Troy. There are a bunch of cops outside sniffing around your truck. My guess is that they'll find something that links you to Cheryl's murder. I'm here to help you because I know you're innocent. You can either go with them or come with me."

"That's bull!" Troy went to take a look. Sure enough, there was a whole army of cop cars in the parking lot and officers surrounding his truck. Fear permeated through his veins and he looked to his strange new friend for an explanation.

"My offer to help expires in thirty seconds. What's it gonna be?"

Troy made his choice when he ran, following behind as the man led him through the women's locker room where they nearly trampled Heidi as she came from a stall. She shouted something after them, but Troy's adrenaline blocked him from hearing what it was. His feet didn't stop moving until he'd gone out of the emergency exit and into the black Acura that was running and waiting. As the guy sped off and Troy attempted to catch his breath, he realized that this was the same car he'd spotted on the security cameras outside of his house.

Chapter 22: Wounded Souls

"Who are you and why have you been stalking me?" Troy demanded to know, pulling out his piece.

"I'm Lloyd Hunter; and I prefer the term 'following' as opposed to 'stalking.' Now will you put that thing away so no one gets hurt?"

"I saw you at the Commons and outside of my home. What do you want from me?" Troy checked over his shoulder to see if anyone was hiding on the back floor. Satisfied that he wasn't being set up to be drugged again, he lowered his weapon.

"Not trying to be rude, Troy, but can we delay the small talk for a few minutes? At least until I know we're safely away from the gym." The man whipped through several back streets before finally jumping on the freeway opposite the direction Troy would normally go to get home. "Don't answer that!" he commanded when Troy's cell phone rang.

It was Shay. When Troy let the call go to voicemail, she sent a text asking what was going on. She'd just gotten to the gym and the "PoPo" were all over the place asking about him. Shay wrote in her message that she was scared. Troy thought about having her share their suspicions about Will with the police, but there was nothing concrete to go on except hunches. He also didn't want to keep putting her in the middle of things so he didn't respond at all. Will had already killed once. Troy thought of Natalie and how concerned she would be about him once she got wind of what had happened. "I need to call my wife."

"No, that's the last thing you need to do. Your home is the first place the cops are going and the less she knows, the better. As a matter of fact, if you don't turn it off, I'll be happy to let you out on the side of the road while you wait for the police to trace your signal."

Troy hated the condescending manner in which Lloyd spoke, but Troy knew he was right. He couldn't bring himself to leave Natalie with a bunch of uncertainties without first reaching out to her. Before turning off the device, Troy sent a text to his wife. "*No matter what, don't worry. I'm okay. I love you.*"

"That's a nice phone you got, man. What kind is it?"

"It's the newest Samsung Galaxy."

"Can I see it?" Troy handed Lloyd his cell only for him to throw it out of the driver's side window.

"What the—"

"It's better that you not have it with you at all. It would be too tempting not to contact anyone. In the words of Adrian Monk, 'you'll thank me later.'"

Troy found little comfort in Lloyd's use of the signature line of a fictional television detective. He still held DJ Rio's number tightly in hand along with his gun and decided to secure them both—the pistol at his waist, the number in his side pocket next to Cheryl's fake diary. "Where are you taking me?"

"To my place." Lloyd must have seen the caution written on Troy's face. "Relax, I'm not going to harm you in any way. I'm actually trying to help you. I know you've been set up for Cheryl's murder."

Troy stared at Lloyd and a new revelation hit him as he envisioned Lloyd without the baseball cap and twenty years younger. Troy had seen a photo of him last night when he was at Cheryl's house. "You're her husband!"

"*Ex*-husband, technically."

"But, Cheryl told me that you were—"

"Dead. Yeah, I've heard that she sometimes kills me off in her world. How'd she tell you I died?"

"In a car accident."

"Humph. That's pretty simplistic. I've heard all kinds of stories. I've been shot by drug dealers in retaliation for a case she'd worked, killed in a boating accident, and I think the most creative one is that I died from a rare genetic disorder. I guess it all sounds better than the truth."

"Which is?"

"We divorced because she let her sister talk her into believing horrible things about me that weren't true."

"Her sister?"

"You didn't know she had a sister?"

"Yeah, but I didn't know Cheryl had found her."

"Oh, Cheryl didn't find Chyanne. Chyanne found her about eight or nine years ago, and ever since that psychopath has been in Cheryl's life, she's done nothing except manipulate and use Cheryl until the point that my wife unraveled. I heard from a mutual friend that Cheryl got fired from the FBI after repeated misuse of her government credit cards. When she and I were married, she was always so conscientious about doing things by the book. Personally, I think Cheryl may have always had some psychological or emotional issues as a result of her childhood that somehow went undetected by the agency, but Chyanne definitely brought out the worst in Cheryl by playing with her need to belong and be loved. I know she's the one setting you up, but like Denzel said in *Training Day*, 'it's not what you know; it's what you can prove.'"

"Why would she do this? I don't know her."

"Ah, but I bet she knows you through the stories Cheryl has shared. You were Cheryl's first love; the one who did irreparable damage to her heart and forever changed the course of her future. No matter how hard I tried, I couldn't erase the damage that had been done to her as a result of the relationship she had with you. I nurtured her; Chyanne used the information to hurt her and you."

Troy was so sick of hearing how he'd broken Cheryl's heart. Nugent reminded him, it was in Cheryl's diary, and now Lloyd was making way more of their relationship than it needed to be. "I don't get how I became such a major player in the destruction of Cheryl's life. We dated a long time ago for like a year and it seems like everyone has made more of our time together than what it really was. She wanted to get married; I didn't. How did that become the end of her world?"

"You really don't know, do you?"

"Know *what?*"

"At the time you broke up with Cheryl, she was pregnant."

The news hit Troy as hard as the elbow James Harden took from Metta World Peace, aka Ron Artest, during the 2012 basketball game between the Lakers and Oklahoma City Thunder. Troy was scared to know, but the question needed to be asked: "What happened to the baby?"

"She aborted it and, unfortunately, there was severe damage to her uterus, which resulted in her having a hysterectomy. I met Cheryl through a mutual friend about a month after it all went down. She was crushed. I tried to encourage her to see a therapist, but she was afraid of how it would look on her application to the FBI. I think we connected so well because we were both wounded souls on the rebound, in search for someone to mend our broken hearts. But, only one of us healed. That baby with you was the only chance she had of having a real family since hers had been murdered, and Cheryl was never able to get over the emptiness she felt. When Chyanne came into her life, Cheryl became someone I didn't recognize and that relationship took precedence over everything…her career, her marriage, and now, apparently even her life."

"What was it that her sister talked her into believing about you?"

Lloyd's jaw line clenched. "I prefer not to talk about it."

Chapter 23: Not Some Fiction Story

Troy didn't say another word as they rode to Lloyd's cabin-like home, which was located on the northern outskirts of town on a country road surrounded by trees. Its long gravel driveway led to a brick house protected by a secured privacy fence. Inside, the living room walls extended to the roof, which contained solar panels. The stairs to the right led to a loft on the second story where Troy saw all kinds of weapon images lined amidst camouflage prints and government paraphernalia. "Who are you?"

He gave a wry grin. "Lloyd Hunter." Troy frowned. "Okay, it's not the time for jokes. I get it. Simply put, I'm an independent contractor who designs weapons for the military. I bet your next question is why I would risk such a good gig to help you. Despite our marriage ending, I never stopped loving Cheryl. Long story short, I want the person responsible for taking her life to pay." Lloyd told Troy that he'd received a call early last Saturday morning saying that she feared for her life. The story she'd told Lloyd was similar to the one Troy had read in her diary about how he and Cheryl were involved in an affair and when she said she'd tell Natalie, he'd threatened to kill her. "That was the first time Cheryl contacted me in years, so I was both skeptical and curious. She sounded so convincing that I wanted to check you out for myself. That's why I followed you to the Commons."

"How'd you find me?"

"I have friends in high places," Lloyd said with that same clever grin. "When I saw you with your family, I didn't peg you as an adulterer or killer. I had a gut feeling that Cheryl was lying and I didn't think anything else about it until after she went missing. Now that she's been murdered, I don't want to see you go down for something you didn't do."

"What makes you so certain that I didn't kill her? Did you?"

"No. I told you; I think Chyanne did. Cheryl called me again last week from a private number after she was supposedly abducted."

"What did she say?"

"She said to remember she was alive as long as no one found her body. I knew then that she had a vendetta against you and when I tried to get her to turn herself in, she hung up on me. A few days later, I received this in the mail." Lloyd threw an envelope at him and began to explain its contents as Troy opened it. "When Cheryl and I first married, we took out million-dollar life insurance policies on each other—"

"Why so much?" A million dollars sounded like a motive for murder. Troy watched Lloyd carefully for his response.

He shrugged. "Because we could. We were two lonely hearts who figured that if one of us died, the other should at least have a right to live worry-free financially. For the twelve years we were married, our policies were well-funded, so the cash values were high. We both changed beneficiaries when we divorced. Apparently, she made Chyanne hers, but look." Troy drew his attention back to the papers Lloyd had handed him. "Cheryl recently cashed out her policy. After twenty years of paying into it, the cash value was well over a half million."

"Okay, so she took the money out and gave it to Chyanne? And?"

"That's the point. I don't think she gave it to Chyanne. I think she hid it somewhere because this key came with it." Lloyd pulled out a gold key that he held close enough for Troy to see, but far enough that he couldn't grab it if he'd wanted to. "In her last phone call, Cheryl told me that as long as no one found her body, she was alive." Lloyd spun his theory of how he believed Cheryl and Chyanne had planned to fake her death together and live off the insurance money, but he believed somehow Cheryl became suspicious of Chyanne and closed the policy. "Insurance companies are reluctant to pay when there's no concrete proof of death, and it could have taken years for Cheryl to be declared legally dead with no body. I bet Cheryl hid the money without Chyanne's knowledge in the event that her sister double-crossed her in order to cash in early."

"You said yourself that you hadn't spoken with Cheryl in years; why would she send you the key of all people?"

"If I had to guess, I would say it's because deep down she knew she could trust me. I didn't leave Cheryl; she left me and I think there's part of her that always knew I'd come running if she truly needed me."

"Do you know where the money is?"

"Nope. I haven't got a clue. It looks like a key to a storage unit, but it would be like finding a needle in a haystack with all the places around Columbus." Troy told Lloyd about Donald Nugent, Will and DJ Rio. "I didn't know Cheryl had started talking to Don again. He had a longtime crush on her and I think he felt slighted when I came into the picture. We used to hang out with him and his second wife, but he stopped coming around after they split up. Cheryl probably reconnected with him to feed him the same story she told me about the two of you having an affair so it would seem real when she went missing. I know Don. He can be a jerk sometimes, but I don't think he's dirty, though. Maybe there's a way we can test him in order to know for sure, but I really think he's just doing his job. I don't know anything about the other guys you mentioned. Cheryl and I have been divorced for over seven years. I'm sure there may be a lot of people in her life I don't know about."

Troy informed Lloyd of the issues he'd been having with Cheryl the last couple of years. "It was eerie the things she knew about me. I really do think there was a bug in that toy car."

"It could have been. If that Will guy is working with them, he could have also planted something in your phone while you had it in the locker room at the gym. Who knows what kind of gadgets Cheryl got from the agency. I bet they also had eyes on you."

Troy decided to take a chance and share with Lloyd the diary he discovered from Cheryl's bedroom last night. He sat quietly while Lloyd skimmed through it.

"Wow! Looks like she pulled an Amy Dunne on you. Well, at least she tried."

"Who?"

"Have you ever read the novel *Gone Girl* by Gillian Flynn?"

"No. Novels aren't my thing," Troy responded, looking at all of Lloyd's weapon creations. Lloyd didn't strike him as a reader.

"Aw, that was a good book. Basically, this lady wanted to frame her husband for murder so she created this fake diary describing how she was scared of him and detailing his abusive behavior. She set him up real good. It was brilliant! They're making a movie out of it this fall and—"

"Can we get back to the real world, please? This is my life, not some fictional story."

"My bad." Lloyd finished flipping through Cheryl's fairytale. "It's a good thing you found this before the cops. Personally, I'd suggest that you destroy it. You can't give it back at this point and there's nothing useful in it. We know Cheryl's dead, so it's not like she can re-create it. Your best bet is to pretend like it never existed."

Troy nodded in agreement.

"Why don't you get cleaned up? I have fresh towels and some things in the bathroom that will fit you. While you're getting yourself together, I'll take care of this."

"No!" Troy quickly snatched the diary from Lloyd for much of the same reason he couldn't release it to Larry. "I'll do it."

"Okay. Suit yourself. I'm starving. I'll whip us up some sandwiches while you freshen up."

Troy made his way to the bathroom with his mind spinning in a thousand directions as all the events from the day collided in his head. He didn't recognize the reflection of the individual staring back at him in the mirror. No longer chasing killers, that person was accused of being one of them and he was scared. No, terrified of what the outcome would be if things didn't work out in his favor. What if he didn't get to see his children grow up? Nate's first high school basketball game? Ean and Ebony's graduation? Ebony walking down the aisle? Angrily, Troy ripped out the pages of Cheryl's diary, tearing them into tiny pieces and flushing them down the toilet in handfuls. When he was satisfied that nothing would come back up, he finally took the much needed shower.

The water washed away his funk, not his fear. In fact, his level of anxiety had heightened and paranoia set in. What if this whole thing with Lloyd had been a setup? For all Troy knew Lloyd could be in on this scheme and the plan all along was to get him out here in the middle of nowhere to kill him as well. He left the water running and stepped out of the shower. With the towel wrapped around his waist and his gun in hand, Troy cracked open the bathroom door. He observed Lloyd sitting on the sofa with his feet on the coffee table eating a sandwich and flipping through the television.

Troy shut the door and leaned against it. *Lord, give me wisdom,* he prayed. He didn't trust himself or his instincts and, at the moment, Lloyd was all he had. But really, who was this dude!?! That night he and Cheryl met at Starbucks, she'd told him her husband had died. Now, in light of how erratic her behavior had been these last couple of years toward him, he questioned everything she told him, including the part about him being her first. "*At the time you broke up with Cheryl, she was pregnant.*" Troy wasn't ready to deal with the weight of that revelation. He hurriedly slipped on the clothes Lloyd had laid out for him and joined his new friend in the living room.

"You're just in time," Lloyd announced and nodded for Troy to focus on the television.

"There's been a break in the disappearance and murder case of former federal agent Cheryl Hunter. Last week, we reported that Hunter had gone missing and that an unidentified Columbus police officer had been linked to her disappearance. We have since learned that the body found late last night at Alum Creek State Park in Delaware, Ohio is that of the forty-six-year-old and that one of CPD's own has become the prime suspect in this murder investigation. Our cameras were there as investigators searched the vehicle of Detective Troy Evans at a local area gym after receiving an anonymous tip. Inside the back of his SUV, officers found a bloody knife, which they suspect may be the weapon that was used on Hunter. Witnesses say that Evans had been inside the gym at the time police initially arrived, but he escaped authorities with the help

of a Caucasian man who led him through an emergency exit and the two took off in a black vehicle. Unfortunately, the man cannot clearly be identified by the security cameras outside the front of the building. We spoke with an employee who arrived at the gym as everything was unfolding. Shay Donovan did not want to appear on camera, but she said that she had a hard time believing any of this because Detective Evans is her friend and is a good guy who kept to himself anytime he was at the gym. Others had similar sentiments, but police say this 'good guy' is a murderer. If you have any idea regarding the whereabouts of Troy Evans or who his mysterious accomplice may be, please contact the Columbus Police Department at 614-555-TIPS. Evans, who led the investigation of the Bible Butcher case two years ago, is considered to be armed and dangerous and should not be approached. If you see him, please contact the police immediately.

"Looks like you're involved in a real-life scandal. Where's Olivia Pope when you need her, right?"

"Who?"

Lloyd sighed. "Never mind. We need to figure out your next move. First, let me ask you, are you considering turning yourself in?"

Troy pondered the question. By surrendering, his fate would be left in the hands of the justice system…the very system he worked for, believed in. Yet, Troy could not bring himself to leave his future, or the future of his family, in the hands of his comrades who were already convinced of his guilt. He needed to be on the outside so he could work the case and clear his name. Thus, his response to Lloyd was "no."

"Good. I think that'll make Chyanne nervous because she knows while you're out, you'll be looking for answers and she'll stay hidden. I'm sure she intended to leave town after cashing in the insurance policy. She's in for a startling surprise when she learns it's been canceled. If we can somehow make her think you have it, it may draw her out in public."

Troy had the same thought coupled with a grave concern. "I don't want to put my family in harm's way. I need to warn my wife so she can get somewhere safe." Thanks to Lloyd, Troy had no way to call Natalie and he hadn't memorized any of the numbers programmed in his phone. When he remembered that he could access his contacts online, he told Lloyd who rejected the idea.

"That's not wise. Your accounts will be monitored. I'll get a message to your wife for you. They'll be safe tonight for sure. Too many cops will be crawling around and probably even watching your place."

There was no way Troy would leave the security of Natalie and their children in the hands of a man he didn't know. He was determined to get a message to Natalie and he figured out exactly how to do it.

Chapter 24: Gone with the Wind

When Natalie received Troy's text telling her not to worry, it increased her level of anxiety even more. She tried contacting him back, but he did not respond to any of her texts, and her calls were going straight to voicemail. When an army of officers swarmed her place demanding to know where her husband was and shoving a warrant in her face allowing them to search the premises, she knew something had gone terribly wrong.

Natalie watched in horror as officers went room-by-room through her family's things. She and the children were ordered to remain in one place and there was nothing she could do while they, including Nate, screamed and clung to her for dear life. The officers' presence had scared them. Natalie also wanted to cry and would have if she wasn't forced to be the adult in the situation. Her babies needed her to remain composed. She tried as best as she could to calm them and placate Nate who, like the police, wanted his daddy whom Natalie had been told had an arrest warrant out on him for murder.

"Ma'am. We're going to need you to come to the station and answer a few questions," one officer said to her. "We can have someone sit with them."

"Whatever you need to ask me, you can do it here. I'm not leaving and no one is taking my kids." Thanks to her husband, Natalie wasn't ignorant of the law. She knew she wasn't obligated to go with them unless she was under arrest. The officer tried intimidation tactics, telling her that Troy was a fugitive and if she was helping him, losing her children would be the least of her concerns. When Natalie didn't waver from her position, he walked away to speak with another officer. It didn't take a high IQ to know that they were discussing her. They kept looking back and as confident as Natalie tried to appear, she was petrified. With hands trembling like she suffered from some kind of nervous disorder, Natalie called the only person she could think of: *Richard*. When he didn't answer, the tears she had held back broke through. She pulled her children in closer to her so she could wipe her face without Nate seeing.

From the living room window, Natalie could see Ann and other neighbors lining the street. A television crew was also present. That's when it hit Natalie—the nightmare she thought she was privately experiencing was being broadcast for the entire city to witness. And when she pulled up the local news app on her iPhone, she understood why her husband had sent such a cryptic message and the extent of how wrong his trip to the gym had gone.

Natalie read and reread the story trying to piece together the situation as best as she could. Did Troy ever confront Will? Who was the Caucasian man helping him? How'd the knife get in his truck? Did she really believe Troy was innocent? She didn't know the answers to the other questions, but when it came to her husband being a killer, Natalie would not make the same mistake she had when she confronted him about the affair. She would take Troy at his word.

When he'd come home from the police station, she hadn't been sure. Had he admitted guilt, it would not have changed a thing about her feelings for Troy. Though no advocate for homicide, Natalie would have understood how her husband could have been driven to such a brink of insanity after all Cheryl had put him, *them*, through. The police could say all they wanted, but in her heart, she knew why her husband ran. It wasn't because he was guilty; it was because he was going to work this murder investigation like she'd witnessed him do so many others.

"Mommy, where's Daddy?" Nate's emotions had calmed down, but not his curiosity. The twins still gripped her with fear.

"Honey, Daddy's working."

"When is he comin' home?" he asked in a whiny voice.

"I don't know, sweetheart. But, we can always pray that it won't be long."

Bless his heart, Nate shut his eyes so tight that it had to hurt and he started saying a child-like prayer for his daddy to come home "right now." As much as Natalie wanted to echo her son's words, it would take a little more time. Thus, she prayed for Troy's safety, wisdom, and revelation. For good measure, she added that she'd like to have him home by their anniversary, which was in five days!

"Sir, I'm going to have to ask you to leave the property. We're conducting official police business." Natalie heard one of the officers say.

"I'm also here in an official capacity and I need to see Mrs. Coleman. I'm sure you won't break the law by denying her representation, will you?" came the response from a voice that Natalie recognized and yet was confused by.

"RJ?"

"Hey, Natalie. Lisa and Chandler are outside in the car. We

knew they wouldn't let us all in. Hey, Nate, give me a high-five, man."

Nate reluctantly obliged the inopportune request and when RJ lifted his hand, Natalie saw the message he'd written for her.

Troy sent me to get you.

She nodded though RJ's note sparked more questions that she wouldn't dare ask at the moment.

"You guys are coming over our house tonight. I'm going to stay right here until after they finish, and then Lisa will come in and help you pack whatever you need."

Natalie wanted to tell him that such measures weren't necessary, that she and her babies would be fine and that it would probably be better for them to stay home so they could have some sense of normalcy, but she didn't argue. Troy had sent him. She trusted Troy, which by default caused her to trust whatever RJ said. Even with his freedom in jeopardy, her husband had made provisions for her. *My protective detective*, she thought and smiled. Metaphorically speaking, she'd done her weeping for the night. Now she would sit patiently and peacefully until her morning came, knowing that somehow, everything would be all right. That night as she lay awake at the Hamptons', Natalie silently repeated the poem she'd written for Troy the night she thought he was out working a triple homicide case.

Now I lay me down to sleep
I pray the Lord my husband to keep
I pray the Lord my husband to protect
May he come home unharmed without any defects
When he finally lays down to rest
May he arise again and be at his best

Troy swore that he could literally hear his heart beating as he walked up to the quaint white house with dark purple shutters. After the news broadcast, Lloyd feared that cops may eventually come knocking at his door. Even if they didn't peg him as Troy's accomplice, as Cheryl's ex-husband, they might ask him questions as they worked to build a case against Troy. "You need to hide someplace where no one, not even your wife, would suspect. There's a vacant house on Dundee Avenue that my friend owns. He lives out of town and I check on the place for him from time-to-time to make sure it's not being vandalized. I would take you there, but you'd be miserable without any furniture or utilities. Let's make that our safe place. If we ever lose contact for any reason or need to meet, we'll do it there." Lloyd gave him the address, telling him that the backdoor was always open. He then asked, "Is there anyone you can call for help who won't turn you in?"

Troy's list of friends was few. The only person he considered was his ex-partner, but for the same reason Troy didn't contact him the night he pretended to get called out on the triple homicide, Troy wouldn't involve him now. The guy had his own issues to deal with and hiding a fugitive wouldn't be an easy feat. It took some doing, but Troy had found the perfect place. His only hope was that this dude could be trusted as they were not friends. They couldn't even be classified as acquaintances.

Troy rang the doorbell, wondering if RJ had been able to get to Natalie and how she and the kids were handling things. Was she mad at him? Would divorce papers be waiting on him after this ordeal ended? Her emotions had been so up and down about the whole situation that Troy wasn't sure what to expect. Natalie was as much a part of him as Eve was to Adam when God created her from Adam's rib. Losing her would mean losing a piece of himself.

When Lloyd shut down the idea of Troy logging onto his account to access his contacts, Troy came up with an alternative. He looked up the number to the rehab center that RJ ran, knowing that even if RJ wasn't in the office, he left his cell phone number on the outgoing greeting of his voicemail. For reasons Troy wasn't sure he wanted to know, Lloyd had a stash of untraceable burner phones and Troy used one of them to contact RJ, telling him that he feared his family could be in danger. "I'm on it," RJ replied, asking no questions, only telling Troy to be careful.

Lloyd dropped Troy off a few blocks from the neighborhood, giving him a thousand dollars in cash and a different burner phone from the one Troy had used to call RJ. "There's a number programmed in there where you can reach me if necessary and I know how to get ahold of you. If you call anyone, the number will register on their end as private, but I don't recommend contacting your loved ones. It's safer for everyone that way. Also, check this out." Lloyd pointed to a red button on the side of the phone. "If you press this during a call, it'll record your phone conversation. If you push it when you're not on a call, it records whatever's going on in the room. This feature could come in handy should you speak with Chyanne or any of her accomplices."

"Understood. I don't know if you're helping me because you feel sorry for me, but whatever your reason, I want to say thank you."

"In the words of Katniss Everdeen after her calf was burned to the bone, 'pity does not get you aid. Admiration at your refusal to give up does.'"

Troy stared at him.

"She's the protagonist in the *Hunger Games* Trilogy." Lloyd sighed in disbelief. "Do you ever go to the movies?"

"Apparently not as much as you."

"All right. I give up. You should get going. If we sit here too long, we'll start to look suspicious."

Troy agreed. "Thank you, again," he said before getting out of the car. "I'll be in touch."

Before Troy could take off, Lloyd rolled down the passenger-side window. "Hey, I know you're eager to contact the deejay, but there's nothing he'll be able to tell you tonight that he can't say in the morning. It's been a long day. Get some rest and start fresh tomorrow. As Scarlett said in *Gone with the Wind*, 'After all, tomorrow is another day.'"

Troy laughed. "Seriously, dude, who are you?"

With the same slick grin he'd given early when Troy had asked that question, he responded by saying, "Hunter. Lloyd Hunter," in true James Bond-ish style and sped off.

Troy shook his head in amusement and jogged to this house where he now waited for the most peculiar man he'd ever met in his life to come to the door.

Chapter 25: Rule 11

It seemed like it took forever for the homeowner to answer. When he finally did, his eyes grew three times bigger as the shock of seeing Troy hit him. "Detective Evans, what brings you to my doorstep at this time of the night?"

"Eric, I'm mean Pastor Freeman"—he caught himself, remembering how hung up on his title Eric was—"I have nowhere else to turn. I don't know if you've seen the news—"

"Yes, I'm quite aware that you're currently Columbus's most wanted. Come in before someone sees you." The inside of Eric's living room was exactly as Troy remembered it—eerily immaculate and more like a mini sanctuary than anything else. Scriptures aligned every wall amidst a white plush sofa and a desk that contained a large copy of the Bible perched on a stand. "Let's go to the den. This room is sacred. If you recall, it's where my heavenly Father wrote messages to me and revealed the location of those dead women."

"Uh, yeah…I remember." Eric was referring to the Bible Butcher case in which he had once been Troy's prime suspect. As Troy followed Eric to another very religiously decorated, but not overly done room, he wondered if there was any place he had overlooked where he could have gone that neither Natalie nor anyone else who knew him would consider.

"Have a seat and tell me how I can help you. I know you're innocent of the murder of which you have been accused."

"How do you know?"

"The Almighty has given me spiritual discernment. You wouldn't be here if you were guilty. You came because you're desperate and in Psalm 51:17, David tells us that a broken and contrite heart God will not despise. I can't despise you, my dear friend. The Lord would be displeased with His servant. Now, once again, I ask, how can I help you?"

Troy got right to the point. "I need a place to hide out while I work this case. It would be a big risk for you because you could face jail time if I'm caught here. I understand it's a lot to ask and—"

"Say no more. You're welcome to stay for as long as you need. I'm not worried about man's laws when there is a divine one that supersedes it. I liken myself to the harlot Rahab who hid the spies that Joshua sent to search out the land after the king ordered his men to seize them. You're a good man, and I will do my due diligence to see that the will of the Father is carried out. However, if you stay here, you must abide by my house rules. If you give me a second, I'll grab them. I keep copies handy in case I have long-term guests."

Troy wasn't sure that Eric was serious until he actually left the room and came back handing him a piece of paper with the words "House Guest Rules" at the top. Troy scanned it. Most were common-sense things such as saying "excuse me" when belching or passing gas; some had to do with good hygiene like being sure to wash hands after using the restroom and before eating, but one was simply ludicrous.

Rule 19: All house guests will arise at 4 am to partake in devotional and prayer sessions that shall be timed at one hour and thirty-three minutes each.

Troy looked up at Eric who stared at him intently. "You can't be serious?"

"Yes, Detective Evans, I am. This is a house of the Lord. Once you stepped through that threshold, you entered holy ground. It's important that we spend quality time with the Lord each morning. The first few days will be hard because I sense that your maturity isn't quite up to the level it needs to be, but you'll get used to it. I'm here to help you, not only with your personal dilemma, but also with your spiritual growth. Feel free to call me Eric. I know the Lord sent you here for my services and I, His anointed servant, shall oblige. Now, please sign at the bottom that you have read and agree to abide by the ordinances of this house."

Troy was grateful for Eric's willingness to help, but the rules made him wonder, once again, if coming here had been the best idea. Like Jesus in the Garden of Gethsemane, Troy prayed for another way, but no other answer was given and so he signed, wondering if Eric was on meds and if he'd remembered to take them.

Eric went to bed around ten and Troy stayed up to watch the eleven o'clock news, which repeated the story it had run earlier about him. He had trouble falling asleep for several reasons. For starters, he was in a strange environment with an even stranger dude and he felt uncomfortable. Yet, this was the perfect place to hide out. No one would ever suspect he was there; he had trouble believing it himself.

Per house rules, Eric awoke Troy early Tuesday morning for devotional and prayer time. The long and precise ninety-three-minute sessions were timed by a buzzer that chimed when each was over. Eric was so much in his own world, he hadn't noticed that Troy kept dozing off or, if he did, he was too caught up to care.

Whether Eric was caught up in *the* Spirit or *a* spirit had yet to be determined. All Troy knew was that he'd missed the morning local news, thanks to the three-hour-and-six-minute event. When it was over, Eric stated that he hoped Troy had gained something from spending the time with the Lord and also had a suggestion for him.

"I feel an unction to direct you to Psalm 57. I believe you'll be able to relate it to your current situation. It was written by David when he was on the run from Saul who was trying to kill him. I recommend you read it," he said, leaving a copy of the King James Bible with him.

Troy, all Bibled out for the moment, told Eric that he'd check it out later and asked if he could use his computer. After being reassured that Troy wouldn't violate rule 11, which forbade the use of any pornographic sites, Eric brought his laptop into the den and created a guest account for him. Eric went on about his daily errands while Troy spent much of the morning reading news articles about himself as the prime suspect in Cheryl's murder. He also did a search for DJ Rio to learn more about the dude Troy was certain was somehow connected to the case. From Rio's social media pages, Troy learned that he had an upcoming gig on Friday night. Troy's initial thought was to attend the event and corner the deejay there. But, Friday was still three days away and he couldn't afford to wait until then for answers. Troy decided to give him a call.

"Hi, my name is Jermaine Coleman." *Not much creativity there, buddy,* Troy thought to himself as he combined his middle name with Natalie's maiden one. "I'm throwing my son a going-away party next month when he goes off to college and I'm looking for a deejay. Someone recommended you."

"Yeah, that's what's up," Rio, who originally sounded half asleep when he answered, piped up. "What date you lookin' at?"

"The exact date hasn't been confirmed yet. If you can do it, I can work around your schedule."

"Oh, I gotchu. Let me look at my calendar and see what I have open."

"Is it possible for us to meet in person to discuss all the details?"

"I can tell you everything you need to know right now. My fee is three-hundred dollars for the first four hours. For each additional hour—"

"Pardon me for interrupting, but I'm old school and I really like handling business face-to-face. I'm willing to pay you for your time. If I decide to hire you for my son's party, I'll give you one-and-a-half times your normal rate."

"Fuh real?"

"Yes, for real, but I like to see people I go into business with. I heard you were good and if you want the job, I'm willing to give it to you. If not, I'll move on to the next deejay on my list."

"Naw, man, I gotchu. When you wanna meet?"

"Is today too soon?" Rio had things to do during the day and wouldn't be available until later in the evening, which was fine with Troy who had to figure out how he'd get to the location. They decided to meet at 7 p.m. at a spot near the OSU campus. At noon, Troy turned his attention away from Rio and to the twelve o'clock news.

"Yesterday, we told you about a police detective, Troy Evans, who is wanted for the kidnapping and murder of his former lover, Cheryl Hunter. Officers searched all through the night for Evans, but so far they have no leads on his whereabouts. We spoke with Troy's attorney, Lawrence Murphy."

A clip of Lawrence, dressed in an Orville Redenbacher-like suit, appeared onscreen.

"What advice do you have for your client?" one reporter asked.

"To call me so we can make arrangements for him to turn himself in and deal with this situation the legal way."

"Mr. Murphy, you have a reputation for accepting only those clients you strongly believe are innocent. Why do you think Mr. Evans has chosen to go on the run if he's not guilty?"

"That's a question only Mr. Evans will be able to answer. Now, if you'll excuse me, I have no further comments."

The newscasters in the studio came back on.

"In an interesting twist, we learned this morning that the lead investigator, Detective Donald Nugent, has been removed from the case reportedly for failing to disclose a relationship that he had with the murdered victim, Cheryl Hunter. An anonymous tip and photos were sent to the police chief."

Larry… Troy thought to himself and smiled.

"We reached out to Detective Nugent who declined to comment. It's important to note that legally, Detective Nugent hasn't done anything wrong. This is a sensitive case and the department wants to make sure it's investigated objectively without bias. We've also learned that William Engelmann, the manager of the gym where Troy Evans narrowly escaped authorities, has not been heard from in over a week. Employees say they thought he was out of town as Engelmann has been known to take spur-of-the-moment trips, but loved ones say that he would have never gone this long without touching base with someone. Authorities aren't saying why they want to talk to Engelmann or if he's linked to the murder case. However, they are asking anyone with information about William Engelmann or Troy Evans to call 614-555-TIPS. You can remain anonymous."

Though he was still mentioned as the prime suspect, watching the news gave Troy a glimmer of hope. The cops were now also looking for Will and maybe, just maybe, they would catch up with him, and Troy would finally be cleared.

Chapter 26: A Quick Hustle

Troy tried unsuccessfully to contact Lloyd and tell him about the meeting with Rio. He left a message, hoping the television/movie fanatic would pose as "Jermaine" so Troy could sneak up behind Rio without the concern of being recognized by the deejay. Plus, he needed a ride to the location. Public transportation was too risky. Being in public, in general, was a big risk, but Troy had to find out the extent of Rio's involvement. He wouldn't be able to do so by phone.

As it got closer to his meeting time, Troy enacted another plan. After eating the burger and fries Eric had been kind enough to bring home for dinner, Troy timidly asked if he could borrow Eric's car after calling the restaurant and leaving a cancellation message for Rio. The quirky pastor was all too eager to help as long as Troy promised to keep the playing of secular music to a minimum. Of all the things Eric could have been concerned about, Troy wondered how in the world music had made the top of the list. He got the keys to Eric's Taurus and headed to the meeting.

Troy sat outside the bar and grill where he'd arranged to meet Rio and waited for him to arrive. Troy had chosen this location because it was busy with a lot of college students who would be too caught up in their own worlds to pay close attention to him. Once Troy witnessed Rio go inside, he pulled the Taurus in front of Rio's car and got out, knowing he'd only have a few minutes before his plan was set into action. Concealed in a baseball cap and sunglasses, Troy knelt down pretending to work on his tire. As expected, Rio soon came out, asking how long he'd be. Troy kept his head down as he responded, "Hopefully not more than ten or fifteen minutes. Would you mind giving me a hand? It'll speed up the process."

Rio's impatience rang loud and clear through his heavy sigh as he bent down to help. As soon as Troy lifted his head, Rio's eyes danced with fear and Troy could tell immediately that the deejay had recognized him. With his gun pointed in the young man's direction, Troy ordered him to slowly get up and get behind the wheel while he himself slid into the backseat. Having a third party drive Eric's car wasn't something the two had discussed. Luckily, it hadn't been one of Eric's concerns. The pastor would be pleased to know that Troy didn't have any secular music floating through his airways. "Try anything funny and I will blow out your brains," he said to the dude before instructing him to drive to a nearby park. Rio tried to plead his way out of the situation by playing clueless, but Troy wasn't having it. "Where's Will?"

"I don't know. I haven't seen him since the last time I saw you at the gym. When I left, he was in the parking lot talkin' to some short chick with long hair. They were arguing about something. Will left and she got into a black truck."

Troy was certain Rio was speaking of Cheryl and it confirmed his suspicions about Will's involvement. "What was your role in setting me up for Cheryl's murder?"

"Man, I don't know nuthin' about no murder, I swear."

Troy pressed the gun harder into Rio's skull. "My patience tank is low. Start talking or I will pull the trigger."

"You're a cop, man, you can't do that."

"Not anymore. Thanks to you and your buddies, I'm thought to be a murderer. What's one more body when my best-case scenario is life in prison?"

Like an accomplice offered a reduced sentence for turning State's evidence, the hard-edged-looking thug sang like a bird. Rio revealed that he'd been approached one day at the gym and offered five hundred dollars and eighty hours of personal training services to keep an eye on Troy whenever he was there. If Heidi, the employee Troy met yesterday, had not told him about Rio getting the most hours of personal training, Troy probably would not have believed him. Still, he questioned Rio's common sense. "That didn't sound weird to you?"

"I didn't ask no questions, man. I was just trynna hit a quick lick. I got a felony on my record and ain't nobody trynna hire a brotha. He said it was a quick hustle and if you confronted me, to play it off like you were being paranoid."

"Who's 'he'? Will?"

"Naw, the old guy that's always there flirtin' wit' all the females."

"*Charlie?*"

"Yeah, that's him. He would text me when you were on your way to the gym and tell me to come."

Troy wondered how Charlie was able to keep up with his whereabouts, but then he remembered Lloyd's theory of them planting something in his phone while at the gym. That made sense considering how much Cheryl had known about him. His insides smoldered at the thought of his privacy being invaded to such an extent. "Tell me what else you know." Troy tapped Rio's head with the tip of the gun as if that would jog his memory.

"That's it, man. I promise. Charlie paid me and hooked me up at the gym. I did what I was supposed to do and went about my business."

When questioned about taking the pictures at the motel and draining all the money out of his and Natalie's accounts, Rio didn't know anything. Thus, Troy was led to believe that it was either Will or Charlie whose image was in the background of the motel pictures and, if Troy was a betting man, he'd put his money on Charlie since he always wore baseball caps. Troy was starting to piece everything together now. Rio had been used as a pawn so that if Troy began to suspect anyone at the gym, it would be him. But, the way it was all looking, it seemed like Charlie was the front man, Will took care of things at the gym, and Cheryl and Chyanne worked behind the scenes. Suddenly, another revelation hit him! *"I bet they also had eyes on you,"* Lloyd had said, and exactly whose eyes had become painfully obvious as similarities between Cheryl and his neighbor were becoming more apparent. Both were petite with a similar skin complexion and long hair. Ann was thirty-six this time last year, which meant she was now thirty-seven. Forty-six, Cheryl's age, minus nine was thirty-seven, the exact age Cheryl's sister would be!

To top it off, the view of Troy's place was crystal clear from across the street at Ann's house. Then, there was Charlie who'd become a frequent visitor of Ms. Harrow's, if that was even her real last name. Both she and Charlie had plenty of opportunities to keep track of his comings and goings. The final element that stitched it all together for Troy was that Ann was at the gym yesterday when he arrived, giving her the perfect chance to call the police and plant the knife in his truck, thanks to the broken alarm!

Troy's first thought was that he was glad RJ had gotten his family safely out of the house. Troy hadn't confirmed it with RJ, but he knew his friend to be a family man himself and Troy trusted that RJ had taken care of things. Troy's second thought was to expose Ann/Chyanne and friends for the murdering, greedy hustlers they were. Troy assumed that Will had taken off because he either had not known about the entire plan to set him up and kill Cheryl or had gotten cold feet about enacting it. The latter would explain why Will had wanted to talk to Troy. Perhaps Will had been trying to warn him after realizing that he'd gotten in with the criminals way over his head. Troy was determined that every last one of them would be held accountable for their actions. To do so, he needed the help of another new friend.

Chapter 27: Number Two

After he'd gotten all the information from Rio, which he learned was short for Mario, Troy made him get out of the car. He left him at the park, telling the dude to use the several-mile hike to think about his future and how he needed to be careful about "quick licks" if he didn't' want to find himself back in the pen. Troy also warned him that his life could be in danger and that he should lay low for a while. Mario was receptive to Troy's advice and even offered a "my bad" apology for the unsuspecting role he'd played in Troy's trouble. Overall, he seemed like a good kid who'd made some bad life choices that came with the consequence of incarceration. If Troy was in a Boy Scout Big Brother sort of mood, he would have taken the time to hear Mario's story. But, he wasn't. He was in a problem-solving mode, ready to crack a case and be reunited with his family.

On his way back to Eric's, Troy tried calling the number he'd gotten for Charlie from the deejay only to learn it was disconnected. Once again, he tried calling Lloyd, still to no avail. He tried not to let his thoughts go wild with speculations about Lloyd's character. The guy had helped him and if Lloyd was in cahoots with Troy's conspirators, Troy was certain that he'd find himself in jail right now.

Eric was kneeling in the "sanctuary" when Troy arrived. Troy tiptoed past him into the den where he used Eric's laptop to look up the number to the gym, hoping Shay would be there. He was disappointed and surprised when someone else answered, but he asked for Shay anyhow.

"No, I'm covering her shift. Is there something I can help you with?" the lady asked.

"This is Detective Coleman. I was one of the officers there yesterday during the incident with Troy Evans." That wasn't a *total* lie. "We're still searching for Mr. Evans. It's my understanding that he and Miss Donovan were friends and I need to speak with her. Is there any way you can give me her contact information?"

It didn't take much prodding, if any, for the lady to cave. She was spooked by the murder accusations flying around and basically said to h-e-double hockey sticks with company policy. Within minutes, Troy had Shay's cell phone number. He thanked her for her cooperation with the "investigation" and hung up just as Eric came into the room.

"How was your meeting?"

"Good. I have a new lead to follow. I'm pretty certain I know who it is that set me up."

"Praise God! I'm glad I took the time to fast and pray for you while you were away."

Praying, Troy could see, but *fasting*...was it really that deep? He hadn't been gone that long. Plus, he and Eric had eaten less than two hours before he left.

"Sometimes I have an evening snack," Eric explained, likely because Troy's perplexity couldn't be masked. "I skipped it tonight so I could spend time with the Lord and intercede on your behalf."

"Thank you," Troy said hesitantly, not knowing what the appropriate response should be. He questioned if it was the right one because silence ensued afterward.

"Well, I'll get out of your hair so you can get back to what you were doing. I look forward to our devotional and prayer time tomorrow."

Oh, yeah...that. "Me, too," Troy replied and immediately dialed Shay as soon as Eric left. Caught off guard by the professional, yet sultry voice of the woman who answered, Troy glanced at the number he'd written down, comparing it with the one he dialed. "Um, hi, I was trying to reach Shay Donovan. Do I have the right number?"

"Yes. May I ask who's calling?"

He thought for a moment. Jermaine Coleman wouldn't get her to the phone if she was screening calls. But, he knew what would. "Tell her it's Southie."

There was a muffled sound of noise before Shay's voice came gushing through the phone. "Oh, my gawd, Troy! What's goin' on? 'Da PoPo were at 'da gym questionin' er'body yesterday. 'Dey called today wantin' me to come to some lineup, but I told 'em I didn't see nuttin' and I don't know nuttin' about nuttin'! I didn't tell 'em we was spose to meet at 'da gym or anything 'bout Will. I didn't know if I should tell 'em 'bout whatchu said 'bout Will, but I did tell 'em you ain't no killer, though. I been callin' yo' phone and it keeps goin' to voicemail. I been so worried 'bout you. You all right? Where you at? You need me to come gitchu?"

"No. I'm good. I do need a favor, though. Is there a way you can talk in private? I'm a little nervous about your friend overhearing our conversation."

"Oh, don't worry 'bout her. She ain't go say nuttin'. She went to 'da bathroom anyway and I think she gotta do number two, so we good. What's up?"

Without disclosing his conversation with Mario, Troy informed her that Charlie was also involved. "The lady I'm accused of murdering had a sister. I think Charlie, Will, Cheryl, and her sister, Chyanne, were all in this thing together to fake Cheryl's death and cash in on her life insurance policy. I also believe Chyanne is the one who killed Cheryl. She's been going by the alias Ann Harrow and posing as my neighbor. I also think Will got spooked after Cheryl's murder and wanted out. Perhaps that's why he was acting weird the last time we both saw him. I think he left town because he got in too deep."

"Ann Harrow… Why does 'dat name sound familiar?"

"She's a member of the gym." Troy described her.

"Okay. I know who you talkin' 'bout now. How you git from 'da Cheryl chick and Will to her and Charlie?"

"I met someone with an inside scoop. Plus, Ann was there when I arrived yesterday and she left right before the police came."

Shay was eerily quiet for a few moments. "If all 'dat's true, 'den on 'da real, Will ain't as innocent as you wanna believe. What if he used me to lure you to 'da gym? Check 'dis out… He been M.I.A. for over a week and all of a sudden he comes to my place sayin' he's leavin' town, but first he goin' to 'da gym. You and me both go, but he don't neva show up. 'Den your neighbor leaves after you get 'dere and all of a sudden 'da PoPo comes. It seems like more of a setup. What if Will only told me 'bout goin' to 'da gym 'cuz he knew I would tell you?"

Shay's theory was plausible. When Troy first enlisted Shay's help, he'd called her from his cell phone, which had been cloned! They'd been keeping tabs on him, thus making his conspirators privy to her involvement. "I think you might be on to something," he said, impressed by Shay's analytical skills and disappointed that he hadn't connected those dots.

"'Dat's why I'm stayin' at my friend's," Shay continued. "On 'da real, I'm a li'l bit scurd. Wit' Will on 'da loose and now you tell me 'bout 'dese otha folks, I don't wanna be at home by myself. He know where I live and I ain't trynna end up like 'dat dead chick!"

Hearing the fear in her voice, Troy felt bad for getting Shay entangled in this mess. "I'm sorry, I should have left you out of it."

"You cool. I'm in now and I can't git out until 'dey all git caught. It is what it is. We in 'dis together. You said you needed a favor. What's up?"

Troy smiled to himself. Shay really was a ride-or-die friend. To think, he'd spent so much time trying to avoid her and now she was one of his allies. Same as Eric. He needed them both and was *almost* becoming fond of Eric's strangeness and Shay's ghetto-fabulousness. They had good hearts, which was more than he could say about Will. Troy laid out the theory about Cheryl cashing out her life insurance policy without Chyanne's knowledge. "I bet by now she's tried to collect the money and found herself in for a rude awakening."

"If you know all 'dis, why you ain't goin' to 'da PoPo?"

"Because I need proof and that's where you come in. I need you to access Ann Harrow's records at the gym so I can get her number."

"I don't understand. Why go through all 'dis if you know 'dis chick lives by you? Why not just go to her house and put her in check?"

"I wish it was that simple, Shay, but I can't get to her house because the cops are probably watching mine. Since I can't get to her in person, I'll contact her. I want her to think I have the money."

"Do you?"

"Let's put it this way, I have a better idea of where it's at than she does."

"I can't git to 'da gym tonight. I called off 'cuz I was scurd after everything, and if I show up 'dis time of night, it's gon' look suspicious. I'll try and git her info for you tomorrow."

"Cool. If, for some reason, you don't have her contact information, get Charlie's. The number I have for him is no good, but I can draw her out through him if need be."

"'Kay. I need a number where I can hitchu back."

"I'll call you say around noon tomorrow. Will that be enough time?"

"Yeah, it should be."

"Be careful. If you see Ann or Charlie, don't let on that they are suspects. What I'm asking you to do could be dangerous and I don't want you to get hurt over this. I'd never get if off of my conscience."

"Aw, Southie, 'dat's so nice for you to be worried 'bout me, but don't worry yo' sexy self. I'll be okay."

"Thanks, Shay. I'll owe you one when this is all over."

"Oooh, maybe you can take me out to dinner!"

"I have a better idea. I'll ask my wife to cook and invite you over for dinner one day. I'm sure Natalie won't mind. She'll be grateful for your help as well."

Shay playfully sucked her teeth. "On 'da real, dat's not how I envisioned our first date, but I guess it'll do 'cuz you married. Shay Donovan don't mess wit' no married men. Uh-uh, hun-nee, God don't like ugly! Like I told you before, Imma respect your vows."

"Okay, thank you. I'll talk to you tomorrow." After they hung up, Troy had a disturbing thought. What if they'd cloned Shay's phone, too!

Chapter 28: Nervous Nellie

It was in the twilight of the night when Lloyd finally got in touch with Troy. "I'm sorry about the delay. Apparently, there was an anonymous tip called in about me possibly being the one who helped you evade authorities." Lloyd told Troy how the police had come to his home late Monday evening to question him. "It's a good thing you weren't here. I know this is Chyanne's doing. If she saw the news stories, it wouldn't be hard for her to put two-and-two together. They put me in a lineup, but no one was able to make a clear identification so they had to let me go. What new revelations you got to share?"

Troy updated him about his conversation with Mario and all he'd learned. "I'm ninety-nine-point-nine percent certain that the lady across the street from me is Chyanne."

Once Troy described to Lloyd the similarities between "Ann" and Cheryl, Lloyd was also convinced, especially after learning she claimed to be a work-at-home IT specialist. He said it was the perfect cover for a computer hacker. "So, all this time she's been hiding in plain sight. I didn't know she had a child though," he stated, "but I know firsthand how that conniving wench can be. I wouldn't put it past Chyanne to have kept her daughter a secret until it benefited her not to do so, or to stoop so low as to pass someone else's daughter off as her own. She isn't above using and harming children to suit her purposes."

Lloyd told Troy a chilling story about how Chyanne had orchestrated things so that Cheryl found pornographic images of children on their home computer when he and Cheryl were married. "It freaked Cheryl out because some pictures were of children in our neighborhood. Children that I used to coach in Little League baseball! I never took any sort of inappropriate pictures of any of them. Chyanne had moved in with us by that time, and I tried to tell Cheryl that her sister had set me up, but Cheryl didn't believe me because she and I were the only ones who had the password. She kicked me out and I left gladly because I didn't want to be under the same roof with Chyanne. Cheryl never turned me in and I think it's because deep down, she knew that I wasn't that type of guy. I quit coaching because I didn't want to catch a case. Allegations can be damaging to a person's reputation and I wasn't willing to take that risk. I really wanted things to work out with Cheryl, but Chyanne got into her head, and my relationship with Cheryl was never the same. I'm telling you, Chyanne is evil. She's like a chameleon. She'll manipulate any situation or person to get what she wants. If I'm right about her calling in the tip, which I think I am, then that means she knows we're on to her. It's a good thing you got your family out of there."

Troy had been thinking the same thing. "I have a connection at the gym getting her number for me. I plan to call Chyanne and make her think I have the money. I'll take your advice and record our conversation. I'm hoping she'll admit to everything. If so, I'll make arrangements with my lawyer to turn myself in and hand over the recording until everything gets sorted out."

"For a guy who doesn't watch a lot of TV, you know that's a classic move. They do stuff like that all the time. Let's hope it works in real life, though. Chyanne is smart and may not admit to anything over the phone if she thinks it's a trap. We need a plan B."

Troy didn't have a second option. One way or another, he had to get a confession from Chyanne and ensure that it got to the police. Hopefully, she'd implicate both Will and Charlie as well. As much as Troy hated to admit it, the betrayal of his longtime acquaintance stung a little. Troy had turned a blind eye to suspicions he had of Will's involvement in possible marijuana distribution. He never called Will out during the times when he knew Will was high. All it would have taken was for Troy to drop a bug in the ear of someone in Narcotics and they would have been all over Will like flies on cow's poop. But, Troy had let him be because he thought Will was a good guy—so much so that Troy had started to feel a slight bit of sympathy for him, thinking that Will had started to regret getting involved with Cheryl and crew and tried to warn him. But, his former academy buddy had played him as well as Jordan played basketball. Wrong or not, there was part of Troy that wanted Will to suffer the most for his duplicity.

Troy's anxiety about everything displayed itself through insomnia. He stayed up until close to three thinking about the entire situation from beginning to end. He had to force himself conscious when Eric awoke him Wednesday morning for the ritual. Eric was disappointed that Troy had not gotten around to reading Psalm 57 yesterday, but was excited that the Lord had given him a different scripture to share on this morning. To ensure that Troy wouldn't miss out, Eric allotted time for them to read it together.

"Are you familiar with Psalm 23?" Eric asked.

"Yes."

Nodding with approval, he added, "I figured you would be. It's a popular passage even to sinners and immature saints." Eric looked at him as if he were trying to determine which category Troy fit most. "When I was communing with the Father, there was a burden on my heart for us to meditate on Psalm 23 during our devotional portion this morning. Here, read it for yourself." Eric handed Troy a Bible already opened to the passage. Troy read anyhow, though he already knew it by heart.

1 *The Lord is my shepherd; I shall not want.*

2 *He maketh me to lie down in green pastures: he leadeth me beside the still waters.*

3 *He restoreth my soul: he leadeth me in the paths of righteousness for his name's sake.*

4 *Yea, though I walk through the valley of the shadow of death, I will fear no evil: for thou art with me; thy rod and thy staff they comfort me.*

5 *Thou preparest a table before me in the presence of mine enemies: thou anointest my head with oil; my cup runneth over.*

6 *Surely goodness and mercy shall follow me all the days of my life: and I will dwell in the house of the Lord for ever.*

"What you're going through right now is designed to kill you," Eric stated. "Your marriage, your career, and your reputation are all facing destruction, but understand that the power this storm is displaying is not real. It's merely a *shadow* of death, meant to make you believe that you're defeated, but as the psalmist said, fear no evil. God is with you." Eric continued his mini-sermon about God being in control of things no matter how long and dark Troy's valley may seem and how the Lord would see to it that Troy's enemies did not triumph over him. Surprisingly, Troy found his level of anxiety decreasing. Eric's words of encouragement had worked. "On 'da real," as Shay would say, Troy felt that Eric's pep talk would have been just as effective in a few hours when the sun rose as it was while it was dark out, but Troy was in no position to argue his point. "Think about how it is you got into this situation and what you can learn from it," the pastor suggested. It didn't take much thought. Troy already knew. Things would have never gotten this deep had he been honest with Natalie about his past relationship and interactions with Cheryl from the beginning. It was all the secrecy that had initially gotten him into this mess in the first place, and it would ultimately be the truth that would set him free.

When the buzzer sounded to signify that the devotional portion had ended and it was time to start praying, Troy meditated on Psalm 23 for a while until he dozed off. He was awakened promptly at 7:06 a.m. by the sharp and condescending tone of Eric's voice, rebuking him for falling asleep like the disciples had done to Jesus when He was praying in the Garden before being taken into custody and ultimately being crucified. Troy let Eric say his piece with no argument. When he'd finished his admonishment, Eric said that he would run out for a little while and that Troy could use his car upon his return. He'd graciously canceled Wednesday night Bible study at his church in Sandusky so that he could "be of service" to Troy. It took great restraint for Troy to stifle his brewing curiosity of wanting to know if Eric's "church" had grown in membership from only being him and his elderly mother.

After Eric left, Troy entertained a brief call from Lloyd who said that he was going to see what kind of dirt he could find on "Ann Harrow." "In the event that a phone confession doesn't work, I'll return the favor of calling in an anonymous tip. Maybe we can get the cops to take her in for questioning on identity theft alone. That should buy us some time if we need it. Call me after you talk to her."

When the call ended, Troy continued to lie on the couch where he drifted in and out while awaiting until noon, the appointed time to call Shay.

"I'm so sorry!" Natalie said with extreme embarrassment to Ms. Fritz, Nate's pre-school administrator, who'd called her Wednesday morning to pick Nate up early after he'd lost his mind!

"Like I said, I know this isn't typical behavior for him. I'm sure you're all under a lot of stress with what's been going on." She paused like she was waiting for Natalie to comment. When Natalie didn't take the bait, Ms. Fritz continued, "There won't be any type of official reprimand on his school record, but I think it'll be best if you don't bring him back on Friday to give the situation a chance to die down. The other mom is pretty perturbed as I'm sure you can imagine."

"Yes, I understand. Thank you for working with me."

"Not a problem." Ms. Fritz bent over to look Nate in the eyes. "You be a good boy for your mommy and I'll see you next week, okay?"

"'Kay," Nate responded softly and Natalie wanted to snatch him up for looking so pitiful.

It was hard for her to tell if his remorse was genuine or rather a result of wondering what his punishment would be. The tears he forced out when they got inside the car infuriated her and she ordered him to *"be quiet and not make another sound if you know what's good for you!"* Apparently, he did know because Nate didn't utter a peep. Natalie checked her rearview mirror and sure enough, that same unmarked cop car was following her like she was going to be silly enough to lead them to her husband if she knew where Troy was! She purposely avoided the highway and took the streets back to Lisa's simply to be ornery, listening to gospel music on the way to calm her nerves.

By the time she made it back to the Hampton household, Natalie had a stream of tears rolling down her face. Songs like "He Saw the Best in Me" and "Never Would Have Made It" by Marvin Sapp had caused her to reflect on the many trials in her life and how God had brought her through them. She was certain that she never would have made it through her childhood had it not been for Him. And, as an adult, when she had become someone others thought was detestable, God still saw the best in her. He saved her. Right now, He was also saving Nate from being on the verge of getting child abused as she couldn't, with good conscience, lay a hand on her son after such a spirit-filled ride.

When they walked into Lisa's, Chandler was playfully roaring like a lion at Ebony and Ean who squealed with laughter. They had that eerie twin thing going on between them again. They'd both cried when she'd left and now neither seemed fazed by her entrance. Chandler asked Nate if he wanted to play with them and Nate mumbled something about not wanting to be bothered with monkey babies. Now, he was being mean! Natalie warned him that he'd better not refer to Ean and Ebony like that again and sent him upstairs to wait for her. "Go in the room I'm in, not Chandler's room!" she added, thinking her five-year-old might try to be witty by going in his friend's room to play.

"Is everything okay?" Lisa asked.

Natalie, who had been too embarrassed and shocked to fill Lisa in on why the school had called, now told her the full story.

"Oh, my gosh! Are you serious?" Lisa covered her mouth with her hands.

"I wish I wasn't. He's not allowed to go back on Friday. I hope I don't see that little boy's mom when I take him next week. I mean, what do I say? 'Ma'am, I'm sorry my son peed on yours?'"

Lisa burst out laughing. "I'm sorry, it's not funny. I can only imagine how you feel."

The story Natalie had been given was that Nate and another little boy were in the bathroom that contained one urinal and two stalls. Both kids wanted to use the urinal, but the other boy got there first and Nate was mad because he said the boy "dished" him. Instead of going into a stall or waiting until the urinal was free, Nate chose an extremely unsanitary approach by peeing on the boy. The other child immediately ran out to tell a teacher and when confronted, Nate claimed it was an accident.

"It's really not funny." Lisa continued trying to contain her laugh as she heard the details. "What are you going to do?"

"Girl, I don't know." This would have been one of those things that Natalie deferred to Troy to handle. "At first I was planning to beat his butt, but I can't bring myself to do it under the circumstances. I'm too emotional. I need to go upstairs before I talk myself into trying that German chocolate cake you made for dinner yesterday since everyone said it was delicious."

"There's plenty of it left if you want some. You want me to cut you a piece?"

"Maybe later when I have a level head. I don't want to get into any emotional eating habits. These hips won't be able to handle it. That's why I didn't have any last night. My skinny jeans are already starting to fit like leggings."

Lisa laughed. "You are so silly. If you want to go upstairs, please feel free to do so without worrying about your babies; I got them. I'm going to fix lunch in a little bit."

"Thanks so much. I really appreciate you and RJ opening your home to us. I wish you would accept money for the extra groceries RJ bought."

Lisa playfully dismissed Natalie's comment by flipping her wrist. "Girl, please. This is nothing. We will forever be grateful for all

Troy has done for us." No additional words were needed. Natalie understood. Troy had met the Hamptons when they were in times of trouble due to former friends of Lisa's turned enemies who sought to ruin both her and RJ's life. The Hamptons felt they owed Troy something, but Natalie knew her husband. He hadn't called RJ to come get them because of some IOU. Troy had called RJ because he saw a man he could trust to look after his family when he couldn't. Natalie smiled as she was going up the stairs to speak with Nate, confident that their current predicament was simply another one of those times when she'd look back and say that they "Never Would Have Made It."

Nate was knocked out when Natalie got to the room. She took the opportunity to lie down with him and stared at the ceiling. This was the room that she and the twins had stayed the past two nights. Nate had slept in Chandler's room with him. Though Natalie had tried not to worry about Troy, her mind couldn't help but wonder where he was. She hadn't seen any reports about him being dead or arrested so that, in and of itself, gave her peace that he was okay. She missed him, and if her heart ached the way it did, she could only imagine what their five-year-old was feeling.

Natalie ignored her mother-in-law's call when her cell phone rang. She wasn't in the mood to respond to questions that had already been asked or to repeat "I don't know" a dozen times to new ones. Staying with Lisa and RJ saved her from playing hostess to Di who was ready to hop on a red-eye from Texas Monday night the moment she learned about Troy going on the run.

"I need to be there to help you with those babies," Diane had declared.

"I appreciate the offer, but I'm staying with a friend and there's not enough room for all of us." Natalie skipped the part about Troy sending RJ after them. Despite Natalie's assertion that she was fine, Diane continued to call multiple times a day to check on her. Though not on purpose, Diane was actually starting to worry her. Her mother-in-law had talked a good game that night she fussed at Natalie about trusting in God when Natalie had been convinced of Troy's infidelity, but now Diane had failed to follow her own advice. When they spoke, Natalie found herself expending energy trying to calm his mother and Natalie didn't have the strength to do so at this moment.

The only other people Natalie had spoken with since Monday evening had been Corrine, Aneetra, and Richard. Corrine was a nervous Nellie like Di, but Natalie had more patience with her daughter than her mother-in-law. Realizing that the last time Corrine was at their house, she'd been left with the impression that Troy had committed adultery, Natalie made sure to clarify things without going into detail about Cheryl's fake diary. With Troy on the run, Natalie was concerned that the cops might have her phone tapped and she didn't want to say anything that could inadvertently incriminate her husband. Natalie's main objective with talking to Corrine was to reassure her daughter that all was well and that she fully believed in and supported Troy.

Bless her heart, Corrine volunteered to take off of work to help with the kids, but Natalie told her it wasn't necessary. She said the same to Aneetra who had made a similar offer. In addition, Aneetra had invited Natalie and crew to come stay at her house and, truthfully, Natalie would have likely been more comfortable there because of the relationship she and Aneetra had. However, she didn't want to offend Lisa or RJ by leaving. Besides, despite his mishap at school earlier, being at the Hamptons' was best for Nate. Chandler was there to play with him and that kept him from asking so many questions about Troy.

Natalie's phone call with Richard was sort of stressful. Somewhat like a father figure to her, Richard had done the protective thing initially. He apologized for missing her call and said that he had been in a meeting at the time. After making sure that she and the kids were okay, he began lecturing her about Troy's actions and encouraging her to tell him to turn himself in.

"I don't know where he is," Natalie had insisted though she doubted Richard was convinced.

"I know he's scared, but this is not the way to handle things."

When Richard suggested that she appear on television with his attorney and plead with him to surrender, Natalie quickly objected, stating that she wasn't going to put her face on camera when the real killer was still on the loose. That was partly true. The other reason was that she wasn't going to be used to get her husband behind bars. Troy knew the risks he was taking by handling things this way and, though she might not have agreed, she trusted him.

Natalie had started dozing off when she heard Lisa's home phone ring. Soon there were footsteps coming up the stairs and a knock on the bedroom door. "I'm sorry to disturb you. Someone named Ann is on the line."

"*My neighbor?*" Natalie asked with uncertainty. Lisa shrugged and handed her the phone. "Hello?"

"Hi, this is Ann, the lady who lives across the street from you. I was told to call this number in case your cell phone was tapped. I have a message for you from Troy."

Chapter 29: What Would Jesus Say

"Were you able to get Ann's number?" Troy asked Shay.

"I didn't find a number for her, but I have one for 'da old-timer." She recited it to him.

"Thu-*ank* you! I owe you one."

"Yeah, yeah… I know, you gon' have your wife cook me dinner. Ooh, I can't wait." Her playful sarcasm made him laugh. "On 'da real though, Southie, if you need anything else, don't hesitate to call me. I want 'dese crazy people off 'da streets so I can go back to livin' my life. You know Imma be in Hollywood one day, right?"

He didn't want to hurt her feelings, so with all sincerity, he said, "I wish you all the best, Shay," and got off the phone to handle business. Seeing that he didn't have Chyanne's number, Troy couldn't get a confession from her, but he had another plan in mind. He'd attempt to turn Charlie against her and what better way to do that than to use the thing that made Charlie, Will, and Chyanne all co-conspirators in the first place…*money!*

Charlie answered on the second ring and Troy began to record their call. "Detective. What do I owe the pleasure of this call?" he said after Troy announced himself.

"Are you alone?"

"Chyanne isn't with me if that's what you mean."

"And Will?"

Charlie laughed wickedly. "He's not here either. Are you going to get to the point of why you're calling or will we play twenty questions?"

"You and your friends have done a good job at framing me. Now, I need your help to clear my name. I want you to help me expose Chyanne for her sister's murder. I know both you and Will were in this with her, but I'm willing to let one of y'all off the hook in exchange for your assistance. Are you in or should I contact Will?"

"Forgive my ignorance, but you're a wanted man and you're talking like you have the upper hand."

"Five hundred thousand dollars says that I do. It's the money from Cheryl's life insurance policy and every penny of it is yours if you follow through. I came to you first because quite frankly, I'm more upset with Will than I am you. He and I go way back and he betrayed me, so you can say that I'm partly motivated by revenge." Truthfully, Troy's conscience wouldn't allow Charlie to go scot-free, though Troy wanted him to think otherwise.

"I must say that's an interesting proposition, detective. If I wasn't in love with Chyanne, I might very well take you up on it. But, I have another option for you. Bring us the money; we'll leave town and never bother you or your family again. Before you hastily reject my offer," Charlie warned, "You may want to reconsider after talking to my new friend. Hold on a sec; I think she wants to say hi."

"Troy!" The sound of his wife's cry crushed him like an elephant would an ant.

"*Natalie!?!* Oh, my gosh, baby! Are you okay?"

"Yes." Troy could hear the tears she was holding back.

"What happened? Are the kids with you?"

"No. Ann called me at Lisa's saying she had a message from you, but it was a trick. I'm so sorry."

"No, babe. I'm sorry I got us into this. I'm going to get you out, okay?"

Natalie was no longer able to hold back her sorrow and Troy's chest tightened with pain as his sobbing wife spoke. "In case we don't get to celebrate our anniversary this weekend, please always remember that I love you."

"Please don't talk like that. We *will* celebrate our anniversary. We still have to get our couple's massage. Remember, you want me to request Brunhilda."

She chuckled slightly through her tears. "One more thing... please tell Lisa I said thank you for making the chocolate cake last night for dinner. Tell her I tasted it and everyone was right; it was delicious."

"What? Babe, that's not important right now."

"*Please.* I may never get the chance to do so myself. They have Charla, too, and Ann is—"

"Whoa! That's enough," Troy heard Charlie say as he snatched the phone away from her, but not before Troy heard Natalie repeat the message he was supposed to deliver to Lisa. Then there was a slap and a frightening yelp.

"*Natalie!*" Troy screamed.

"Are you starting to like my offer a little better now, detective?" came the sound of Charlie's creepy voice.

"You bas—"

"Now, now, watch your mouth," Charlie said patronizingly. "I thought you were a Christian man. What would Jesus say if He heard such filth come from you?" He then laughed with an evil undertone that made Troy shudder.

"You better not lay another hand on my wife or you'll be meeting Jesus sooner than you think!"

"Yeah, whatever. I don't judge people for believing in mythological characters. Here's the deal: bring me the money and you get your wife. Don't bring it and you become a widower. It's that simple. According to the conversations we've tapped into between you and your gym girlfriend, you know where it is. And since you brought Shay into this, bring her with you. She talks too much and we need to tie up that loose end as well. All of you can stay here until Chyanne and I leave town."

Troy may not have had his badge, but he still had his oath and cops never intentionally put civilians in harm's way. "No! I'm not giving y'all another hostage. Leave Shay out of it. I'll come to you, but I'm not bringing anything until you let Natalie and Charla go." Troy knew these psychopaths would kill whether they got the money or not. They'd have to settle for his life; not his wife's, or Charla's who didn't need to add this craziness on top of the issues she already had. "When I know they're safe, I'll reveal the location of the money, but not beforehand."

In the end, Charlie and Troy had struck a deal. Troy was to call back in three hours to get the address where the exchange for hostages and a half million was supposedly to take place. "Oh, and detective, if you're smart, you'll leave the cops out of this. The minute I hear sirens, I'll pull the trigger."

Chapter 30: Cray Crays

"Call the police!" RJ said when Troy called to warn him that he needed to get Lisa and all the kids out the house. RJ had already been one step ahead of him. Lisa had called him after Natalie left. At the time, Lisa had no idea where Natalie had gone, but she knew something wasn't right. Natalie's car was still at their house and she'd gone out the back, through their neighbor's property. Lisa believed those were the instructions Natalie had been given by the caller in order to avoid being trailed by the cops.

When Lisa got on the phone with her tearful apology about not being able to stop Natalie from leaving, Troy explained to her that she wasn't at fault. "With all she's going through, Natalie wanted me to tell you that the cake you made for dinner last night was good." Troy hoped that relaying that message would ease some of Lisa's guilt.

"But, I don't understand. She didn't have any cake. We talked about it, but she didn't want any at the moment. She went to lie down and then she got the phone call."

"Well, she must've had it without you knowing because she specifically said that she tasted it and to tell you that it was delicious."

Lisa was confused and Troy didn't have the time or mental capacity to debate the matter. His wife's life was on the line and his three hours to come up with a plan had been cut to two and a half by now. He got off the phone with the Hamptons and called Lloyd who also thought that he should involve the police.

"You can't play games with these people," he warned. "If I knew where the money was, I'd tell you, for real. This is a dangerous situation you're in. Sooner or later, they'll figure out that you don't have the money and kill Natalie."

"I know, but if you will help me get Natalie away from them, it'll never come to that." Troy presented his plan to Lloyd in detail.

"I might work. It reminds me of a movie I once saw—"

"Not now, Lloyd!"

"Okay! My bad. I just can't shake this feeling that something doesn't fit right. We know that Chyanne is the ring leader. I don't understand why she would let Charlie do all the negotiating like he's in charge. I bet she has a trick up her sleeve."

"So do I, my friend. So do I."

Troy had been all set to turn himself and the recording over to the police, but he had to ensure his wife's safety first. To do that, he'd use the criminals' ability to listen in to his phone conversations against them and called Shay, knowing they were eavesdropping on her line.

Shay seemed surprised to hear from him so soon, but listened intently as Troy laid out his entire conversation with Charlie.

"I don't understand. Why was he askin' for you to bring me?"

"They think you know too much. It's a trap to get us all in one place and kill us, but don't worry. I wouldn't dare have you come with me. I'm calling to tell you to leave your friend's house immediately. They've been recording your calls so they know where you're staying."

Shay cursed. "Are you for real?"

"Yes. Get out of there now!"

"Huh-nee, you ain't gotta tell me twice." It sounded like Shay grabbed her car keys that very moment. "Whatchu gonna do?"

"I'm going to meet Charlie, but I'm not bringing the money with me. First, they have to let Natalie go and when I know she's safe, I'll lead them to the cash."

"But, won't 'dey kill her if you don't show up wit' 'da money?"

"If they have Natalie, the money and me all in the same place, death is pretty much a guarantee. If their ultimate plan is to kill us, I'll make sure they do it broke. If they want the money as bad as I think they do, they'll let her go. In the end, I'll probably get killed, but that's a risk I'm willing to take as long as my wife remains unharmed."

"Wow! I admire 'da love you have for your wife. 'Dat's deep. On 'da real, I'm scurd as I don't know what, but Imma help you however I can 'cuz 'dey trippin' trynna kill er'body. How you gon' git to Charlie's?"

If Eric was back in time, Troy was going to use his car. If not, he'd ride with Lloyd since his incognito friend had already planned to meet him at Eric's house and follow behind him. The plan was for Troy to leave the place and lead Charlie on a wild goose chase, while Lloyd worked on getting Natalie and Charla to safety. Both he and Lloyd were banking that Charlie would not risk escorting Troy alone and that either Will or Chyanne would go along for the ride. Troy would put his money on Will so there could be additional muscle, but Lloyd said he bet Chyanne would be the one to accompany Charlie because she wouldn't trust anyone else to collect that much money outside of her presence. Knowing that someone was listening in on their conversation, Troy didn't want to say any of that on the phone. Instead, he told Shay that he was going to ride the bus.

"You ain't gotta ride no bus. Imma come gitchu."

"No. I don't want you involved."

"I already am. The minute 'dese cray crays started tappin' my phone and wantin' to kill me, I was already in. I ain't trynna go witchu to meet 'dem, but you can take my car if you want and Imma hide out somewhere else. I can't say where since people wanna use me and be all up in my business!" She intentionally got louder, like she wanted to make sure Chyanne and friends were aware that she was on to them.

Troy gave her proposal some thought. Having a sure ride was better than the uncertainty of not knowing when Eric would be home. It was also smarter that he and Lloyd drove separately rather than ride together. There was only one problem with hooking up with Shay: Troy didn't want to reveal Eric's address to her during this monitored phone call. He told her as much. "I'm sure they won't come here since I don't have the money with me. Still, I'm not willing to put anyone else in danger."

"I don't know how I can help you, 'den. There's no place for us to meet without 'dese mutha—"

"I know!" he said, cutting her off before she could fully get it out. Troy suggested they meet at the local precinct of the suburb in which Eric lived. He didn't say this, but it was only a few blocks from Eric's house. He chose the location for three reasons. The police station was the last place criminals willingly went, the likelihood that civilians would be around was slim, and even with the manhunt out for him, Troy was certain no one would be looking for him there. Troy instructed Shay to go someplace that Will would least suspect and stay there until he contacted her. She agreed, jokingly asking if, by helping today, that meant she had two dinner invitations coming. She tried to sound calm, but Troy heard the terror in her voice. "Shay, if Natalie and I make it out of this alive, you can come to our house for dinner for an entire week if you want."

She laughed nervously. "All right, Imma hold you to 'dat, Southie," she said before hanging up. Afterward, Troy called Lloyd to update him.

Chapter 31: Bucket List

As suspected, Charlie wasn't pleased with the alternate arrangements Troy had made on his own, and he threatened to blow Natalie's brains out on the spot if Troy didn't bring the money with him.

"You won't do it," Troy called his bluff, though it terrified him to gamble with his wife's life. "You won't kill her because, if you do, you get nothing and I'll have a half million dollars at my disposal to hunt you down until I find you. When I do, I'll torture you to the point that you'll welcome death."

Reluctantly, Charlie agreed to release his hostages upon Troy turning himself into his conspirators and gave Troy an address where they were to meet. He warned again that if he heard the cops, Natalie would be as good as dead. Troy believed him, which is why he vehemently refused to get the police involved when Lloyd suggested it again after Troy told him of the meeting place. Troy had a feeling that it wasn't going to be as easy as Charlie made it seem. There was no honor among thieves or killers, and Troy would be a fool to take Charlie at his word. That's why he'd brought Lloyd into the mix.

The suspicious part of Troy believed that Lloyd was keeping something from him. Maybe it was paranoia about trusting a stranger, especially with the well-being of his wife. But, Troy had to admit that, in the forty-eight hours, he'd known his new friend,

Lloyd had proven to be trustworthy thus far. Prayerfully, the TV/movie buff would come through now that Troy needed him the most. Natalie's life was on the line.

Eric got home shortly before Troy was about to leave to meet Shay. "Your countenance is different than it was before I left. Is everything okay?"

Not willing to drag Eric further into the situation than he already had, Troy simply told him that there was another lead. "If I don't make it back tonight, I'm either dead or in jail," he said bluntly.

"Where are you going? Do you need to use my car?"

"No. Someone is picking me up, but I appreciate the offer. Thank you for everything. The fact that you so willingly opened your home to me under the circumstances will always mean a lot."

Eric stood proudly with his chest out and his shoulders squared. "Proverbs 17:17 says that 'a friend loveth at all times, and a brother is born for adversity.' I believe the Lord had us meet for such a time as this. It has been my honor to be a vessel, serving both you and the Lord."

Despite the staunch manner in which he spoke, Eric also appeared sad that Troy was leaving. It was hard to imagine this dude having any real friends considering all of his weird mannerisms. It seemed like he led a very isolated and lonely life. Troy wondered if being here was as much a blessing to Eric as it had been to him. "Thanks, man. I'm not sure what I would have done without you." As Troy walked through the sanctuary to the door, Eric called out to him.

"Don't be afraid, my friend. Remember what we talked about this morning. This situation is merely a shadow of death. Fear no evil, for God is with you. Though it looks threatening, it won't kill you in the natural or the spiritual."

Getting killed was the least of his worries. Death was a risk he'd willingly signed up for when he became a cop. It was Natalie he was most concerned about. As he left, he started to recite Psalm 23 to himself, but thinking about his wife. *The Lord is my shepherd; I shall not want…*

Troy spotted Lloyd parked alongside the street about a block from the station. Shay pulled in minutes later in a dark reddish-brown sedan. "You drive 'cuz I'm too nervous." She slid into the passenger's seat and Troy hopped behind the wheel.

Her claw-like nails were gone and her blonde hair with its multi-colored tips had been dyed jet-black. She looked nice with the ghetto turned down a notch of two. Troy didn't tell her that. Instead he said, "I see you changed your appearance."

"I told you 'dese people got me freaked out. I'm trynna blend in wit' 'da general public."

"I'm really sorry for getting you involved. Where am I taking you?" he asked as he drove off.

"To a friend's. Imma stay wit' her 'til you call me. Drive like you goin' to 'da gym. She lives near it. I'll direct you when we git closer." It was about a fifteen-minute drive from the local precinct in Eric's suburb to the side of town where the gym was located. Troy checked the rearview mirror to make sure Lloyd was behind them. Shay stretched her neck to glance back. She'd changed her appearance, but not the way she dressed. The shirt she had on showed her cleavage and then some. Troy couldn't avoid seeing her tattooed breasts if he tried. "Is someone followin' us?"

"Yeah. It's the guy who helped me escape at the gym. He's going to make sure Natalie gets to safety."

"Cool. How you know him?"

"I don't really. He's the ex-husband of the lady I'm accused of murdering."

"*Shoot!* I forgot to tell my friend 'dat we on our way. Let me text her real quick." Shay pulled out her phone. "So you think 'dese people really gon' let your wife go?"

"Like I told you on the phone, if they want to kill her, they'll do it broke."

"I hurd 'dat! 'Dey betta do whatchu said 'den 'cuz five hundred thousand dollars is a lot of money. If I had 'dat much cash, 'da first thing I would do is take a trip somewhere I've never been. What aboutchu?"

"How'd you know how much money there is?"

"You told me. When you was tellin' me about 'da chick 'dat lives across 'da street, you said she killed her sister for the insurance money and 'dat it was a half million dollars."

"Hmph..." There were two things about Shay's statement that bothered Troy. When he spoke of Ann, he could have sworn that he referred to her as his neighbor, never specifying where she lived. He knew without a doubt that he never mentioned the amount of the insurance policy to *anyone* except Charlie. So Shay was in on this, too! *Danggit!* Now they all knew about Lloyd. Luckily, Troy still had an ace in his pocket; no one knew that he didn't really have the money. As long as he kept it that way, Natalie had a chance of surviving.

Natalie... Troy thought about his last conversation with his wife. "*Tell her I tasted it and everyone was right; it was delicious*," Natalie had requested he relay these words to Lisa who was certain that his wife hadn't had any cake. Yet, Natalie was insistent that he deliver the message. She'd even repeated it when Charlie snatched the phone from her. Troy eyed Shay who was still in her own world, reciting her bucket list of all the things she'd do if she had that kind of money. Her overly exposed breasts sat high with the help of a push-up bra for all of creation to see the word she had branded on her chest, and that's when Natalie's message started to make sense. "*It was delicious.*" Natalie had been trying to warn him of Shay's involvement!

The cell phone rang urgently and he answered, hoping to God that he hadn't been tricked by Lloyd, too! "What's up?"

"I had a buddy of mine run the license plates. Dude, that vehicle is registered to Chyanne Donovan! You're in the car with Cheryl's sister!"

As the newest bombshell exploded, Troy looked over and saw Chyanne smiling and pointing a gun in his direction. He hung up the phone being sure to hit the outside button so that anything Chyanne said to him in the car would be recorded.

Chapter 32: A Safe Place

"You might not believe this, but I actually like you." Magically, Chyanne's urban accent faded instantly and out came the smooth sounding voice of the woman who'd answered "Shay's" phone yesterday when Troy had called. "I can see why my sister had a thing for you. It was so hard to talk her into this plan at first. She really thought that you still held a spark for her." Chyanne sighed. "She could be so dumb when it came to men. I tried to tell her that you would never love her the way you love Natalie. I mean, for real, you and Natalie withstood some tests. Your marriage survived us hacking into your home computer and deleting her work files, the hotel pictures, taking your money, and being accused of murder. I'm impressed!"

"Shay's" absence of urban diction was replaced by lack of couth, in general. Troy wanted nothing more at that moment than to lodge a bullet in her throat, but his gun was tucked in his hip on the right side. There was no way he could get to it without her seeing and shooting him first. "So, who'd you really text a few moments ago? Charlie?"

"Yep. I had to tell him about our friend back there so he could be prepared. Having Lloyd trail you was an awesome idea. I didn't see it coming though I suspected he might have been the one to help you when Heidi described the man she saw. Now, I wish I would have gotten him arrested for child porn when I had the chance instead of only having Cheryl find it. The plan you and Lloyd had was brilliant. I have to give it to you, Southie. I can still call you that, right? I mean, we do have this love-hate thing going, but hopefully you understand that it's nothing personal. It's all about the money."

"Then why don't y'all let Natalie and Charla go? You have me now, and I meant what I said earlier; I'm not giving up the money until I know my wife is safe. There's no negotiating that. Let Lloyd get her and I'll give you every dime I have."

"How do I know Lloyd won't get to the money before we do?"

"He doesn't know where it is. Seriously, Chyanne, do you think I'd risk telling him where I hid five hundred thousand dollars? He'd get it and take off. The only reason I got him to help me is because I promised to cut him in. This was before I knew you'd taken my wife as a hostage, of course."

Chyanne contemplated for a moment. "Okay. You have a deal," she said reluctantly and pulled out her phone. "Hey, we have to let them go…*because* Troy won't give up the money if we don't… I don't like it either, but we have to. Harming her will only piss him off and now that people are on to us, we need to get out of town a-sap. *Yes*, I'm sure. Now get out of there. Lloyd's on his way and the police might be as well."

While Chyanne was distracted by arguing with Charlie about whether or not freeing their hostages was a smart move, Troy took the opportunity to try and get his gun. He kept his right hand on the steering wheel and crept his left one across his lap. He managed to touch the tip of the magazine when Chyanne caught him.

"I wouldn't do that if I were you!" He grimaced when she jammed the barrel of her gun into his rib before ripping his piece from his waist. Chyanne gave Charlie instructions to hide out somewhere until he heard from her and then had Troy call Lloyd and he could go get "the hostages." Soon Lloyd veered from behind them and Troy was ordered to drive to another location where they switched into a different vehicle in case Lloyd tried anything funny like sending the cops after them.

"So where are Ann and Will?" Troy asked while driving around aimlessly waiting to hear that his wife was okay before taking Chyanne to the money.

"Will's dead, honey. We killed him when he started playing detective on his own." According to Chyanne, Will had seen Cheryl get into the back of Troy's truck the day she drugged him and took those staged photographs with Charlie's assistance. Will confronted Cheryl about being in Troy's vehicle and she claimed it was part of her investigation and made him leave. Dissatisfied with her explanation, he came back later that night and started going through the records and questioning Shay about the use of Troy's credit card being billed for an excessive amount of personal training services for a different member. She played it off as a billing error, but Will still had his suspicions. "He started asking too many questions," Chyanne complained. "Then, we saw that text he sent to you about wanting to talk and we knew he had to go. He and 'Will Do' are resting peacefully at the bottom of a lake." Troy learned that Will had never been involved in the scheme to set him up. Will had been tricked into letting Chyanne work at the gym by believing he was part of an undercover FBI sting operation into the unethical corporate dealings of the gym franchise. Charlie, who'd been a member of the athletic facility for years, was well aware of Will's extracurricular activities involving marijuana. Though she'd already lost her job at the FBI, Cheryl pretended to bust him in the middle of a transaction and made a deal that, if he helped with her investigation, she'd see to it that charges were not officially filed against him. Thus, the plan was set in motion.

"Shay" was introduced as an FBI agent whom Will "hired" as the administrative assistant, giving her access to confidential client information. Her position also afforded her the opportunity to plant a cloning chip in Troy's cell phone that he stored during workouts in the lockers for which she had a master key. Upon learning that Ann was Troy's neighbor, Charlie hooked up with her and made frequent visits to her place so he could keep an eye on the comings and goings at Troy's house. Ann being at the gym the other day was a mere coincidence. In actuality, Charlie and Chyanne were a couple and the sole masterminds behind this entire scheme.

"I can't tell you how tired I was of pretending to be Will's dumb girlfriend. First of all, he is *so* not my type. I like my men to be edgier. Will was too soft. He cried like a little punk when he thought Cheryl was going to arrest him." She took a heavy breath. "I'm so glad that's over. I see the years I studied acting in college paid off, though, because I fooled you. In case you're wondering, the tattoo *is* real. It was Charlie's idea," she added like Troy really cared. He was busy processing her revelation about Will's murder. That news was going to be detrimental to Will's mother and especially his young nephew who already lacked positive male role models in his life.

"Why'd you kill Cheryl? I know you wanted the money, but why not fake her death and all of y'all live happily ever after off of her insurance."

"That was the plan, but she was too wishy-washy. One day she'd be all like 'yeah, I'm gonna make him pay for ruining my life,' and the next she'd be feeling bad. I didn't have time for her to keep taking me through all of those emotions. I knew she would blow the whole thing when Charlie discovered that she didn't leave the diary like she was supposed to do. The diary was supposed to incriminate you because of the lack of other physical evidence, but she chickened out and messed up everything. I had to sneak into her house and leave it for the police to find. When we saw your text that you were going over there, we thought about calling the cops and having them bust you going through her things. But we'd already decided to get rid of Cheryl by that time and we thought planting the knife in your truck would hold more weight than you being discovered at her house. But, I did call Donald Nugent the next morning pretending to be a neighbor who saw you at Cheryl's house the night before."

That explained the questions Nugent asked during the last interrogation. "You set me up to go in the gym so you could hide the murder weapon in my truck, huh?"

"Yep. I knew jacking up your alarm would work in our favor. Charlie is an expert mechanic and knows how to do all that stuff. At first, we were going to plant hairs and drops of blood, but when Cheryl started acting crazy and we were forced to kill her, the knife seemed more logical. Cheryl could still be alive right now if she would've listened. I kept trying to tell her that things were going much better than we'd planned. You helped us without even knowing it. We knew you would flip after she met with Natalie, but when you came over to her house and went off the way you did, oh, that was perfect! We had to seize the moment! You were so mad that you didn't even know I was there. She had an attitude because I didn't come out to help. I hid in the closet until after you left and then staged the scene a little and coaxed her into calling nine-one-one like we'd planned. Charlie did a great job impersonating you in the background, don't you think?"

Shut up! Troy wanted to say as he remembered the maroon car parked on the side of the street that he'd almost sideswiped that day. It was the same car that Chyanne had picked him up in. He also recalled Charla's words about a purple car. "So it was you who drove Cheryl to my house?"

"Yeah, we did that to mess with you. It was Cheryl's idea. I thought it was too risky, but she thought it would be funny. See what I mean about her being wishy-washy?"

"How'd you get Ann to go along with tricking Natalie?"

"Now that was easy! We had her and that googly-eyed daughter of hers chained up in the same room opposite one another and we put a bunch of food near Charla. As I'm sure you know, she has Prader-Willi Syndrome. It only took a few minutes of Ann watching her daughter eat like there was no tomorrow and she caved like the twin towers on nine-eleven. You should have seen the way Charla stuffed her face." Chyanne let out a screeching laugh. "It was so funny!"

This woman is sick! Troy thought to himself as he answered the ringing cell phone.

"*Troy!* Baby, I'm okay!" Hearing those words from Natalie was as soothing as a cold Popsicle on a hot summer day. "The police are here and this man is telling them everything he knows. Ann is too! And I hear that they caught the man who was holding us hostage a few blocks away. His car had run out of gas! You're going to be cleared, baby. Where are you? Are you on your way?"

"No. I still have some unfinished business to handle. I'm glad you're safe, babe. If I...," Troy found himself getting choked up and paused for a moment to clear his throat, "I may not make it home to celebrate our anniversary this weekend. Please never forget how much I love you." It pained him to hear her wail, begging him to come home. The only comfort he had was knowing that she was finally safe and when Lloyd got on the phone, Troy thanked him for all that he had done. "Do me a favor, please, and continue to look out for my family. I'm about to take Chyanne to the money and we both know she's going to kill me."

Chyanne squealed. Troy wasn't sure if it was a result of him mentioning the money or his death.

"Don't worry. As Michael told Leigh Anne in *The Blind Side* when she was a little scared about being in an unfamiliar neighborhood, 'I got your back.' You take care of yourself and try your best to get to a safe place."

"Okay," Troy responded before Chyanne ordered him to hang up and take her to get her money now that he knew the "missus" was safe. He did so with a smile in his heart having fully understood Lloyd's cryptic message. Troy didn't know why, but he knew exactly where the obsessed movie buff had directed him. Off to the vacant house on Dundee he went. Troy contemplated on whether or not to tell Chyanne that her boyfriend had been apprehended. Ultimately, he did after secreting making sure the phone call hadn't interrupted the recording. He thought it might spark some remorse. He was wrong. Chyanne's response was "so what?" She'd planned on killing him anyhow.

Chapter 33: A Little Shame

It was a few minutes before five when they pulled up at the small blue house that sat empty on Dundee Avenue, off of Hamilton Road on the city's east side. Troy drove the car all the way to the detached garage and turned it off.

"Whose house is this?" grilled Chyanne.

"A friend of mine owns it. He lives out of town and I check on the place for him from time-to-time to make sure it's not being vandalized," Troy repeated what Lloyd had told him verbatim. "It's vacant. This is where I hid the money."

"You better not be playing games with me, Troy. Don't think your wife or children are completely out of my reach. No one, not even Lloyd, can watch them twenty-four-seven. I got to Natalie once. I'm sure I can do it again."

"Shut up!" Troy didn't try to mask his irritation. There was a good chance he was about to die and he was determined to do it fearless. As Lloyd had said, the backdoor was open. Troy went in, looking around the cracked wooden floor, wondering what the next step was in his friend's grand plan.

"Where's the money!" Chyanne demanded, waving the gun at him. If she was a few feet closer, he could maneuver it away from her.

"I'm about to show you. If you will indulge me for a moment, please, I have one question for you first. How long have you been planning this?"

"For about a year or more. It was after Cheryl lost her job. I was at her house helping her go through some paperwork and I found the insurance policy listing me as the sole beneficiary. Imagine my surprise at the policy itself, *and* that Cheryl had kept it a secret from me. I was sure she told me everything, but I see she was better at keeping things than I thought. I didn't know she'd cashed it out until after we killed her. I would have preferred a million dollars, but five hundred thousand is still a nice chunk of change."

"Your sister loved you. Why would you manipulate her to the point of destroying her entire life?" As Chyanne talked, he inched closer, hoping to be able to take the weapon.

"By the time we met, I was beyond developing relationships. I learned I was adopted when I was fifteen. I overheard my parents, if that's what we want to call them, talking about how they regretted the day they brought me home. I admit, I was a hellion. I used to do things like pee in the lemonade and put itching powder in their shoes," Chyanne chortled. "I *loved* to see their reactions. They were fed up with me, though. They'd refused to give me my allowance one week, so when they were gone, I took all of their jewelry and sold it at a pawn shop where the owner was known for not asking questions. I got over three thousand dollars and spent every last dime at the mall. Don't look at me like that." Troy's disdain must've been apparent. "It was their fault. They raised me to think I could have and do whatever I wanted, but when I became a teenager, they all of a sudden wanted to have rules because they thought I was too spoiled and out of control. What-*ever!* Anyhow, when I heard them discussing the possibilities of what to do with me, I decided to take matters into my own hands. That night, I waited until they were sleeping and set the house on fire. Poor mom and dad didn't make it because *someone* had taken the batteries out of the smoke alarm." She gave an exaggerated sigh.

"I was an orphan for the second time around and went from foster home to foster home, learning how to hustle. When I became an adult, I went to college. At first I was going for computer forensics, but it was boring. I'd already learned everything they were teaching me and then some on my own. I tried acting for a little while because I thought it would be fun. I would've gotten my degree except the classes were too expensive and I ultimately had to drop out. That's when I made it my mission to find out about my birth family. I learned their tragic story and that I had a sister and I searched for Cheryl until I found her. I didn't expect to have a relationship with her; I was curious like anyone would be, and I was hoping to hit her up for a few dollars. I was broke and didn't have a place to stay and figured I could use the "we-are-blood" card for sympathy. I finally found Cheryl about ten years ago and she was *so* pathetic. All she did was cry and say how much she loved me and she'd never gone a day without thinking about me. I was looking at her like, 'Seriously, you don't even know me!" But, I could tell right away that she was like my adoptive parents, so eager to please that she didn't use common sense. When she heard my sad story, about how my other parents died and how I lived a rough life since the age of fifteen, I had her hooked and she'd been wrapped around my finger ever since."

Troy was dumbfounded. Chyanne was a bona fide psychopath!

"Okay, enough about me. Now give me my money," she demanded, turning on her "Shay" voice. "'Cuz Imma 'bout to blow yo' brains out if you keep messin' around."

Troy felt confident enough that he could get the pistol away from her, and as he was about to make his move, a male voice came from the side. "Put the gun down!" Chyanne turned to face Don Nugent and obediently laid her gun on the floor. "Move out the way, Troy!" he ordered.

"Well, well…look at the roly-poly my sister rejected in high school coming to save the day. Too bad your efforts are in vain." Chyanne reached from behind her back and grabbed the gun she'd confiscated from Troy, but she wasn't quick enough. Before she could pull the trigger, Nugent shot her straight through the heart.

Troy's head was reeling from all the commotion as he watched Chyanne's body go limp and crash to the floor.

"Lloyd called me earlier," Nugent explained. "He told me how they had your wife and that you were going to exchange her freedom for the money. He was planning to send you here and wanted me around to have your back. He thought I'd jump at the opportunity to redeem myself since I've been embarrassed by getting removed from the case."

Troy let out a big exhale. "Thanks, man!" He'd had a suspicion that Lloyd had been keeping something from him. This was it. "Oh, and about you and Cheryl, I wasn't the one who contacted the chief. I promise."

Nugent shrugged. "It doesn't matter. A half million dollars is worth a little shame, don't you think?"

"Huh?"

Nugent now pointed a gun Troy's way. "Where's the money?"

"You can't be serious. If Lloyd told you the plan, then he obviously told you that I don't have the money. I was bluffing."

"Bull. Lloyd said no such thing. You two are planning to split the money, but neither of you deserve to cash in on Cheryl's death. You played her like a rag doll and he left her. I'm the only one who's ever truly loved Cheryl and I should get that money. Once you show me where it is, my story will be that I got here too late. Chyanne killed you and I killed her in retaliation. I'll be long gone by the time forensics sorts things out and the cops learn about the money. As you can see, our friend Lloyd likes to keep a low profile, so I don't expect him to come forth with details anytime soon."

Troy had had enough! Nugent was standing much closer to him than Cheryl had been and without giving it a second thought, Troy did a maneuver that knocked the gun out of Don's hand to the floor and the two of them wrestled until Troy eventually got the detective pinned to the ground. Hoping the sirens he heard were coming their direction, Troy maintained his position until the cops burst in with their weapons drawn and ordered Troy up.

"Thank goodness y'all are here!" Nugent exclaimed. "That is Troy Evans, the fugitive wanted in connection with the murder of Cheryl Hunter, the former FBI agent. He killed this young lady here and was trying to kill me, too."

Troy saw the cell phone Lloyd had given him lying on the floor. It must have fallen during their struggle. "Our whole conversation has been recorded. Check it out; you'll see which one of us tried to kill the other."

One of the officers picked up the phone while another ordered both him and Nugent to turn around and get handcuffed. "We'll sort this out at the station," he barked.

Troy obliged the request without complaint, knowing he'd eventually be a free man.

Epilogue

Sometime in the future…

As Troy sat in the basement going over case files, he smiled at the sound of his children's feet running across the floor and his wife yelling at them to "stop!" It was a scenario that repeated itself every so often, and it was usually Nate who set off the chain of events during his horseplay with the younger ones. Troy stopped for a moment to look at the recent photo on his desk of him, Natalie, their children, and Corrine. Taking professional family pictures wasn't really his thing. He did it more to appease Natalie, but this particular photo gave him so much pride for reasons he couldn't explain. There was nothing overly special about the photograph except that their outfits were all coordinated. Again, Natalie's doing! Perhaps it meant a lot to him because of the genuine smiles on their faces. It could have possibly been the memories of eating ice cream at the park immediately after the photo session. Maybe it was simply that the picture served as a reminder of how blessed He was. His marriage, his family, and his finances all remained intact and had survived the craziness brought on by Cheryl and friends. Whatever the reason, Troy took great pride in the portrait and it was the first thing he saw every time he sat at his desk to work.

That day on Dundee sparked a change in him. As he rode in the back of a patrol car to the station, Troy thought about his family and their future. While waiting for hours for the cops to sort out the details and sitting quietly through the chastisement from Mr. Murphy about how he handled things, followed by a wink from Larry on the side, Troy came to a decision; one that would forever alter the course of his life.

His decision was confirmed the first time he saw his family after being released from the station. Between Nate's "*Da-dee!*" squeal, Ebony's and Ean's bouncing and babbling, and Natalie's tears of joy, Troy felt every bit of the superstar treatment that Natalie often teased him about whenever he came home after being gone any length of time. Everyone was amped up on adrenaline and it took forever for him and Natalie to get the kids to bed that night. When they did, Troy gobbled her up with hugs and kisses. They made love until they were both expended and had nothing left to give. That weekend, they celebrated their anniversary. As they lay in bed at the Hilton, Troy finally shared his thoughts with Natalie, seeking her input.

"I think it's a great idea," she'd said. With his wife fully on board, once Troy's suspension was lifted, he retired early from the CPD after twenty years and went to work for himself as a private investigator. Troy called upon B.K. Ashburn, a well-known and respected veteran investigator with whom he'd worked on a special case in Houston. B.K. provided suggestions that helped Troy start his own company. By the fall of that year, Evans Investigations was up and running!

News coverage about his case with Cheryl worked in Troy's favor. People seemed intrigued by the "cop gone rogue" in order to clear his name. When the locals reported that he'd started his company, the phone started ringing. Maintaining good relationships with officers on the force helped Troy when it came to being privy to some information that the average investigator might not have access to. Overall, his company was doing quite well. During the early days, Troy accepted all kinds of cases—missing pets, runaway teens, cheating spouses—but nowadays he could afford to be more selective thanks to a plug about him in a book about investigative techniques B.K. had written.

The honor of Troy having his name connected with B.K.'s wasn't enough to stop the inconsistent cash flow of being self-employed. Some months were more plentiful than others. Luckily, during those lean times, the Evanses had a nice reserve to fall back on because of Lloyd's sharing spirit. Somehow Lloyd found the money Cheryl hid from her life insurance policy and several months after Troy started his company, he received a pretty healthy stack of cash via UPS with a note inside that read, *"I'm applying a lesson taken from Season 1, Episode 9 of Barney & Friends, 'Caring Means Sharing.'* ☺ "

Though there was no signature or valid return address on the package, Troy knew it was from Lloyd. He shook his head in amusement that the dude had really quoted Barney! Of course, the money came in handy. Troy took care of some household essentials, bought a new truck, and then he and his family took a trip to Houston to visit his parents. It was a nice visit. Troy was pleased to see that his mother displayed signs of spiritual growth. She still wasn't ready to fully jump on board with the whole Jesus thing, but she admitted to praying more. In addition, her swearing had been reserved to times when someone excessively worked her nerves or violated a major superstition.

Another thing Troy and Natalie did with the money they'd received was help Will's mother set up a memorial fund in his name for kids with incarcerated parents. Sadly, Will's body was never recovered. With Chyanne dead and a lack of evidence directly tying Charlie to any murder, including Cheryl's, he refused to talk. Thus, the only charges brought against him were for abduction and fraud. Further investigation proved that Don Nugent hadn't been involved in any of the plots and could offer nothing regarding the murders of Cheryl and Will. Troy made it his personal mission to one day locate Will so his mom could get closure. Telling Nugent about the money had been Lloyd's way of testing Don's integrity. Troy suspected that Lloyd would have given Don a cut of the money if Nugent had proven himself loyal. In the end, the dumb prick lost his job and further damaged his reputation because of greed.

After all their spending, Troy and Natalie had not depleted the monetary gift from Lloyd. Instead of putting the rest in the bank, they installed a wall safe in the basement where the remaining cash, along with Lloyd's humorous note, hid behind decorations.

With the sender of one mystery package identified, the person behind the presents for Nate and the kids remained unknown and the gifts continued. Even Corrine had started to receive items for her birthday and the holidays. Natalie believed it was someone from her father's side of the family in Jackson, Mississippi and thought it was "cute" that the individual did not want to be identified. "That's how it should be when we give," she'd argued. Troy wasn't convinced, but he promised his wife that he wouldn't do his "detective thing" by outing the anonymous benefactor, so he let it go… *for now.*

Troy was intently reviewing his case notes when the doorbell rang. He'd been expecting Mario to come by and pick up some material. Troy occasionally hired the deejay to do legwork for him. Despite his criminal background, Mario proved to be a decent guy. A couple of weeks after Troy was cleared of any wrongdoing, Mario contacted him with a real apology for having any involvement with his troubles. He'd even offered to pay for the personal training sessions that had been charged to Troy's credit card. Troy listened to Mario's spiel about wanting to do "the right thing," and felt sympathy for him. After Evans Investigations was established, Troy presented Mario with an opportunity for piecemeal work, which he graciously accepted.

"Honey, can you come up, please? Someone's here to see you," Natalie yelled from the basement door. That's when Troy knew it wasn't Mario who had rung the bell because Natalie would have sent him down. It had to be Ann, who, after learning that he helped negotiate her and Charla's freedom, quickly forgave him for tempting Charla with food that day he was trying to get information from her. She also apologized for luring Natalie out of Lisa's house and into harm's way. All was squashed and they'd been neighborly ever since.

Charla didn't sneak over to their house much anymore because Ann had tightened security around her place. The experience with Charlie freaked her out so that she became paranoid about every new person she encountered, and Ann kept an even closer eye on her daughter than she had before. She continued to work from home, which allowed her time to have the news channels playing nonstop and peep out of her blinds excessively throughout the day, taking down license plates and descriptions of anyone who seemed out of place and passing that info along to Troy. He was certain he wouldn't miss anything that happened in their neighborhood, or all the world for that matter, as long as Ann Harrow was planted across the street.

"I'll be up in a sec," Troy responded to his wife's summons. Since it was nearly time for dinner, Troy decided to call it quits for the day. He tried to have evening meals with his family as often as he could, which averaged out to be at least three, sometimes four, days a week. Other times, duty called in the form of interviews, leads, or surveillance missions. Troy went up the stairs, bracing himself to meet Ann with a straight face. Last time she came over, she reported that their mailman looked like a fugitive she'd seen on an old episode of *Unsolved Mysteries.* She wanted Troy to check it out and he did to appease her, only to discover that the guy featured on that show had been caught nearly twenty years ago and died in prison.

"Would you like to stay for dinner?" Troy heard Natalie ask. The real shock came when the declined invitation came from a male's voice. It wasn't Ann at the door as Troy had thought.

"*Eric!*" Eric Freeman was someone whom Troy kept in contact with occasionally because he was eternally grateful for how the pastor had helped him out. The two had become friends in an extremely loose sense of the word. Troy could only take Eric in small doses. Whenever being around his spiritually eccentric pal became too much, Troy would distance himself from him. It was sort of like Natalie did with his mama's phone calls whenever she started to get on his wife's nerves. Sadly, Troy didn't know who was crazier sometimes—his wildly superstitious mother or his over-the-top, Bible-thumping buddy! "What brings you by this evening?" Troy asked after the astonishment wore off.

"Something bad has happened. I've been praying all day for the Lord to bring clarification and my spirit has led me to you. I hope you will hear me out and take my case."

The Pastor Eric Joshua Freeman of the Tabernacle of Jesus was coming to him for help. *Did his Bible go missing?* Troy swallowed the laugh that tried to fight its way out at the thought. After the way Eric had been there for him, Troy felt obligated to indulge. "Sure thing, my friend. Have a seat and tell me what's on your mind." As Troy also sat down, he took a deep breath and braced himself for the details of a case that was sure to be like none other.

Book Discussion Questions

1. Robert mentions that one should never keep secrets of his/her spouse? Would you agree or disagree? Why or why not?

2. Is "the Lord works in mysterious ways" a scripture or something that has been passed down orally as scriptures such as "clean liness is next to godliness?"

3. Money issues can play a huge part in marital strife. Do you think that a couple's decision not to combine their income is rooted in mistrust? What are some pros and cons of couples combining their income?

4. Were you a working mom or stay-at-home mom? What factors influenced the decision that was made for your household?

5. Have you ever been jealous of the attention that someone else is showing your spouse or vice versa? How was that handled in your relationship?

6. Do you know what scripture in Romans Natalie is referring to in Chapter 2?

7. Do you agree with how Troy handled things Saturday morning in Chapter 4? What would you have done differently?

8. Do you think Troy was really protecting Natalie in Chapter 5 as he claimed or was he protecting himself from having to fully disclose everything?

9. Do you think Natalie handled the situation well in Chapter 6? Why or why not? Is there anything you would have done differently?

10. If you're not familiar with the Betty Broderick case, google her name and click on any of the links that display. Do you think her ultimate reaction to her husband's betrayal was over the top?" Is there any part of you that empathizes with her story?

11. Do you have a friend on whom you can call in times of despair? If so, what makes that person trustworthy?

12. In Chapter 9, Troy and Natalie have an argument and he accuses her of running away instead of facing the issue. Do you agree with his assessment? Why or Why not?

13. How do you feel about Troy's actions in Chapter 10? Do you think it was a natural response considering the circumstances or should he have handled things a different way?

14. Also in Chapter 10, Natalie is tormented by negative thoughts, reminding her of her past mistakes. How do you combat such reminders about things you used to do or be?

15. Have you ever heard of Prader-Willi Syndrome?

16. In chapter 14, Natalie talks about how karma is coming back to get her while Aneetra tries to encourage her to remember God's grace and that she's been forgiven for her past behavior. Do you believe in the concept of karma *after* salvation? What's your take on the reaping and sowing principle mentioned in the Bible? (See Galatians 6:7)

17. Do you think Troy's tactics for getting information from Charla were too much? Why or why not?

18. Have you or anyone you know ever been a victim of identity theft?

19. Cheryl is found dead and Troy is suspected of her murder. Do you have any idea who really killed her?

20. Have you ever disliked someone so much that you secretly wished he/she was dead? How did you get past those feelings?

21. Lloyd is introduced in chapter 22. What do you think of him so far? Do you believe his story about Cheryl?

22. Do you have rules for your house guests? If so, what are they?

23. Under what circumstances, if any, do you think it's okay for Christians to disobey the law?

24. In Chapter 27, Troy connects the dots of his conspirators. Did you see these connections before he did?

25. Troy attributes his situation to his lack of honesty with Natalie about all that happened before. Do you agree? Why or why not?

26. Do you have a favorite gospel song? If so, what is it?

27. Do you think Natalie was too soft on Nate's misbehavior at pre-school? If so, what would you have done differently?

28. Were you surprised at who the culprits were that conspired to set up Troy?

29. What do you think about Troy's decision mentioned in the epilogue?

30. Do you have any speculations about why Troy's help was requested in the epilogue?

ABOUT THE AUTHOR

Yolonda Tonette Sanders holds two bachelors degrees from Capital University in the fields of Criminology and Political Science, and a masters degree in Sociology from The Ohio State University. After working for the State of Ohio for a short while, she took a leap of faith by resigning from her job to focus more on writing. It was a leap that she has never regretted as she became a traditionally published author and also started her own company, Yo Productions, LLC, which specializes in literary services and theatrical entertainment. Yolonda has had six novels published so far, including *Wages of Sin* and *Day of Atonement*, which were the first two books in her *Protective Detective* series. Currently, Yolonda resides in Columbus, Ohio and is the loving wife of David, proud mother of Tre and Tia, and joyful caregiver of her mother, Wilene. Visit the author at www.yoproductions.net, www.yolonda.net, www.facebook.com/yoproductions and on Twitter @ytsanders